Why Did God Make the Tree?

Praise for *Why Did God Make the Tree?*

"A mystifying but endlessly absorbing tale blending surreality and issues of mental health . . . surprisingly cohesive, thanks in large part to the author's deliberate pacing and unambiguous transitions."

—*Kirkus Reviews*

"Compelling debut . . . explores madness, devil worship, human monstrosity, and the way stories and nature affect our own conscious reality . . . [Gregg] weaves these braided tales into a psychological procedural best suited for readers who relish humane scares over vivid gore . . . [and] toys with expectations throughout, favoring suggestion and mystery over spoon-fed exposition, trusting readers . . . to feel their way through the murk."

—Editor's Pick, *BookLife Reviews*

"A journey through madness, love, and self-forgiveness in a modern-day gothic ghost story elevated by wit, rich characters, and proliferating mysteries . . . A master storyteller, Gregg implants exposition into the midst of powerful emotion . . . [and] deftly holds mirrors up to real-life horrors in this twisted, dark and deeply immersive tale."

—Starred Review, *BlueInk*

"Filled with otherworldly encounters delivered with engaging conundrums for added value, *Why Did God Make the Tree?* is a delightfully unpredictable foray into psychological horror that is thoroughly absorbing from start to finish."

—D. Donovan, Senior Reviewer,
Midwest Book Review

"A winding novel that delves into complex subjects through a dark, thought-provoking narrative lens . . . Some of the most haunting parts aren't just monstrous in the story; they reflect real-world horrors. Gregg crafts one of the most thought-provoking portraits of a monster I've seen, one that leaves a burning, searing imprint on the conscience. It's a raw, unflinching look at the darkness that exists both in the mind and in the world around us."

—Renae M. Richardson, *Dead Talk News*

"Thought-provoking and haunting, this modern gothic tale presents psychological depth, humor, and poetic prose that will have audiences biting their nails in anticipation."

—*The BookLife Prize*

Why Did God Make the Tree?

A Patrick Denny Novel

TAMMY GREGG

Cemetery Hill Publications

Why Did God Make the Tree?
A Patrick Denny Novel
Tammy Gregg

Copyright © 2025 by Tammy Gregg
All rights reserved.

This is a revised edition of the work originally published as *The Tower, the Monster, and the Tree*, copyright © 2014 by Tammy Gregg, ISBN 9781497309845.

This is a work of fiction. Names, characters, places, and incidents either are the product of the author's imagination or are used fictitiously. Any resemblance to actual persons, living or dead, events, or locales is entirely coincidental.

No part of this book may be reproduced or transmitted in any form or by any means, electronic or mechanical, including photocopying, recording, or by any information storage and retrieval system, without the written permission of the publisher, except where permitted by law.

Published in the United States by Cemetery Hill Publications
Methuen, Massachusetts

First Edition: April 2025

ISBN: 979-8-9923271-0-6
Library of Congress Control Number: 2025900234

Cover design by David Rines

Printed in the United States

*For
Dad*

TABLE OF CONTENTS

PART ONE •	The Tower	3
PART TWO •	The Monster	71
PART THREE •	The Tree	153
Epilogue		279

"The bird a nest, the spider a web, man friendship"
—William Blake, *The Marriage of Heaven and Hell*

Part One

The Tower

CHAPTER ONE

Sam stared out the window. She gazed past her own reflection, past the giant maple that flamed orange and yellow in the late-day sun. Her eyes moved past the almost deserted parking lot and up the steep slope of Tower Hill Cemetery. They continued their ascent until coming to rest upon the top of the hill, where yellow-gray headstones jutted up, a misshapen grin encircling the red brick giant that penetrated up into the darkening sky.

"Sam," Dr. Denny spoke from behind her.

"Yes," she responded without moving from her spot in front of the window, the customary post she took up at the beginning of their sessions.

"What are you thinking about?"

She shrugged. "Not sure. Nothing really."

The wind kicked up and the branches of the maple reached out to her, tapping and scratching against the glass. A whirlwind of leaves rose around the headstones, giving them the appearance of motion. They danced about the tower, a Sabbath dance in honor of their master, an offering of the souls carved into their stone bodies. Sam let out a long sigh, her breath fogging the glass and blotting out the scene.

"Why don't you come away from the window and have a seat," the doctor coaxed.

"Okay." She turned toward the mahogany desk. Behind its great expanse sat a fortyish-looking man, his short, wavy blonde hair framing a tanned face, his blue eyes sparkling even in the dim light of the desk lamp. She curled up on the oversized armchair across from the desk and wrapped herself in the wool throw blanket that had been draped over the back. A chill hung in the air of the drafty, high-ceilinged room. But despite the cold, she felt safe and warm, secure within the sphere of the desk lamp's protective light.

Dr. Denny smiled at her. He always smiled. Not the same smile, but myriad variations on a smile. At the moment, he was exhibiting his patient, *take-your-time* smile. From anyone else, Sam would have found his perpetual pleasantness insincere—or at least incredibly annoying. But in the short time she'd been his patient, she had concluded he was genuine. Strange, no doubt, but genuine. And she couldn't help but like him.

"Have a peppermint," he said, sliding a candy dish across the desk toward her and snatching one for himself.

Sam rolled her eyes at the ritual. "Today it's peppermint," she said as she grabbed one of the shiny pink and white sweets and popped it into her mouth.

He nodded. "I felt like Christmas today. Peppermint always transports me to Christmastime." He examined the candy, gave it a sniff, smiled with childlike glee, and popped it into his mouth, cheeking it so he could continue talking. "Candy canes, red and green and gold wrapping paper, twinkling lights. I think I'm seven years old. My mum has just finished baking cookies—gingerbread. And my dad is snoring in his recliner by the tree." His eyes gleamed at the memory, and for a moment, Sam almost believed he'd transported himself back in time. She observed his happy reverie until he came back to the present.

He let out a contented sigh and refocused his eyes on her. "So, what about you? Where does peppermint take you?"

Sam shrugged, her usual way of answering his questions, and crunched on the hard candy until it was gone.

"Try," he said. "Close your eyes and use your imagination."

She did what he asked, squeezing her eyes shut as if in deep thought.

"Good. Now, what time and place does peppermint take you to?"

"Hmm. I'm eight years old. My mouth is numb. The dentist is drilling into my tooth to fill the cavity I got from eating too much candy."

"Okay." The doctor appeared somewhat disappointed, but despite her negativity and lack of imagination, his perpetual enthusiasm was not diminished. "So, my friend, how'd you sleep last night?"

Sam winced and wriggled deeper into the chair cushions, attempting to get as far from the question as she could.

"Not good?"

She shook her head.

"Hmm," was the doctor's only response.

The wind howled outside the window, its view now a mirror

of the room against the darkness. The ancient radiator, a giant, twisted monster along the wall, pinged and hissed, its warm, dusty breath mixing with the sweet scent of peppermint.

"Why Christmas?" Sam asked, desperate to leave behind the topic of sleep. "Why not Halloween? Or even Thanksgiving? I mean, have you been outside today? For Christ's sake, it's a classic New England fall day out there!" She thrust her hand toward the darkened window, her movement abrupt and agitated.

Dr. Denny repositioned his candy to the other cheek and replied, "No reason. I just felt like Christmas when I woke up."

That didn't surprise her. At their last session, he felt like summer and handed her a grape popsicle when she walked through the door, despite the chill of the late October day. He had a cooler full of them. Just grape. He didn't *feel* like any other flavor. Sam accepted the treat, shivering as she ate it, the temperature outside having dropped below forty degrees.

No, Dr. Denny's oddities didn't surprise her anymore.

"What do *you* feel like today?" he asked, folding his hands on the desk and leaning more into the light.

Sam's eyes fell on the wrist brace poking out from his left sleeve. *How had he injured himself,* she wondered. *Did he play sports?* He appeared athletic and in good physical shape. *Very good.* She wouldn't bother asking him though. He never offered details about his current life. Only snippets of his past that came with his little sensory trips through time and space. His mum, his dad, his favorite boyhood things.

"What do I feel like today?" she repeated his question. She stared straight into his expectant eyes. He was very handsome. Tall and fit and all-around good-looking. A little old for her, but not so old that he couldn't feature in one of her harmless romantic fantasies. Yes, she would probably have a massive crush on him if she wasn't so damn tired and he wasn't . . . well . . . such a freak.

He waited for her response, a glimmer of anticipation in his eyes.

"I feel like shit," she said. "What flavor is that?"

Dr. Denny blinked and sat silent for a moment. Then, with an amused tilt of his head, he broke into one of his smiles. Rolling back his chair to stand, he slapped his desk, laughed, and pointed at her. "Samantha," he said, "you are a clever one. Even with no sleep. How long has it been?"

"This time?" She hesitated before answering, her stomach tightening and the panic rising in her chest. "About ten days," she said, her voice almost a whisper.

"Ten days?" he repeated. "Is that all? Oh, you've gone longer than that before." He turned away from her and searched for something along the wall of shelves behind his desk. "Read any good books lately?"

"What?" she asked, confused by the sudden shift in topic.

He glanced over his shoulder with a mischievous grin. "Have I got an amazing book for you. Just what the doctor ordered."

She groaned at his bad joke. "No, really, Dr. Denny. I can't read a book right now." The thought of looking at a page full of words made her temples throb and her bloodshot eyes sting.

He seemed to ignore her as he searched up and down the rows. "Now, where did you get to?" he mumbled.

"Maybe . . . maybe it's time to give medication another try," she suggested, her immediate need for sleep overpowering her resolve to avoid being drugged once again.

"Where did I put it?" He pulled a book from the top shelf. "*Eat, Pray, Love*? I keep forgetting to return this to Dr. Philbin."

"I don't think I can keep going through this." She tried to keep the quiver out of her voice. She didn't like to show too much emotion. It made her feel weak, and all the other doctors seemed to prey on that weakness. Especially Dr. Dilby. Her face burned at the thought of that pompous, condescending man. He'd given her so many medications, a rainbow of pills, the side effects from which she was only now recovering. But she had to sleep. Nothing else seemed to matter anymore. "Maybe we can try another benzo?"

"Aha! There you are." He bent down and pulled a dusty, leather-bound book from the bottom shelf. With a triumphant smile, he held it out to her.

"Are you even listening to me!" she cried.

"Yes. No benzos. No meds. No more whining. Now, please take this book. Quick, it's heavy."

Ripping the blanket off, she stood and snatched the book from him, unprepared for the object's weight. She gripped it tightly with both hands and glared at the doctor. "This won't help me! You shrinks never listen," she snapped and plopped back into the chair.

The doctor took his seat and chuckled. "It's been a while since anyone called me a shrink. Very retro. Now open it," he said gleefully as if he had just given her a present.

She set the book down on her lap. It seemed ancient, the leather cracked and musty smelling. There was no title, no writing, no markings of any kind on the covers or the spine. She looked up at the doctor, who waited expectantly. "Fine," she huffed, opened the book to the flyleaf, where she found a handwritten inscription, and read it out loud. "This is the Diary of Alfred D. Cummings, Master Builder and Architect, Waylingbrooke, New Hampshire, twenty-third of September, eighteen eighty-seven." She frowned. "It's just an old diary."

Dr. Denny nodded his head enthusiastically.

Flipping through the pages, Sam found that the entire book was in the same old-fashioned longhand as the inscription.

"Why would I want to read this?"

"Because . . ." the doctor stood up and, keeping his eyes on her, crossed the office toward the window. "Mr. Alfred D. Cummings, Master Builder and Architect, was the guy who designed and built *that* tower." He pointed out into the darkness in the direction of Tower Hill, the outline of the imposing structure just barely visible in the distance. His eyes seemed to radiate their own light, and Sam half expected him to giggle.

Frowning at the book in her lap, she repeated, still confused, "Okay . . . but why would I want to read it?"

He stepped toward her quickly. "Because Mr. Alfred D. Cummings' tower is no ordinary tower." Taking the book from her and placing it on the desk, he flipped through the pages until he found the passage he wanted. "Thirty-first of October," he read. "My dearest Virginia, I must confess that I have resolved to put an end to this dreadful phantasmagoria. I can no longer deny the presence of a force that beckons me, nay, compels me to complete this tower with an inhuman rapidity; I cannot sleep, I cannot eat, I cannot think of anything but the completion of this brick-and-mortar abomination. Indeed, I find myself utterly consumed by its bewitchment, unable to break free from its unearthly grasp. It has ensnared me in its diabolical clutches and demands the very lifeblood from my veins." The doctor stopped reading and eagerly awaited Sam's response.

She rose from the chair and walked to the window. Icicles pricked at her spine and her cheeks burned red hot. No longer able to see past her reflection, she stared at the distorted face of her twin, who was evidently quite angry. "Are you CRAZY!" she shouted, turning on the overgrown child in whom she had put her last hopes.

Dr. Denny closed the diary and sat on the edge of his desk, apparently aware that a loud, lengthy rant had just begun.

"I can't sleep! And I have night terrors when I do! Why would I want to read that?" She pointed accusingly at the diary. "How could you possibly . . . I mean . . . I thought you were supposed to be helping me, not driving me more insane!" She paced in front of him. "I might as well check myself back into the asylum and let them drug me into oblivion. At least then," she jabbed a finger against her head, "my brain could get a rest from the constant thinking about sleep or not sleeping or . . ." Her voice trailed off as she dropped back into the chair and slumped forward.

The doctor remained silent.

The wind shrieked against the window and the radiator hissed.

"I thought you were going to help," she murmured.

He held out the book to her once again. "Trust me."

She wasn't sure why—whether it was just her desperate need to trust *someone* or a genuine faith in the man—but for some reason, she did.

The Tower

• • •

Sam trudged down the steps of the Old Meeting Hall building with the diary of Alfred D. Cummings tucked under her arm. The wind thrashed the trees that lined the street and charged her already agitated nerves with a blast of chilling cold. A torrent of fallen leaves skittered across the sidewalk, accumulating in a mound at the bottom of the steps where Sam paused to zip her jacket up to her chin. She glanced back at the renovated, two-centuries-old building, wondering if Alfred Cummings had ever been inside.

Most of the building's narrow windows were dark, but a solitary light shone from Dr. Denny's office on the second floor. She pictured the doctor sitting at his desk, writing up the notes for their session: *Samantha Perez, 19, pathological whiner.* Her face flushed with embarrassment at her childish outburst. It wasn't the first, of course, but each time it happened, she wanted to kick herself for behaving so in front of him.

The bell from St. Michael's tolled the hour, and Sam set off on the short walk home, sticking to the diffused glow of the street lamps that hung from poles every twenty or so feet. She looked up at the quaint reproductions made to resemble the old gas lamps from the turn of the century. "Damn historical society," she grumbled. In her present agitated state, she would have preferred the former fluorescent lights that lit up the sky like a night game at a football stadium. Then there would be none of the shadows in which the monsters of her imagination now lurked.

She plunged ahead into the path of murky light and shadow,

moving like a machine, her arms held rigidly at her sides, her strides even and rhythmic. The streets were deserted. All the businesses closed shop at five sharp, leaving the heart of the town empty and quiet. The sound of the church bell rang out through the lonely night, calling people into a community of prayer, a reminder that they were not alone. But for Sam, each echoing toll was a death knell, announcing the end of day and the beginning of a long, sleepless night.

The diary dug into her ribs, but she couldn't stop to adjust it. She had to keep moving, sure that even the slightest hesitation would invite attention from whatever lingered in the shadows. The bell struck its sixth and final toll, and Sam's nerves lurched into overdrive. She rushed forward, well aware that even in the warmth and safety of her childhood home, no relief was waiting for her. No comfort. No sleep. Yet still, she raced homeward, away from the anxiety and fear, attempting to escape the inescapable—the torment of her sleep-deprived mind.

She turned a corner and caught her breath. Halfway down the deserted road, a streetlight was out. Her determined pace slowed, and she stared wide-eyed into the dark chasm before her. Each step she took was now accented by a sharp surge of fear, her heart pounding in her chest as the silence pressed in around her.

Just yards from the gap in the lights, she came to a stop. She stared intently, unwilling to blink lest something in the shadow might take that instant of opportunity to make its move. The cold air stung at her eyes and tears rolled down her cheeks. The darkness wasn't opaque. She could still see through it to the light on the other side. And the more she scrutinized its murkiness, the more she was sure there was something inside it. Yes, something was there, churning up the emptiness, skulking about, and waiting for her. She took a step back. Maybe she could find another way home. Her mind raced through the possibilities. She took another step back. But the only feasible route would send her by the entrance to Tower Hill Cemetery. She took a step forward. Maybe if she hurried, held her breath, kept her eyes focused on the light, she could slip by—

It moved—a mass of amorphous black that undulated and roiled and slunk toward her from the shadows. Her mind ceased to analyze possible routes home. Instead, it shrieked for her to run, and she obeyed, sprinting back toward the center of town. She rounded the corner in a wide arc, nearly crashing into one of the street poles, hoping to see the light in Dr. Denny's office. But as she approached the Old Meeting Hall building, her heart sank. Except for a dim light in the lobby, the front of the building was completely dark.

Maybe he's in the parking lot? she prayed, stopping in front of the building and scanning the lot across the street. But it, too, was empty. Dejected, terrified, and unsure of where to turn next, Sam's eyes were drawn from the parking lot up to the top of the hill. The tower glared down upon her, and the words from Alfred D. Cummings' diary boomed in her head. *"I cannot sleep, I cannot eat, I cannot think of anything but the completion of this brick-and-mortar abomination."*

Mesmerized by its awfulness, its power to dominate the night sky, she stumbled toward it. And it seemed to grow before her, pushing itself upward and outward until it loomed overhead, crushing her into the ground, pushing her under the earth, a live burial, an eternity without air or light or warmth. She suppressed the primordial scream that rose from deep inside her. Her knees buckled, and as she crumbled to the street, the diary tumbled out in front of her, its pages flapping in the wind, shrieking up at their master.

"Samantha?"

The sound of her name was all it took for her strangled cry to be loosened upon the night, a throat-shredding wail of terror that echoed through the empty street.

"Jesus, Mary, and Joseph!" exclaimed the old man. "What is the matter?"

Sam looked up at the frightened priest, who shook with the aftershock of her scream. She glanced back up at the tower. Somehow, it had shrunk to its normal size and receded into the darkness upon its hill. The diary had settled down, its pages fluttering gently in the cold night breeze. She snatched it up and let Father Owen help her to her feet. As the elderly priest bent forward, a large gold crucifix dangled from around his neck, and Sam involuntarily averted her eyes.

"I . . . I guess I just got spooked."

He glanced around the deserted street and up at the cemetery and tower. With a nervous laugh, he said, "I guess I can't blame you. It's one of those spooky nights when one wishes to be in the company of other people, preferably somewhere well-lit." He raised his bushy eyebrows to emphasize the point and offered her his arm. "Why don't I walk you home?"

She took his arm and nodded with relief. They stepped onto the sidewalk, and she tucked the diary close against her once again. If only he could come home with her, sit up all night keeping watch, and never leave her side. Then she might find the relief she so desperately sought. But she doubted Father Owen would be up for such a job.

He led her back in the direction from which she had just come.

"Can we take the long way?" she implored as she tugged him back.

"The long way?"

"By . . . by the cemetery," she stuttered, now willing to endure the unpleasantness of that route.

"That's three times the distance!" Father Owen protested in a high-pitched voice.

"Please," Sam pleaded, her eyes darting past him toward the shadowy presence she feared still approached, almost certain she could hear the dull echo of footfalls moving toward them from inside the darkness.

"Well, okay," he agreed, somewhat displeased, yet let her lead him on the longer route.

Trying to walk at the old priest's excruciatingly slow pace, Sam caught him eyeing her. It seemed as if he wanted to say something but wasn't sure if it would be okay.

"Is there something you want to ask me, Father?" She was somewhat surprised by his reticence. Being the family's pastor since before her birth, he probably knew more about her than she knew about herself. He'd baptized her, given her first communion, confirmed her, and would most certainly officiate if she ever got married. He was there through both of her parents' illnesses—and deaths. And she had vague recollections of him praying over her when she lay in a drug-induced stupor in the hospital. Not last rites, she thought as they walked along. No, the sacrament was really called the Anointing of the Sick. Not as hopeless-sounding a phrase.

Her memory flashed back to the worried priest leaning over her at the hospital, his large gold cross dangling from his neck and glinting in the cold white light of the observation ward, the disturbing sounds of her fellow inmates rambling and groaning and giggling from all around. "May the Lord who frees you from sin save you and raise you up," Father Owen had blessed her as he anointed her forehead with Holy Oil. The echoes of those words sent a wave of guilt through her as she waited for him to ask his question.

He paused their walk, cleared his throat, and, with a tinge of anxiety in his voice, asked, "Have you heard anything more about the investigation?"

Sam's chest tightened at the mention of the investigation, but she tried to maintain a neutral expression. She shook her head. "No. I think that's all over now. After the coroner's report, there wasn't much else for them to investigate. And Detective Foret has stopped contacting me."

Anger distorted the priest's usual calm demeanor. "That man! He should never have involved the coroner. Insufferable, sacrilegious bast—"

"He was just doing his job," Sam interposed gently, trying to allay Father Owen's protective indignation. "With both of them dying so close together, he had to do his job, Father." Her heart ached at the memory of her parents' illnesses, the long-suffering, and the inevitable outcome. But she didn't blame the policeman's suspicions. How could she after—

"To accuse you of such unspeakable acts!"

"He was just doing his job," she repeated.

But Father Owen continued unabated, "I told him you were incapable of such a horrible sin. It's against all the tenets of our Faith. And even suggesting that your parents, God bless them, would ask their child to do such a thing! But that heartless, selfish man kept pushing and pushing!" He had to stop for a moment, the force of his angry outburst leaving him winded.

"Father, it's over now. Please don't worry anymore."

"But—"

Sam placed a hand on the priest's hunched shoulder.

His eyes widened and his face softened as he realized he had lost himself in his own resentment for the policeman. He patted Sam's reassuring hand. "You're right. The investigation is over now," he said, a hint of uncertainty still lingering in his voice.

She retook his arm and they walked on. "Besides," she said with a half-hearted attempt to lighten the mood, "I *am* the sole heiress to their entire estate. That automatically makes me a suspect, doesn't it?"

Father Owen looked up to the heavens wryly. "Oh, yes. A house in ill repair and a mountain of medical bills."

Bittersweet sadness tugged at Sam's heart. "Well, at least I still have the house. Let's hope I can keep it."

A flicker of concern crossed his face. "Any luck finding work? I could put in a word with some people I know?"

Sam shook her head. "No, no. I've got applications in at a bunch of places. I'm just waiting to hear back." But that was a lie. She hadn't been trying to find work. And she was far too embarrassed to tell him just how completely dysfunctional she had become.

As if reading her thoughts, he asked, "So you're doing better now, aren't you? The new doctor is working out?"

"Dr. Denny is a little . . . well . . . different. But I like him."

"Yes, I've heard he's a bit unorthodox, but if he is helping you . . ." He left the thought unfinished and patted her arm. "Your mother would be very proud of the progress you've made. I'm sure of it."

Sam sniffed. "Yeah, Mom would be so happy her daughter escaped the nuthouse."

"Now, Samantha," Father Owen said sternly, "you shouldn't think of it that way. It was a brief hospital stay, and you worked hard to get well enough to be discharged. Anyone put under the kind of pressure—well, a young girl shouldn't have to bear so much responsibility all alone. Two sick parents, school, a job, and that damned investigation!" Sam could see him winding up for another tirade against Detective Foret, but he caught himself and cleared his throat. "You did a remarkable thing taking care of them the way you did. It's no wonder you got sick afterward." He ended his speech with a self-affirming huff.

They turned off Hideaway Lane, and Sam was relieved to see cars and people and fluorescent lights again.

"Maybe I should move to the city," she said absently.

"Hmm. Better job prospects," Father Owen responded. "But we'd miss you here." He smiled at her kindly and patted her arm again.

She wasn't sure to whom *we* referred but was glad at least one person in the world would miss her.

They approached the entrance to the cemetery. Sam stayed at the side of Father Owen closest to the street, though she could still clearly read "Tower Hill Cemetery" arched in bold bronze letters over the gate. It was an old graveyard, and now that Dr. Denny had given her the diary, she had a better idea of just *how* old. But there was still ample room for new tenants, and she could almost pick out her parents' headstone about halfway up the long slope of the hill.

"You must miss them terribly," Father Owen said, and Sam realized she had stopped them right before the entrance.

"I can't believe it's already been two years," she said, her voice barely above a whisper. The day of her mother's funeral, almost exactly two months after her father's, was a cold fall day, much like this one. The shadow of the tower fell across those gathered for the interment as her mother was lowered into the earth. Few people attended. Sam had no time for friends, having to work and care for her long-sick parents while trying to keep up with school. With no extended family and her parents being housebound, Father Owen was the only person present who knew her. He stood by her at the wake the evening before to greet the strangers, mostly obituary watchers who showed up at every local wake and funeral as a matter of practice. And he had said such beautiful things about her mother at the Mass, unable to keep the emotion out of his voice.

She'd remained stoic throughout the ordeal, resolved to move forward in the world on her own, even though she was just seventeen at the time. It wasn't until a month later, when she was informed that her parents' bodies were to be exhumed, that her resolve had faltered. She watched the caskets being lifted out of the hard, cold ground, the smell of dirt, the tower looming above against the gray sky of the coming winter. That very night in her big empty house, imagining her parents' bodies lying side by side on the cold metal slabs of the coroner's autopsy room, that was when it all started.

She moved Father Owen and herself on their way again. "Sleep deprivation is a form of torture, you know," she said to him as they left the cemetery behind.

"Still having a lot of trouble with sleep?"

She nodded. "Have you ever had insomnia, Father?"

"Oh, I've had my troubles with sleep. In my line of work, you tend to hear a lot of people's problems, and sometimes that sets the mind racing."

"How do you deal with it?"

"Well, of course, prayer eases the mind, but if I'm still having trouble, a snifter of brandy helps," he whispered conspiratorially. "But don't tell anyone else."

"Alcohol just makes me sick."

"Pity. Well, after that scream you greeted me with, I will probably follow my own advice when I go to bed tonight."

Her pulse quickened at the mention of bed, and she was sure Father Owen sensed her distress as the muscles in her arm tightened. They walked the rest of the route in silence until they came to her street.

Her house sat in the middle of a row of identical nineteenth-century Victorians. But hers stood out. Tall and intricately detailed, its clapboard siding was a dusty pink rose, the scrolling trim work purples, yellows, and greens of all shades. An oversized dollhouse, possessing the unburdened joy of a child, with the more serious adult houses around it looking on sternly.

The porch light spilled its warm glow over the front steps

like a welcome mat, and she knew she had to let the priest go. St. Michael's parish house was a few blocks back, and she didn't want to make the elderly man go even more out of his way. "I'm okay to go the rest alone," she told him, relinquishing his arm.

He looked relieved and gave her a peck on the cheek. "Goodnight, Samantha."

"Thank you, Father."

He started on his way, paused as if to say something, thought better of it, and commenced once again toward his home. Sam watched the priest, her only friend—her only family—amble away until he disappeared around a corner. Reluctantly, she walked toward her house and climbed the front steps, careful to avoid the loose board that needed fixing.

Her happy house was tired. The paint was peeling, the porch was leaning, and the yard was overgrown with weeds. It needed a lot of work, but she had neither the money nor the energy to do much about it. She peered into the night, and somewhere, a distant neighbor's dog barked, probably enraged that someone dared to walk by its house. Her heart sank a bit. She knew she would eventually have to give the house up, that someone else would call it home. The dog barked again and she understood its torment.

CHAPTER TWO

"So, Dr. Denny, how you settling in?" a friendly voice inquired from behind Patrick.

Glancing back, Patrick found Dr. Philbin's pleasant smile greeting him.

"Adjusting," he answered through a mouth full of stuffed mushrooms.

"Hope you're feeling welcome here at Everston," Philbin said as he poked around the hors d'oeuvre tray, grimacing at his choices.

Patrick scooped up another mushroom and crammed it into his mouth. He found that a constant mouthful of food made it easier to avoid conversations with his new colleagues.

Giving up on the food, Philbin grabbed a glass of wine from the tray of a passing server. "I'm surprised Estelle didn't arrange your welcome reception sooner."

"That would be my fault," Patrick sputtered, attempting to catch the bits of food that flew out of his mouth. "She's been trying to pin me down on a date, but I've been swamped." In truth, he had avoided the director's assistant as long as possible. Social gatherings like this made him miserable. Lousy food, cheap wine, phony chit-chat, and puffed-up egos. These people simply didn't understand the concept of a good time. But Estelle was relentless. Despite his repeated evasions, she persisted until he reluctantly agreed to a date and time.

"Odd time, though," Philbin commented as if he had read Patrick's thoughts, watching with fascination as his new colleague emptied a tray of questionable-looking shrimp in rapid succession. "Nine-thirty on a Tuesday night?"

Estelle wasn't too happy about that either, Patrick thought impishly. "Food's great, though," he said, holding up the last shrimp. He left Philbin behind to follow a server and load up his plate. As he did so, he noticed that the entire attention of the room had suddenly shifted toward the entryway. He followed their captivated gazes to where Helen had just made her entrance.

The red cocktail dress was tight in all the right places and tailored to reveal just enough of her striking physique without crossing over into lewdness. She stood in the doorway, posing for her audience—a tall, blonde Norse goddess in four-inch red spikes.

Grinning widely, Patrick abandoned his plate and met her at the door. He loved her entrances. "You're late," he said to her with a peck on the cheek.

"Business," she answered and scanned the crowd. "What a room full of duds."

Patrick concurred with a nod. "Well, it's a psychiatric hospital. What did you expect?"

"Tell me again why you're doing this," she said as they glided into the room.

"I don't need to," he answered, still grinning but now with a noticeable tightness in his jaw. "You know why. We've been through it over and over again."

"You don't need a job. Just write another book. Then we'll both make a ton of money." She was baiting him as usual. But he'd just ignore her. Their relationship worked well as long as he retained that particular skill. "Get me a drink," she said, wrinkling her nose at the dried-up stuffed mushrooms and crumbling mini crab cakes offered to her by an overly enthusiastic young man with a tray. As Patrick raised his hand to wave over a wine server, Helen's eyes lit up. "Your wrist brace! You *are* writing a new book!" She exclaimed delightedly, and he could almost see the dollar signs in her eyes. "What's this one about?"

"Oh, nothing you'd be interested in, I'm sure," he said, tugging his coat sleeve over the brace.

"Well, that's true. None of your books interest me. But I love the shoes they buy me." She lifted her long, shapely leg and admired her red, shiny, and obscenely expensive Louboutin stiletto. "So, introduce me to people."

Patrick held out his arm and she took ownership of it like everything else he had. He led her around the room, making his introductions.

"Dr. Philbin," he greeted the bookish little man, who was still attempting to find something decent to eat. "I'd like you to meet Helen Olssen, my significant other."

Philbin dropped the finger sandwich on which he was tentatively nibbling and brushed the crumbs from his hands.

"Oh, hello," he said awkwardly, struck nearly dumb by the beauty and stature of the woman standing over him.

"It's very nice to meet you, Dr. Philbin," Helen said and held out her hand.

Fumbling a bit, Philbin reached for her hand and looked up at her, too bashful to meet her striking gaze directly. "Archibald. You can call me Archibald."

"Well, Archie, what do you do around here?" she said with a playful tilt of the head.

With fascination, Patrick watched her do her thing. For behind her pleasantries and charm, a machine was at work, calculating and assessing the potential author and cash cow that stood before her.

Philbin laughed nervously and tried to force a more grave tone into his voice. "Oh, I work with the geriatric patients. It's difficult sometimes," he said self-importantly. "Mostly dementia and Alzheimer's. Very sad. Very, very sad."

Helen nodded knowingly. "Well, they're lucky to have you watching over them." She stroked his arm, causing the timid man's face to flush a deep red.

"He's a good man," Patrick laughed and gave his flustered colleague a hearty pat on the back. "Okay, Helen, there are others to meet." And they left Philbin behind, staring after her.

"Vamp," Patrick whispered into her ear.

Grinning wickedly, Helen strutted alongside him, drawing eyes from every corner of the room, including those of a giant of a man who conspicuously looked her up and down several times.

"Who is *that*?" she asked.

"Oh . . . *that* is the boss," he answered coolly and steered her to where Alexander Anderson, the Director of Everston Psychiatric Hospital, stood among his underlings. He was tall, a full head taller than Patrick, and towered over the others like a king looking down on his subjects. With an almost imperceptible wave, Anderson dismissed the throng of fawning sycophants, who scattered, leaving him to wait for Patrick and Helen to come to pay their homage.

"Dr. Denny, good to finally see you," Anderson said loudly, reaching out his large hand to Patrick and ignoring Helen with obvious intent. "Welcome to Everston."

Patrick accepted the proffered hand. "Thank you, Director."

With an excessively firm grip, the director pulled Patrick closer. "I hear you gave Estelle quite the runaround." He gestured to the sour-faced woman who stood alone by one of the meeting room's enormous Palladian arched windows and watched the party with a disapproving scowl.

Patrick's electric blue eyes sparkled defiantly as he squeezed back. "I'm not big on social events. Very time consuming."

Anderson leaned uncomfortably close to Patrick's face and dropped his voice to a low growl. "Remember our arrangement. When I want you to show up and be seen, you'd better show up and be seen."

"Of course," Patrick said unflinchingly. "But just remember your side of the agreement."

The two men stood locked in their staring contest for a few more moments before Anderson, as if suddenly realizing Patrick would not yield, released his grip and stepped back. "Well, who is this lovely lady?" he asked, abruptly turning to Helen, the shift in his demeanor disconcerting.

But undeterred and not waiting for an introduction, Helen reached forward and said, "Helen Olssen, Patrick's better half."

Anderson took her hand, cupping it between his, and leered down at her. "I'm jealous."

"Most men are," she replied coyly, reclaiming her hand and looping it through Patrick's arm.

"Director," a disapproving voice broke into their banter, causing them all to start. "It's almost time for that overseas call you've been waiting for." At some point, unnoticed by the three, Estelle had joined them, seeming to defy the laws of space and time by transporting herself from one part of the room and materializing behind them. She stood impatiently, her arms folded across her chest, brows knit together into a deep frown.

Anderson's expression once again morphed, revealing a not-so-subtle abhorrence for his assistant. "Thank you, Estelle," he said without bothering to look at her.

"Hello, Estelle. How are you this evening?" Patrick greeted the slightly hunched woman, who glowered at them all in silence.

"Well, I have other things to attend to. Please excuse me," Anderson said, looking Helen up and down once again. He headed toward the door with Estelle trailing close behind.

Helen watched Anderson swagger away and let out a long breath. "Boy, what a creep."

"Which one?" Patrick said with a smirk.

She stared at Patrick with suspicion. "Are you going to tell me what that little exchange was about?"

He kissed her cheek. "Nope." Then he proceeded to introduce her to the rest of his colleagues, some of whom he hadn't even met himself before that night.

After they made a torturous tour of the room, Helen leaned into Patrick and whispered, "Sorry to say, you're the only superstar here."

"Lucky them. They don't have to deal with all the fan mail."

"Speaking of fan mail, darling . . ."

"I asked you not to go through my desk."

"The letters were lying on top. And as your agent, I like to keep my eye on what your fans have to say."

"You're not my agent anymore. You're my girlfriend."

"Whatever," she said dismissively. "One of them seemed pretty disturbing to me. I think it's time for a restraining order."

"Michael?"

"Yes, I think that was his name."

"Stop reading my mail."

"But—"

"Finally!" Just then, to Patrick's perverse delight, Clifton Dilby strolled into the room. "Someone should restrain this guy," he said, ditching his wine glass. "Stay here," he ordered Helen, who glared at him indignantly but obeyed. Patrick stalked across the room right up to the man, who, unperturbed by the aggressive approach, nodded his head to acknowledge Patrick's presence.

"Denny."

"Dilby."

A fat, white-bearded Englishman, Clifton Dilby wore a pretentious tweed suit and, in contrast, a Halloween-themed tie intended to amuse his patients. Patrick would have found that touch of whimsy delightful, but he knew all too well that most of Dilby's patients were drugged beyond the ability to see his face, let alone his tie with the little dancing skeletons and witches.

"So, I hear that Amelia Dearborne's family has asked you to look into her case," Dilby said casually as he glanced around the room.

"Yes," Patrick responded. Dilby was quick. Patrick had just gotten off the phone with Amelia's parents only a half hour before the party started. *Too bad he isn't so quick when his patients are spiraling*, Patrick thought bitterly.

"She's a very sick woman," Dilby said, fixing a cool gaze on Patrick.

"She has problems," Patrick conceded.

"I think it would be a mistake to interfere with her medications."

Patrick knew he would think so.

Dilby regarded him over his glasses. "It's dangerous taking these people off their meds, you know."

"These people? To whom are you referring?"

Dilby didn't answer. He just stared at him disapprovingly.

"You know," Patrick said, the exhilaration of battle welling up in him, "it's equally dangerous to put people on medication they don't need."

"Have you read her case file?" Dilby asked.

"Not yet. But in my experience, I've found many, if not most, patients do better with other forms of treatment."

"Experience?"

Ah, he's going there, Patrick thought. "I was a practicing psychiatrist before I started publishing fiction."

"Well, that was a while ago," Dilby dismissed him. "These people are very sick and need to be medicated."

Anger and pleasure surged in Patrick's chest, and his voice grew louder. "There it is again—*these people.*"

Dilby waved him off.

Patrick's sardonic laugh was loud enough to make others nearby take notice. "So, it is your contention that all these people need to be medicated."

"According to accepted psychiatric practices," Dilby said, his composure unchanged by Patrick's theatrics.

The buzz of conversation about the room had grown quiet, and Patrick felt the eyes of the spectators upon them.

"Of course, each diagnosis has its own standard treatment," Dilby continued.

Patrick scoffed. "But all with the same result. Zombification. That's if we're lucky."

Dilby stood silent, still unaffected, and let Patrick continue.

"If we're not lucky, though, and we haven't completely neutralized these people, we all know that some of them *will* snap, killing themselves or a whole bunch of other people," he exclaimed bitterly, his voice rising with each word, too fueled by adrenaline to curb his indignation.

Helen was now at his side. "Okay, boys, let's break this up. This is supposed to be a party."

"These are sick people," Dilby repeated evenly. "You shouldn't interfere with their treatments."

"So, what's the result? What's the best we can hope for with your treatments? Medication for life? Or let's call it what it really is—medication until death."

"In some cases," Dilby answered.

"How many is some? Twenty percent? Fifty? Ninety? Tell

me, Dilby, how many of your patients are on medication until death?"

Dilby's eyes flashed with satisfaction as he gestured to the displeased faces that stared at them from around the room. "Why don't you ask the rest of our colleagues the percentage of their patients on medication? My guess is that the number is rather high."

Patrick turned to the crowd of vexed onlookers and sighed, realizing that once again, fueled by the heavy burden of his own baggage, he had allowed his zeal to get the better of him. With a subtle bow to his adversary, he acknowledged the minor victory. "Well, we all have our methods," he said, attempting to inject a lighter tone into his voice. "Thank you, everyone, for this warm welcome. I really appreciate it." He made a quick check of the imaginary watch on his wrist. "But I have a *very* early appointment tomorrow, so we'll have to be on our way."

He paused, nodded to Philbin, the only sympathetic face among the unfriendly crowd, and then led Helen to the door.

"Way to make nice," she whispered to him.

"At least I livened up the party."

CHAPTER THREE

Shadows rippled across the ceiling above Sam's bed, expanding, contracting, and contorting until they spilled over the edge and poured down the wall. Not yet prepared to close her eyes and attempt sleep, she watched the next tide of passing headlights filter through the open mini blinds, a fleeting detour on their travels through the chilly October night. With the blankets clutched up to her neck, she lay on her back, her body as rigid as a corpse, and listened intently to the sounds of the night. The muted whistle of the wind through the cracks and crevices around the window frame. The whoosh of passing cars. The heaving and sighing and creaking of her old house settling down around her. All was as it should be. Nothing to fear. She took a deep breath and shut her eyes. The ritual had begun.

Empty. Empty. Empty. She repeated the mantra in her mind. She pushed all thoughts and fears away and breathed out. She took another deep breath and focused on not thinking. *Empty . . . Empty . . . Empty . . .* The mantra, no longer a steady rhythm, began to slow, each *empty* echoing in her mind with increasing drowsiness. She was drifting off, feeling the weight of her thoughts fading.

But the instant she realized sleep was in her grasp, it fell apart, too fragile to withstand even the slightest bit of attention. Keeping her eyes shut tight, she wriggled under the heavy covers. Her sweat-soaked pajama top stuck to her back and an unreachable spot between her shoulder blades itched and she could feel the anxiety welling up in her chest and—

"No," she said out loud, refusing to lose control. She pulled the covers more tightly around her neck and started again. She breathed out and relaxed her clenched muscles. *Empty. Empty. Empty.* She breathed in and tried to ignore the pool of sweat that saturated the pillow beneath her head and the clump of matted hair stuck to the back of her neck. How she longed to roll over, to stretch out her stiff body and flip her pillow to the cool, dry side. But that would leave her too exposed. She breathed out. *Empty . . . Empty . . . Empty . . .* By sheer force of will, she compelled her mind to dispense with all thought. Slowly, the veil of sleep fell. Consciousness melted away—

A violent rumble shook the world and her eyes snapped open. The house quaked from the basement to the attic as the furnace kicked on, roaring to life and angrily announcing its presence.

Ripped from her almost sleep, she peered furtively around the room, searching for any newly materialized boogeyman. No headlights cut through the darkness, but she could still make out the familiar objects of her childhood—the collection of porcelain dolls in the corner, the vanity where she used to sit while her mother brushed her hair, the dollhouse her father had built with his own hands. Everything was in its spot. Nothing had changed.

"Goddamned furnace," she hissed through clenched teeth and listened as the radiator by the window ticked, shuddered, and rattled, forced to life by the beast in the basement. She hated that thing, that ancient metal monster that lived in the dirtiest, darkest corner of her house, plotting, planning, and gnashing its teeth, tainting her otherwise bright childhood imagination with the foul, oily stench and filth of the things that crept up the basement steps while her family lay sleeping—

"No, no, no! Empty, empty, empty!" she chanted out loud, desperate to stop the uncontrollable cascade of more and more horrifying imaginings. But it was too late. They crawled out of the darkness, black, soulless forms that slunk along the floor toward her bed. She sat up, rigid with fear. They weren't real. She knew they weren't real. But the wider she opened her eyes and the harder she tried to see that they weren't really there, the closer they got. Too afraid to move, blink, or even breathe, she sat petrified, sure she could hear their voiceless, frenzied murmurings, accusatory and vengeful. She trembled as they closed in around her.

Then, as if driven by some primordial part of her non-thinking brain, her arm darted from beneath the blankets. The bedside lamp clicked on, the force of her movement causing it to rock back and forth, casting a wavering light across the room.

It was empty.

But even though her eyes could see this, her trembling body wasn't so sure, and a burst of nervous energy propelled her from the bed, only to be snatched back by some invisible force that coiled around her legs, sending her headfirst toward the floor. Half-suspended above the plush pink carpet, she had no choice but to look under the bed.

There they were, hiding from the light, the contorted faces of pain, suffering, and rage with their sunken, hollowed-out eyes accusing her, their mouths voiceless, gaping holes silently crying out for justice. She let out a strangled cry and kicked her legs free until the tangled blankets released her, and she rolled onto the floor. When she peered back under the bed, the faces were gone.

Her whole body trembled as she inspected the room, turning on every light, searching in the closet and behind any object big enough to conceal hidden danger. Again and again, she checked under the bed, but the horrible faces never rematerialized. Once satisfied that she was alone, she stood in the middle of her room and groaned. The night was ruined. She wouldn't sleep now. She'd have to wait until the next night to try again.

Pulling a sweatshirt over her head, she padded down the long hallway toward the bathroom, her socks muffling her steps against the hardwood floor. She lingered at her parents' bedroom and gazed down on the ghost of her younger self, curled up against the closed door, also too afraid of monsters to fall asleep. But the sound of their cheerful voices, a reassuring presence in the darkness, would lull her to sleep, and then, by some miracle, she'd awaken in her bed the next morning.

The voices were gone now, and all that remained behind that door were boxes of clothing, waiting to be donated, and dismantled furniture stacked against the walls. That's as far as she had gotten after her mother died and before Detective Foret's

The Tower

investigation had unearthed the guilt that now haunted her every waking moment.

Overwhelmed by conflicting emotions, she hurried to the bathroom. She splashed her face with cold water, but nothing could wash away the mask of exhaustion. As she stared into the mirror, an old hag stared back. She poked at the dark, puffy bags beneath the eyes and raked her fingers through the tangled, lifeless hair. "Who are you?" she asked this pale stranger, who to her relief did not answer back.

I'm losing my mind again, she thought as she dried her face on the towel hanging from the hook on the back of the bathroom door. But it wasn't the bathroom door anymore. It was the door to the locked inpatient ward at Everston Psychiatric Hospital, with the sign that warned visitors not to bring in sharp objects or shoelaces or matches, not to touch the patients or speak too loudly or look them in the eyes.

Then she was on the other side, her clothes stripped off, her arms and legs in restraints. She could feel the cold metal sting of the needle in her arm as the stony, unsympathetic face of Dr. Dilby leaned over her. "You're a very sick girl," he said, and she was sure she would never leave.

"No!" She flung the towel to the bathroom floor. She had to do something. She wouldn't let them take her back to *Foreverston*. She rifled through the bathroom cabinets, sure she still had some. Ripping one of the drawers open, she pulled it out of the cabinet. Its contents clattered to the floor and rolled this way and that across the white tile. She dropped to her knees and searched through the mess, pushing aside toothpaste tubes, combs, and cotton balls until she found the plastic prescription bottle. It appeared to be empty, but she shook it by her ear and heard the rattle of the few pills that remained. The ones that calmed her, that turned off her mind.

Dr. Denny had overseen the weaning process while she was in the hospital and made sure she left with no medications. And, per his request, she had dutifully turned over everything she had at home. She must have forgotten about these though—or so she tried to convince herself.

She twisted off the cap, shook the tiny yellow pills into the palm of her hand, and stared at them. They *would* put her to sleep. They always had before. But it wasn't real sleep with dreams and that delicious feeling of waking the next morning restored. Black sleep, that's how she used to think of it. A temporary death. Her mind would just stop. And when she woke from it, nothing would have changed. It was like quitting life for a little while and then being born right back into the pain and misery from which she was trying to escape. A temporary suicide. It had been so painful weaning off these awful things, but a hellish night stretched out before her now. The minutes would tick by so slowly, her mind fatigued but fully alert, completely aware of each passing second. Waiting, waiting, waiting for the sun to come up. She closed her hand around the pills. These could make it go faster, help her skip to tomorrow. But it would only be a temporary relief. And how would the next night be any different? Or the next? Or the next?

"Dammit!" she cried out, and with a flick of her wrist, she dropped the pills into the toilet, flushing them before she had time to change her mind.

The Tower

...

The diary waited patiently by the front door where Sam had deposited it hours before. She picked it up off the floor, ashamed that she had shown it and Dr. Denny so little respect, and took it into the front parlor. The room was oppressively dark, and though she tried to keep her rising anxiety in check, her free hand shook as it groped along the wall for the light switch. After what seemed an eternity, her fingers brushed against it. She flipped the switch, fully expecting the room to flood with light. But nothing happened. Flipping it up and down several more times in growing agitation, she stared into the unyielding darkness as panic gripped her chest.

She stumbled toward where she thought the floor lamp should be, colliding with the coffee table, nearly falling over the sofa, until her hand brushed the leaded edges of the tiffany-style lampshade. With a desperate tug on the chain, a vibrant mosaic of colored light burst forth, dappling the walls and chasing away the darkness. She let out the breath she hadn't even realized she was holding and settled herself in the chair closest to the lamp with the diary on her lap. Summoning all her willpower, she forced herself to ignore the shadows that still lingered in the corners of the room and focus on the object before her.

The leather cover was cold against her fingertips as she ran them across the edges. With a tingle of anticipation she hadn't expected to feel, she opened to the inscription and read it once again:

Why Did God Make the Tree?

*This is the Diary of
Alfred D. Cummings
Master Builder and Architect
Waylingbrooke, New Hampshire
23rd September 1887*

*To my Beloved Virginia,
I pen this diary as an account of all the moments during which we are separated, until at last I have returned to your gentle presence and can share with you each and every second of our time spent apart.*

*Your devoted husband,
Alfred*

Sam grimaced at the cloying sentimentality of Alfred's inscription. Yet still, there was a curious allure in the idea of a husband expressing himself to his wife in this manner. "You better not have a mistress on the side, ya bastard," she muttered to the diary and flipped the page.

*23rd September
I met with the Town Council today to discuss their plans for the Tower. In truth, I cannot comprehend why they are so desperate to have this eyesore looking down over their Town. Of all the projects I have undertaken in the past, the design of this Tower is the most dull and unappealing object I have ever encountered; the measurements are absurdly contrived, and its shape is that of an elongated tin can with a hat-like roof plopped on top. I dare say I shall have to spend the next several*

days convincing them that changes must be made; otherwise, I will go mad with boredom.

I also met with my Foreman today, a Mr. Argus Riley, a man of few words but impeccable qualifications. He resides in a neighboring Township but seems familiar enough with Waylingbrooke to procure reliable workers from the local population. I am certain you would find Mr. Riley quite disagreeable, my love, in that his hygiene and manner are less than sufficient for polite circles; however, I have the impression that he is a decent, hardworking fellow, and I am pleased to have him leading my workforce. My hope is that under his stalwart command, the endeavor will be executed with all possible swiftness.

I so regret taking this contract that brings me away from your tender embrace, especially now, since the construction will give me none of the usual pleasure I take in my work.

24th September

The oddest thing happened today, my love; I was approached by a small cadre of Townswomen, a clucking group of feisty hens, if you can imagine, who agree with me about the design of the Tower and who have an abundance of suggestions. Some of these ideas are quite feasible, and they are determined to approach the Town Council this evening on my behalf. It will not surprise me if they succeed in revamping the whole of the project ere tomorrow's first light.

I investigated the intended construction site today, and discovered that the ascent to the top of the hill is much steeper than I anticipated, necessitating a strong crew to transport the materials. But today, for the first time, I experienced that tingle of excitement I get at the commencement of a new project. If my lovely little hens do their part, perhaps this will not be so torturous an endeavor after all.

"Yep. There it is. You'll be banging one of those lovely little hens by the time your tower is erected," Sam scoffed, attempting to ground her anxiety in the more mundane. But beneath this, if she were honest with herself, lurked a deeper fear—that something far more ominous than Alfred cheating on his wife was about to unfold in the coming pages.

25th September

In the most peculiar turn of events yet, I was summoned to the Meeting Hall today by the Town Council; my hens were not only able to get them to make changes to their insipid Tower design but somehow prevailed upon them to turn the whole of the new design over to me. Ah, Virginia, I cannot express to you the rapture of designing from foundation to finial that which I will build with my own hands. The day could only have been more satisfying if you were by my side. Now, I must set to work designing this Tower, ensuring that its presence shall be felt by the entire Town, watching over them from its lofty perch.

Sam raised her eyes from the page and let them close. Though there was nothing in the diary to suggest anything about his appearance, a picture of Alfred started forming in her mind as she read. He was tall and thin with thick, dark hair, longish on top and in the back. He wore small round glasses—*they probably*

The Tower

would have called them spectacles—and his eyes were coal black. She saw him standing at the top of the hill, gazing down over the cemetery, the wind blowing his long coat, an expression of intense concentration creasing his handsome face. She smiled wistfully as she turned to the next page.

1st October

I offer my sincerest apologies for the gap in my entries; however, I have done nothing all these days except conjure the plans for my Tower—never have I been so overcome with such fervor for my work as I have for my Tower! My brood of hens has kept an almost constant vigil here at the rooming house, bringing me the most delightful food, while keeping the Councilmen at bay as I work tirelessly on the designs. I can scarcely sleep; the overwhelming excitement of the task ahead of me keeps my eyes from closing for more than a few moments before a new inspiration rouses me from bed to drafting table. Gertrude, the top hen as I think of her, has been supplying me with a special potion that she swears lays out her husband cold for a full ten hours; though I am sure, being an old man, he has less resistance than I to the narcotic effects, since it only gives me a few raucous hours of the strangest dreams I have ever experienced. In my fancy, the Tower is the chief actor in these nightly performances, which is no surprise since every second of my waking thoughts is dedicated to its realization.

Last night's Dream was the strangest yet; for in it, the Tower spoke to me—most peculiar since I saw no discernible mouth; however, as funny as dreams are, I questioned not that it was my Tower speaking to me. Even more peculiar was

*that it told me the manner in which it is to be constructed—
elevations and geometries of diabolical complexity—yet,
I understood and recalled them when I awoke and have
actually incorporated the suggestions of the dream Tower into
the designs of the real Tower. The human imagination is a
funny thing, is it not, my love?*

"I'll say," Sam agreed emphatically as she pictured the tower as it stood today. Its oppressive stature, its long dark windows at the top, glowering over Waylingbrooke. She could almost hear its voice, deep, booming, commanding. *"Look at me,"* it ordered. *"I am here."* Sam shifted in her chair, the springs creaking beneath her as she turned the page, her eyes momentarily flicking toward the three-paneled bay window as if expecting to see the tower looming outside her house.

Tucked into the crease between the pages was a pink ribbon, pressed flat and frayed on the ends. *Was this Alfred's placeholder? A keepsake given to him by his adoring, young wife?* Sam felt the silky material. A faint scent of lavender, barely discernible, lingered on the ribbon. She held it to her nose and drew in a long, slow breath, initially calmed by the delicate fragrance but then suddenly suspicious.

She frowned. "Subtle, Dr. Denny," she exclaimed. "Trying a little aromatherapy? You'll need something a little stronger than lavender to knock me out. Maybe a rag full of chloroform!"

She tucked the ribbon back into the crease and continued reading, torn between envy and anxiety over Gertrude's miraculous sleeping potion.

The Tower

2nd October

Ah, Virginia, I am destroyed! Today, I presented my design, my beloved future Tower, to the full Council in the Meeting Hall. At first, I took their silence for awe in the face of my genius, but as I stood at the front of the room, my heart swelling with pride as I gazed upon their faces, my sketches and plans tacked to the wall with every ounce of my conviction, I realized that their inability to vocalize was born of horrified stupefaction.

Councilman Stevens crossed himself with the gesture of the Catholics and Councilman Hertford averted his eyes. Then, with a vitriol I have never encountered, the lot of them began to shout and jeer, their faces contorted with rage, and verbally attack me with such unbridled hatred that I felt their words as strikes from a whip. I am not sure how long I endured their onslaught before my legs gave out, and I found myself on my knees, all my precious designs ripped and thrown to the floor around me in tattered pieces. And then, as if angels on wing, my hens broke into the meeting hall and rescued me and my designs from the ungrateful mob. They have brought me back to the security of my room, and even as I pen this, Gertrude has dashed off to fix me one of her calming tinctures. I feel without it my heartbreak and frazzled nerves will forever prevent me from peaceful respite again.

5th October

Gertrude's remedy worked beyond my expectations; not only did it plunge me into a sleep so deep I would not have known it from Death itself, but it kept me there for several days, during which time my hens worked such magic, it is almost beyond belief. During my slumber, they transformed the aversion of the Town Council to my plans into acceptance. A begrudging acceptance, granted, but an acquiescence nonetheless. In addition, these preternatural ladies have managed to mobilize a workforce beyond my best expectations, as well as secure the delivery of the necessary materials, which are expected to arrive within the week. My Foreman, Riley, only shook his head, his expression as solemn as ever, when I enthusiastically conveyed my wonder at the workings of these ladies. Truthfully, Virginia, they are either my guardian angels or demons trying to bargain for my Soul—either way, my heart and everlasting gratitude belong to them, whether it be for Heaven or for Hell.

My newly acquired workforce has begun excavating the foundation, and soon, I will see my Creation reaching into the heavens.

Sam shifted in her seat again. Gertrude's miraculous remedy, the town's sudden acceptance of Alfred's plans—something was about to go terribly wrong. She could feel it, and hanging over each word was the knowledge that Alfred would soon be referring to his *creation* as an *abomination*, the words of Dr. Denny's recitation from earlier that day echoing in her agitated mind.

9th October
The materials arrived this morning, many days earlier than expected, and my crew has commenced the arduous labor of hauling them up the hill. First, the timbers, the very

The Tower

skeleton of my brainchild, were dragged one by one. Initially, they attempted to employ the use of horses, but the poor beasts, unable to maintain their footing, were soon abandoned in favor of a more astonishing solution; the men themselves, in an act of unparalleled dedication and inexhaustible perseverance, strapped on the harnesses and dragged each timber up with their own strength. Gertrude attributes this remarkable display to my leadership and the genius of my design, and more and more, I am won over by her argument.

Riley, ever cautious, worries that the eagerness of the men may prove hazardous and has striven to temper their zeal; however, Gertrude assures me that the men she has chosen are ideally suited for the task at hand.

10th October

We lost a man today—the first Sacrifice to my Creation. One of the tremendous support timbers, having come loose from its deck, rolled down the hill and struck the poor fellow when his back was turned. Riley, who had secured the chains and shackles himself, is beside himself with Grief. The man's name was O'Brien, and I later discovered that he was husband to one of my hens. I feel a profound Sorrow for this loss, yet his missus shed no tears; instead, she displayed only pride—pride that my Tower was being built and that she had made the ultimate Sacrifice in service of its construction.

I realize it may sound peculiar to you, my love, but such is the atmosphere surrounding the construction of my Tower. Among these determined people, no Sacrifice seems too great; indeed, they see it as a tremendous honor that O'Brien will be the first burial in the Cemetery that will surround my Tower, a fact of which I was entirely unaware until now. Though, for reasons I cannot fully articulate, it seems strangely fitting. My mood has been very peculiar of late, and things I would have found highly irregular before coming to Waylingbrooke now seem quite matter-of-fact. I fear I have been too long away from your gentle influence.

12th October

Three more of my men have perished today. While laying the foundation, an unexpected tremor in the ground toppled half the wall, smiting the poor wretches on the inside: Phelps, Granger, and—to my astonishment—Councilman Stevens, all gave up their lives to my Tower. I was utterly unaware that Stevens had volunteered to take O'Brien's place, and now he, too, will rest with the others around the foundation of my Creation.

I find myself thoroughly exhausted, my love. Never have I felt so drained of vitality, so overcome with weakness. Yet my mind and body are still driven by some unnatural force to see this project through to completion. The Grief I felt today after losing my men was so wretchedly overwhelming that Gertrude had to shake me back to my senses; this uncanny woman has been my rock throughout this trying ordeal, and I know not how I would have gotten this far without her—or my other hens. But please, do not mistake my affection for anything but gratitude; they are wonders to me, but you, my love, are my heart, and I yearn to be in your presence once again. How I wish you could come to me now, in this hour of darkness and tribulation! Your serenity and gentle light would be a balm that these other women, devoted though they are, cannot provide!

As for Riley, he was utterly inconsolable, to the point that he halted construction for the day and has since vanished from the site. I am certain he has holed up somewhere to grieve the loss of the men, but Gertrude assures me that his despondency will pass quickly and that the project will recommence tomorrow.

Increasingly, I hear rumblings about town, whispers from those who feel the Tower project should be abandoned, that some supernatural Force is at work, and that what stands should be torn down and burned. Perhaps there is some wisdom in this sentiment. For now, I think I shall try to sleep.

Alfred's grief and exhaustion weighed heavily on Sam, making it difficult for her to hold the cumbersome book. As her eyelids grew heavier, her mind drifted to the empty graves on the hill, just above where her parents had been buried and then unceremoniously exhumed and reinterred. She'd never really thought about the rest of the occupants of the cemetery, the other people—mothers and fathers and sons and daughters—who populated her parents' final resting place. O'Brien and Phelps and Granger. Her head lolled forward, and the book fell from her grasp, startling her awake. She bent down and picked it up from the floor. The pink ribbon placeholder slipped out from between the pages, the sight of the frayed edges triggering a bittersweet memory that Sam quickly suppressed. She forced her tired eyes back to the page.

Why Did God Make the Tree?

13th October

I awoke this morning to a most disquieting discovery. It appears that some interloper has stolen into my room during the night, for upon rousing from my slumber, I found the contents of my secretary in disarray, as if subjected to the rummaging of a curious hand. Most peculiar of all, within one of the small gallery drawers, a trinket had been concealed—a rather beautiful Rosary, adorned with intricately detailed, many-colored cloisonné beads that call to mind the brooch I bestowed upon you on the morning of our nuptials . . .

Sam stood up, fully awake and seething. "He has some nerve!" she shouted and slammed the diary onto the chair, storming about the room in a rage. "A bookmark and rosary beads and the cemetery! Oh, I see what he's up to, I see! None of these doctors can be trusted. They're all the same. Constantly using your words against you. I see. Yes, I see, Dr. Denny." Her head spun dizzily from the fit of rage, sending her to her knees. She propped herself against the chair with her elbows and glared down at the diary. Yes, she'd told him about the bookmark she'd made for her mother as a child and her father's favorite set of rosary beads that her mother had given him on their wedding day. *At least . . . she thought she had told him.* Forcing herself to think, she tried to work out how he had done it. But her mind was too muddled to put her suspicions into any rational order. The book before her was old, certainly written well before she and Dr. Denny had ever met. Perhaps he had selected it because of these coincidences with the details she had shared with him. But for what purpose? After a few moments of confused reflection, she picked up the diary, crawled back into the chair, and gazed around the shadowy room.

Her fury had burned itself out and gave way to exhaustion and embarrassment once again. "Delusional and paranoid," she mumbled, searching the pages until she found her place. "Not everything is about you, Samantha Perez," she said, now determined to read the story without interruption, genuinely curious to learn the fate of Alfred and the truth about that tower that had now come to haunt her waking dreams.

> *. . . I am tempted, my darling, to keep this treasure safe for you, as the beads are of exceptionally fine quality, and the Crucifix, despite the ghastly image of torment it depicts, appears to be crafted from solid gold.*
>
> *I have my suspicions that the proprietress of my rooming house, a kindly little Italian woman by the name of Signora Giapetti, may be responsible for this mysterious addition to my belongings. She is a very superstitious woman, as are most of her lot, as evidenced by the large Crucifix that hangs in every room of her establishment. Why she felt I was in need of this extra talisman is beyond my understanding, and I am quite perturbed by the thought of her creeping into my chambers as I slept. However, I am certain that her actions were guided by her profound devotion and concern for my well-being. As such, I have resolved not to confront her about this incident, and upon my eventual departure from her lodgings, I shall discreetly return the beads to her possession. Henceforth, I shall take care to secure the latch on my door each night before*

retiring, so as to prevent any further intrusions.

On a separate note, there is still no sign of Riley. Should he fail to make an appearance at the worksite on the morrow, I shall have no choice but to seek him out myself and ascertain the reason for his prolonged absence.

14th October

Once again, my love, an unpleasant morning greeted me upon waking. I drew back the drapery from my window and nearly cried out. It was evident that a deluge had descended upon the Town as I slumbered. Gertrude's sleeping potion must have put me into a temporary Death, for I heard no rain nor wind against the roof. Yet the ground outside has been turned into glutinous sludge, and a heavy fog has set about the place; the Tower has wholly vanished behind the miasma. I have been forced to halt construction; to allow my men to work on such treacherous terrain would be to court disaster, and I will not tempt further Tragedy.

A late-night convocation of the Town Council has been announced, and I am summoned to appear. Riley remains absent, and I fear the Town's business this evening concerns the aforementioned man and the recent worksite fatalities.

15th October

The Town Council has terminated my Foreman, Riley. They have determined that his recklessness and inability to maintain control over the workmen were the cause of the fatalities. I protested, of course, believing that each incident was beyond mortal control, but the Council had already

The Tower

decided. I would have preferred to bid him farewell, but he has already been sent on his way.

In addition to this distressing turn of events, the weather has decided that it, too, dislikes my Tower, dumping an ocean of rain on Waylingbrooke for a third day straight. I do not foresee construction resuming until this ungodly flood ends and the ground has had time to drain and dry.

I believe Signora Giapetti has taken to creeping about my room again. When I returned from the town meeting last evening, I noticed that the Crucifix had been removed from above my bed. Perhaps she has taken it for cleaning. Nothing else has been touched, though. The Rosary remains tucked away in the secretary. I must have a word with her regarding her uninvited entry into my chambers.

20th October

I apologize for the lapse in my entries, my love, but as soon as that infernal rain stopped, we began construction again in earnest. It has consumed so much of my time of late that I have scarcely had a moment to eat or sleep; however, it has been worth every missed morsel and wink. I still cannot believe my eyes. As I sit here looking out the window of my room, I can at last gaze upon my Tower. Not complete, but growing closer and closer to its ultimate form every hour. Gertrude has the men working night and day now. The sound of the trowels slice and grate through the darkness. She has kept the pressure on me as well, incessantly demanding adjustments to the design of the roof, the windows, and the brickwork. They all must be perfect, of course.

Why Did God Make the Tree?

There are eight graves now. Nigh half my hens have sacrificed with the blood of their husbands. I have taken to help with the layout of the graves, though the Cemetery is not part of my contract, but Gertrude feels that there should be a symmetry to their placement around the Tower. She has instructed that one should rest at each of the five corners of the walls and five should rest an equal distance from the center of each, making a circle within a circle. Though I must say, planning ten graves when only eight bodies await burial seems to invite more Tragedy to my building site.

The weight of fatigue grows more burdensome with each passing day; Gertrude's remedies seem to work less and less, and I require more to achieve only a fraction of the sleep I once enjoyed. I fear that the man who shall return to the love and comfort of your embrace will be but a Shadow of the young, vibrant groom who departed from your side a mere two months ago. There are moments when I wonder if Gertrude sees something in my future and has reserved one of the extra graves for the enshrinement of the Tower's Creator.

21st October

More rain fell last night. The tempest raged so violently and loudly this time that even Gertrude's magic could not keep me asleep. I lay awake, listening to the rain's relentless pounding upon the roof above my bed and the wind's fearsome thrashing against the building, rattling the casements and shaking the very walls until the late hours of the evening. By the time it subsided, my nerves were so keyed up that I could not drift off. Though I must have at some

The Tower

point, for I remember having the strangest Dream. A chilling Phantasmagoria that possessed such an air of Reality that I failed to recognize it as a mere Dream until the following morning, when the sun broke across my room and Reason returned to my mind.

Believing I was awake, I walked to the casement and threw back the heavy curtains. This somnambulism must have in reality occurred because, indeed, when I awoke this morning, the curtains were still parted. As my dreaming mind peered out into the night, it noted how the storm had passed and the clouds had parted. My half-finished Tower stood out against the dark sky as a moonbeam illuminated it. And down at its base, I could see figures, women in the likeness of my hens, but berobed in white and barefooted. Can you imagine? Respectable Townswomen, running about in the mud, bereft of shoes or stockings! As if to further propel the phantasm into the realm of the inconceivable, they began to dance, not the proper dance that one would see at a church social, but a writhing, contorting, and convulsing display of such unimaginable depravity that my mind recoiled in horror. Then, to my shame, they let their robes fall to the ground and continued around the Tower in their demoniacal gyrations, naked as the days they came into the world. My dream self knew that he was witnessing something unholy and retrieved Signora Giapetti's Rosary from its hiding place in the secretary. And as I began reciting our Lord's Prayer and clutching the beads, I watched in horror as a man, resembling in every detail my former Foreman, Argus Riley, was led to one of the open graves and thrust down into it. I let out a shriek of such piercing intensity that it tore at my throat, leaving it raw and burning—even now, the pain lingers, a testament to the fact that I must have cried out in my sleep—I spun around and tried to exit my room. I needed to sound the alarum, to gather the aid of the other residents, and save the man. But my door would not budge, somehow locked from the outside. I struggled to open it, shrieking and banging on it until, exhausted, I collapsed dead asleep on my bed.

Needless to say, when I awoke, and on remembrance of the night's murderous events, I once again rushed to the door, but this time found it unlocked. My sudden and disheveled appearance in the hallway, clad only in my nightdress and wearing what I am certain was a wild expression of terror, was met by the astonished gaze of Signora Giapetti, who was busily mopping mud from the steps. Still clutching the Rosary in my hand, I must have appeared quite alarming to the little woman, who crossed herself and fled back down to the first floor, muttering in some obscure Italic dialect.

I have since gotten hold of my frayed nerves and have concluded that it was all just a terrible Nightmare, most likely brought about by my fatigue and the unnatural violence of last night's storm. Of course, I plan to investigate the scene of the imagined Crime later today when the sun has dried the ground a bit. I am confident that once I have verified with my own eyes that the events of last night were nothing more than the machinations of an overactive imagination, the lingering shred of unease will dissipate entirely.

I have decided to stop taking Gertrude's tonics, as I believe these are the cause of my hallucinatory manifestations.

The Tower

22nd October

It appears, Virginia Cummings, that you have married quite a silly man. I went up to the worksite to investigate the imaginary Murder, examining the ground like a Poesque character out of one of his 'tales of ratiocination,' when I came upon a procession of footprints around the circumference of the Tower. As you might expect, that lingering seed of apprehension from the previous night's events began to grow and flourish, and before long, I found myself on hands and knees scrutinizing the evidence. Most of the prints could be explained quite easily, of course, the identifiable pattern of work boots making up the majority of impressions. But I was certain that some of the smaller, more shallow prints were that of the barefooted sorceresses. In my consternation and fervent desire to uncover the Truth, I quite forgot my surroundings and ventured perilously close to one of the remaining empty graves. With the ground still being unstable from the rainstorm of the previous night, my weight and movement caused a landslide of sorts, and in the blink of an eye, I found myself submerged in muddy water inside the grave. After a brief moment of contemplation regarding my predicament, I stood up and tried to climb out. Well, as you can imagine, the earthen walls of the grave were as unstable as the ground above, and I made no discernible progress in extricating myself from the Death pit. It is at this juncture, my dear, that I must confess, with no small measure of embarrassment and concern for your perception of my masculinity, that I began to shriek in a most hysterical manner. The memory of the Nightmare grew painfully clear in my mind as I hollered and begged for someone to help me. I imagined that at any moment Riley's corpse would float up from the muddy water, eyes alive, but body quite dead. Though I am not typically prone to such fancies, I found myself in an absurdly emotional state, utterly unable to rein in my faculties. As I looked up into the rectangle of blue sky above me, I believed that at any moment the faces of those witches would suddenly appear, cackling and chanting their wickedness, and then they would begin to fill in the grave with shovelfuls of unhallowed Earth, delighting in my live burial. I am at a loss to say how long I remained in that wretched pit, for my hysteria escalated to such a fevered pitch that all sense of time abandoned me.

This shameful display of femininity was rendered all the more humiliating when, all at once, a rope unfurled from above, striking me squarely in the face, and Argus Riley's head, very alive and healthful, appeared over the edge. Quite calmly, and to my mortification, said he, 'Seems like ya got yerself stuck, Master Cummins.' Thankfully, my face was so entirely covered with mud that the man could not see the humiliation that burned at my cheeks.

Evidently, Riley had not left Waylingbrooke at all but had been staying with distant relations at the edge of town. He said he did not feel right about leaving and was worried about my well-being. When I pressed him for an explanation, he simply shrugged and told me to mind my safety. I should have pressed him further, but, caked in mud as I was and shivering with cold, I could think of nothing else but returning here to the rooming house and taking a long hot bath.

The Tower

Words fail me in describing the look of utter bewilderment on Signora Giapetti's face as I trudged up her pristine staircase, leaving a trail of muddy smudges on each and every step.

25th October
Today, I feel a renewed vigor. The timbers for the roof have been hoisted into place, and the completion of my Tower is now but a matter of days away. It is my most ardent desire that you come, my beloved, and stand beside me in celebration. Gertrude has arranged a ceremony of some sort, and she agrees you should be by my side at the dedication of my Tower. As I pen this entry, I do so with the knowledge that a letter is winding its way to you at this very moment, bearing instructions for the day and time of your departure. As I look back through my journal entries, I am filled with shame upon reviewing the hysteria and overreaction that marked my responses to the typical tribulations that all construction endeavors must inevitably face. I am convinced that the Melancholy born of our separation has painted even the most minor of setbacks with the hues of Catastrophe. But now that the end is in sight and your physical presence will soon be with me, I feel only elation.

Sam's eyes fluttered shut. She blinked, fighting to keep them open, struggling to focus on the words, but her lids were so heavy and Alfred was so happy. He sat at his desk writing, and she could see over his shoulder the long ink strokes, the joyous swirls of his letters.

A noise in the darkness outside startled them. They peered out the window, past the maple tree, and up the hill. The tower stood against the dark blue sky, roof rafters exposed in the moonlight. Down at its base, the gravestones were dancing. No, not the gravestones, but people. And they weren't dancing, but fighting.

Jumping to his feet, Alfred flew from his desk and down the staircase of the rooming house. He burst through the front door and onto the rutted dirt road, Sam a shadow at his back. Up the hill they stumbled, passing by the spot where Sam's parents would one day be buried. A deep longing pulled at her heart, but she couldn't linger. Tethered to Alfred by some dreamlike cord, she was towed helplessly behind him.

They hurried to the top of the hill, closing in on the brawling mob, and with a glance over her shoulder, Sam looked out over Waylingbrooke. She could see the Old Meeting House building, a candle burning in one of the windows, and the silhouette of a dark figure watching the scene unfold.

"They're trying to burn the tower down!" someone screamed to Alfred, who plunged into the fray, his fists and elbows flying as he fought to reach the tower. Feeling Alfred's terror and desperation as he fought side by side with his workmen against the raging townspeople, Sam watched in horror as a few of the rabble-rousers slipped through the defenses.

"No!" Alfred shrieked as they entered the tower, their torches flaming by the windows as they wound their way up the spiral staircase toward the unfinished roof. "Gertrude! They'll burn it down!" he bellowed.

Suddenly, a woman appeared. Tall and imposing, Gertrude

The Tower

stood beside Sam and Alfred, grinning her yellow, misshapen teeth. "Have faith," she said calmly, and they followed her gaze to the top of the tower where the torch-bearing attackers tried to set fire to the exposed timbers. Above them, angry clouds rolled in and blocked out the moonlight. Rumbles shook the sky and big fat raindrops began to fall. "See," Gertrude said with satisfaction. "Nothing can stop us now."

The wind whipped up and rain flooded down upon the townspeople, extinguishing their torches and knocking them back down the stairs. The tower was safe. And just as Sam was about to cry out in relief, she felt herself take to the air, propelled by the wind, higher and higher until she hung suspended directly above the tower. Her link to Alfred had been severed. With horror, she looked down upon the freshly dug graves that spiraled out around the tower in the shape of a pentagram. Two remained empty in anticipation of what was to come. Sam watched as the defeated townspeople retreated down the hill in terror, and Alfred fell to his knees at Gertrude's feet.

"Behold," the wild-eyed sorceress directed with delight, pointing to the bottom of the hill. One by one, Alfred's hens ascended the slope in a long, snaking train. Each carried a candle, miraculously burning despite the raging tempest of wind and rain. Each wore an expression of pure ecstasy. And following up the rear, a young woman staggered along, a look of confusion written across her innocent face.

"Virginia!" Alfred screamed and raced down the hill.

Floating above in her mid-air perch, Sam watched, powerless to act, as Alfred embraced his young wife, as he led her to Gertrude, as the rest of the tower's acolytes gathered and the ceremony began. Under Gertrude's direction, Virginia and Alfred were separated, roughly pulled from one another, and forced into the awaiting graves.

"Stop it!" Sam hollered over the roaring wind, but no one seemed to hear.

The couple vanished into the earth, and with uncanny swiftness, the hens and workmen showered them with shovelfuls of dirt. In a matter of seconds, the task was complete, and headstones erupted from the ground, marking the freshly made sacrifices.

"Wake up, wake up," she ordered herself, but the sleep she had been desperate for would not relinquish her so easily now. All over the hillside, headstones sprouted up, until the Tower Hill Cemetery that she knew was laid out before her. She willed herself not to look, but she couldn't stop her eyes from searching it out. Her parents' headstone jutted up more prominently than the rest, and to her horror, there Gertrude stood, her wide, yellow grin a beacon through the wild storm.

"You got your wish!" the evil woman cackled, her eyes blazing with triumph at Sam. "They belong to us now!"

Sam gasped and dropped from the sky, sucked down back to the earth, dragged past the tower and over the graves, and flung to the ground at the base of the hill. She scrambled to her feet and looked up toward her parents' graves. There they stood, her mother and her father, living and breathing, yet somehow still lifeless. Between them was Gertrude, directing them into the freshly dug graves.

"No, not my parents!" Sam screamed at the diary that was now in her hands. She stared at the pages, at the long flowing strokes from Alfred's pen that twisted and wriggled and coiled around her parents, binding them up in black shrouds of ink. "Stop it!" she shrieked and fought to untangle her immobilized parents.

As she struggled, Detective Foret materialized from the shadows, a specter from the waking world. His dark, intense eyes bore into hers, accusatory and unyielding. "Give me the book," he commanded, startling Sam into losing her grip. "It's evidence." The diary slipped from her grasp as Foret tugged at it. The tangles of ink tightened, constricting her parents further until they disappeared into the darkness of the page.

"No, not again!" she bellowed as the detective took possession of the diary and faded away. The storm still raged over the cemetery, and Sam bounded up the hill, determined to save her mother and father before it was too late. Faster and faster, she pushed herself to run. But the hill grew too steep and then she was tripping up the staircase, laboring up each step of the tower's twisted spine until she made it to the top and sprinted down the hallway toward her parents' room. Standing before the closed door, she blinked with the confusion of waking suddenly from the dream.

"Momma? Daddy?" she whispered and leaned her forehead against the door. Her heart thumped in the silence. She took hold of the cold metal doorknob. They couldn't be on the other side, she knew. But what if she were still dreaming . . .

She turned the knob and charged inside. It was just as she had left it. Boxes were piled up in the middle of the dusty floor. Furniture stacked against the wall. Their disassembled bed leaning against the window. Their disassembled lives sprawled in front of her. She stared at the belongings of her deceased parents that had been packed up and forgotten. Overcome with shame and anger at herself, she lunged at the boxes, tearing open the tops and rifling through their contents.

This one held her father's possessions. The familiar smell of his aftershave instantly transformed her into that little girl sitting on his lap, safe in his arms, as he read to her from one of her favorite books. She choked on a sob and groped blindly inside the box until her fingers brushed against her father's rosary beads. Collapsing to her knees, she ran her fingers along the pearlescent beads to the golden crucifix, clutching it until it hurt. Her entire body trembled, and she fought for breath amidst the torrent of sobs. She had left them in that box for so long, left them in the darkness, unable to look at them with the knowledge that they would never be held by her father again. He would never hold anything again, never smile, never help her with her homework, never call her his angel. "Daddy," she cried out hoarsely and slipped the rosary around her neck and under her shirt, pressing the crucifix against her heart.

She crawled across the floor to another box, one containing her mother's belongings, marked PERSONAL ITEMS in large, bold letters. Ripping it open, she recoiled at the odor. The smell of sickness and antiseptic still clung to the contents, and she had the awful notion that it still clung to her mother's remains, entangled with the atoms of her decomposing body. Holding her breath, she dove in and retrieved her mother's bedside prayer book. Her hands trembled as she turned the worn pages until she found the homemade bookmark—a tattered piece of cardstock with an asymmetrical heart in red and pink crayon, its purple tassel frayed and missing most of its strands. A birthday gift from six-year-old Sam that her mother had always kept close at hand. "Please don't be dead," Sam cried hoarsely and clasped the bookmark to her chest. "Please don't be dead. Please, please, please," she begged, tears streaming down her face. "I didn't mean it. I take it back."

You got your wish. They belong to us now! Gertrude's voice jeered from the dark recesses of her mind. She pictured her parents being shoved into their graves, no one there to help them, taken by the tower, that awful beast that glowered out over the town. It held them, imprisoning them in the cemetery with its spike-topped fence and padlocked gate, keeping them beneath the frozen earth to rot and disappear into nothingness.

"No, no, no," Sam refused, unable to accept their fate and the part she had played. She dashed out of the room and down the staircase, flinging open the front door. A frigid blast of wind struck her face and wailed past her into the house. She peered out into the cloudy night. Shadows lurked everywhere. But she didn't care. She flew down the front porch, leaving the door wide open. Her lungs ached as she sucked in the icy air, her stockinged feet painfully beating against the pavement. The shadows chased her, trailing behind her, reaching for her, but she ran too fast for them to catch her.

Her father's rosary beads banged against her chest with each stride, her mother's bookmark crumpled in her balled-up fist. The streets were empty. The moon fought to break through the clouds, beams filtering through in some places, briefly lighting her way. She rounded the corner and a gust of wind tried to push her back. But she fought against it, right up to the cemetery gates.

The tower loomed over everything, moonbeams illuminating it in a ghostly glow of silvery light. The trees around the cemetery flailed in the unrelenting wind. Sam tugged at the locked gates, shaking them violently, and cried out, "Let me in, you bastard!"

She could see the grave, the moon momentarily shining a spotlight on it as the clouds rolled by. Without thinking, and in an act more daring than anything she'd ever undertaken before, she heaved herself to the top of the gate and swung a foot over the side. It was only once she found herself hanging from the top that she realized just how high she was. "Bad idea, bad idea," she scolded herself. She glanced back over her shoulder at the street and started. Something was coming toward her. An inky dark shadow that pinched itself off from the night and now crept toward her.

Instinct pushed her over the gate, and she fell hard onto a patch of frozen grass. But she jumped up, fear propelling her forward despite the pain, not daring to glance back at whatever followed. The grass crunched beneath her feet, cold and brittle, as she sprinted up the hill.

She stopped before their headstone, realizing that this was the first time she'd laid eyes upon it since her parents' exhumation, too devastated to be there for their re-entombment. She read their names. "Francis C." and "Margaret A." She read their birth dates and their death dates. She read the epitaph, which ensured the world knew they were loving parents. Touching the rosary around her neck, squeezing the bookmark tighter in her hand, she dropped to her knees and lay down upon their graves.

The clouds moved in front of the moon and a cold darkness wrapped around her. "Momma. Daddy. I miss you so much.

The Tower

I'm so sorry! I should never have . . . but you were in so much pain and so tired." Then she shook her head. "No! It was my selfishness. I wanted . . . I wanted it to be over *for me*. I was selfish and weak and so tired. I just couldn't take it anymore. I wanted to be free. *It was for me*!" she wailed. "And I'm so sorry!" she cried. And cried. And sobbed. And shook with convulsions of grief and guilt until she was entirely spent and there was nothing left to confess.

. . .

The clouds had parted and moonlight blanketed the hill and tower in a peaceful glow. When he wrapped the blanket around her, she stirred, mumbling "I love you, Daddy," and started to snore softly. It had been a long night, and Patrick could feel the cold earth against his backside as he sat next to Samantha, keeping watch until daylight or until she awoke, which might not be until the next nightfall or another daybreak. It didn't matter. She could sleep as long as she needed.

He tried to make himself comfortable, leaning against an adjacent headstone. "No disrespect," he whispered to the occupant beneath him. He pulled the collar of his jacket up around his ears and stretched his arms. The wrist brace began to bother him, so, as quietly as he could, he pulled the velcro fasteners apart and rotated his ink-stained hand. He gazed up at the tower with a silent chuckle, his blue eyes gray in the moonlight.

Part Two

The Monster

CHAPTER FOUR

Patrick pulled on the heavy oak doors, fighting against the wind and hail, until they gave way with a screeching crack. As the doors opened, he stepped forward and peered into the darkness of Waylingbrooke's Great Organ Hall. Chilling gusts swept past him, sending bits of dead leaves and pine needles skittering across the marble floor. Urged by the wind at his back, he took a few tentative steps into the hall, barely able to see past the vestibule in the dreary midday light. A thousand ghostly voices greeted him, the hollow, tubular sighs of a lonely, forgotten chorus. Slipping Michael's keys into his coat pocket, he flipped on his flashlight, tucked it under his arm, and turned to shut the doors. Rain and ice pelted his face as he heaved at the giant doors, closing himself into the darkness with an eerie, final-sounding thud.

His light cut across the gloom as he scanned the vast emptiness of the place. "Hello," he called out, expecting to hear his voice echo back. But only silence answered him. He tried again, raising his voice to a shout, but the completeness of that silence stirred in him a desire to leave as quickly as possible. "Is anybody here?" Again, he paused to listen. But his voice disappeared into the darkness, absorbed into an invisible void. Pushing forward, he turned toward the main part of the hall, illuminating gossamer webs that stretched between the pew-like benches. In the stillness, the air was stale, unmoving, possessing the heaviness of a gothic cathedral. But this was no church.

Father Owen had told him that the now-derelict building, constructed over a hundred years before, had once been part of Brookfield College's music school. After the institution closed its doors, the hall stood vacant for decades until it was acquired by a foundation for the arts. In its prime, it was alive with the music of famous visiting organists from around the world. But now, silent and forsaken, the once-vibrant space exuded the eerie atmosphere of a giant mausoleum.

As he examined the walls with his flashlight, Patrick discovered thick brocaded panels on the upper portions. "Soundproofing," he sighed with relief, now understanding the unnatural silence. He continued up until his light reached the vaulted ceiling, and there above him, naked cherubs flew and danced to silent music. He walked down the center aisle, following the angelic dancers in their swirls and leaps until he stumbled against a set of steps that led up to the dais on which the organ console was housed. He had to quell the urge to cross himself, the long-forgotten altar boy in him reemerging, and, with an amused chuckle, he wondered what other reflexive actions still lurked deep within his catechized psyche.

Up above, he caught the glint of enormous burnished pipes

and understood even more the need for the soundproofing. The sheer size and number of the pipes hinted at the immense volume this instrument must have been capable of producing, and he had a desperate, childish urge to bang on the pedals and keys and make the building shake. He smiled and trotted up the steps, directing his light down from the pipes. "Jesus!" he exclaimed, struck motionless by the scowling face of a man. Not an actual man, he realized. But the bust of a man, *of the master*. Its head protruded in sharp relief from the dark walnut housing, watching over the organ in all its German baroque sternness. To each side of Herr Bach, the half-naked forms of behemoth men—*no*, Patrick realized—of muscular, bare-breasted women held up pillars that, in turn, supported the great organ pipes that reached up to the ceiling. But even the might of these Teutonic goddesses was not enough to protect the organ console itself.

Its electrical innards, with its keys and knobs and buttons and pedals, had been ripped from the housing of the console and strewn haphazardly across the floor. As Father Owen had related, some time ago a spring deluge occurred, the likes of which the region had not witnessed in living memory. The brook that ran alongside the building and throughout the whole town had risen and flooded the entire area. Although the building survived with minimal damage, the organ console suffered ruin, and the concerts ceased.

Sweeping his light back over the benches, Patrick scanned the hall for any sign of life, but it was empty. The thought of the basement loomed in his mind, and he rubbed his forehead. The idea of wandering around in the dark and damp bowels of the building held little appeal. "I need a sidekick," he muttered as he searched the dark for a way down. Off to the right, on the other side of the hall, a door caught his eye. The moment he shone his light upon it, Michael's urgent words flooded back to him—the pronouncement that had set all the events of the past month into motion: *"I did it. Just like you told me to. I trapped the monster."*

For a moment, Patrick stood in the silent, dark space, staring at the spotlighted door, almost too afraid to confront Michael's "it." But too much had happened and too much time wasted to hesitate any longer. Determined to finish this once and for all, he marched at the door—and right over the edge of the dais, falling with his hands and knees into a pile of building debris.

"Dammit!" he growled, trying to free himself from the tangle of wire, broken boards, and glass. "Jesus!" he cursed again as a sharp pain cut into his hand. Recovering his flashlight from the pile of debris, he examined the jagged shard of blue-green glass that protruded from his palm and sparkled in the light. With a swift, decisive motion, he yanked it out, wincing as blood dripped down his arm and splattered onto the floor. He gritted his teeth, trying to ignore the throbbing pain. Improvising with the materials at hand, he slipped off a shoe and removed one of the expensive silk socks Helen had given him. He wrapped the sock tightly around the wound, watching as the blood seeped through the beautifully woven fabric. He wanted to revel in the sock's ruination, to find satisfaction in the destruction of his ex-girlfriend's gift, but his bitterness was fleeting.

With the bleeding sufficiently stanched, he picked himself up and brushed away any remaining debris. "To the basement," he announced loudly after he slipped his shoe back onto his bare foot and walked slightly off balance toward the door. It was locked, of course. Holding the flashlight between his teeth, he fumbled in his pocket with his good hand, searching for Michael's keys. Trying each one on the ring, he finally heard the click of success, and the door creaked open. He peered down the steep, winding stairwell and frowned. "Perfect. I'm in a horror movie."

He laughed and couldn't resist narrating the scene. "The good doctor knew it was foolish to venture forth into the dark recesses of the building's basement by himself. But something compelled him against all his better instincts. With extreme caution, he proceeded into the depths of the hellish abyss, leaving the protection of the angels above to dance to their ghostly music. But it was his . . . his *duty? mission? responsibility?* Crap! Helen's right. I am a talentless hack." His face flushed with anger at the memory of Helen's spiteful description of him, and the bitterness he'd been struggling to grasp earlier came without effort. "Vindictive bitch," he spat and walked forward, missing a step, catching his sockless foot on the next step, and losing his shoe. He stumbled down into the darkness until he slammed into a door at the bottom of the staircase.

Somehow, he'd managed to keep hold of his flashlight, and, slumped against the door, he pointed it around, trying to get his bearings. Realizing the absurdity of the situation, the absurdity of his life, he laughed, the sound echoing in the confined space. What a ridiculous man he was, trying to play the hero, like one of the absurd characters from his absurdly written books. "Idiot," he said as he heaved himself up.

"Is someone there?" a small voice called out from the other side of the door. It was so low and muted that, for a moment,

Patrick wondered if he had imagined it. But then, something began to claw frantically against the wood. "I'm in here. Let me out!"

☙

ONE MONTH EARLIER . . .

Michael stood in line outside of the bookstore and danced back and forth in his spot. Every minute or so, he would stand on tiptoe and try to see inside. But there were too many people, and the posters on the storefront windows blocked the view. He let out a frustrated grunt and whispered to himself in a way that made the people immediately in front and behind him move away. He held his copy of the book close to his chest, protecting the sacred document. His thumb flicked at a torn corner of the dust jacket, and he continued to whisper loudly to himself. "I did it. I did what he told me. I have to tell him. He's going to be proud of me." The line snaked forward and he felt a jolt of excitement. He was closer now. "Almost there. ALMOST THERE!"

The elderly couple in front of him seemed to decide that waiting at the back of the line wasn't such a bad idea, and Michael was able to move forward again. "Thank you," he called to them with sincere appreciation. He was almost at the door. The next people who waited in front of him were talking about the book, and he wondered if they, too, had been recruited to complete a task.

"I love this book," said a scruffy young man to his companion. "I wish he'd write another one. You know, I heard a rumor that he had a nervous breakdown or something."

The Monster

"No. I heard he was sick of the publishing business and went back to being a psychiatrist. I'm just glad they released a new edition, and he's doing book signings again. I thought I'd missed my chance to meet him in person," said a young woman in a dreamy voice.

The scruffy guy snorted. "I'm sure he's got some kind of security, so try not to jump across the table at him."

"Ha, ha," said the dreamy girl. She opened her brand-new edition of *The Monster* and gazed at the author's headshot on the back sleeve. "Look at him. He should have armed guards around him," she teased.

Michael peered over her shoulder at the book. It wasn't right. The cover was all wrong. "That's not right," he said, pushing in between the two. "That's not the real book. See. This is the book." He held out his battered hardcover copy to the young couple and waved it back and forth.

Scruffy Guy exclaimed, "Wow, dude, is that an original edition?"

Dreamy Girl got excited as well. "Is there a different picture of him in there?" She tried to take the book, but Michael snatched it back and eyed the two suspiciously.

"You didn't get the message. You're not one of us." He stepped back and started whispering to himself again. "I did it. I did what he told me to do."

The young couple exchanged a look of bewilderment, turned back around, and continued their conversation as if uninterrupted.

"I think I'll ask him to sign my shirt."

"I think I'll ask him if he really did crack up."

She punched her companion in the arm. "Don't embarrass me!"

He laughed. "I'm sure you'll do a fine job of that all on your own."

The line moved forward and Michael grew even more excited. He was through the door. He could smell the new books and coffee and hear the indistinct murmur of people talking. And even though there were dozens of conversations going on, he was sure he could hear *his* voice over it all. Again, he tried to sneak a peek. He could just make out the front of the line, but too many people were blocking his view to see who was sitting behind the table. What he could see, though, was a large poster of the book's new cover serving as a backdrop for the signing area. For a moment, Michael became transfixed by the enormous black eyes boring into him—the empty, soulless, all-consuming eyes of his nightmares. He forced his attention away, turning his gaze to the tall blonde woman who leaned against the poster and looked out over the activity within the store. *She's probably one of us*, Michael thought excitedly. She was scanning the crowd, and Michael was sure she was searching for him and others like him—all who had gotten the message.

As the queue continued forward, Michael's excitement grew almost uncontrollable. He was only a couple places away from the front of the line, from standing before him, from telling him that he had accomplished his mission. He bounced up and down like a child trying not to pee his pants. "I did it. I DID IT!" he blurted out uncontrollably.

Scruffy Guy and Dreamy Girl glanced back with curious expressions. Behind him, a hushed voice warned, "Don't get too

The Monster

close to this guy."

And then he saw her notice him. The tall blonde woman had straightened up and fixed narrowing eyes upon him.

She sees me! She sees me! he thought, his excitement spilling over, causing him to collide with the couple in front of him.

"Hey! Buddy. Back off," Scruffy Guy warned. And he shoved Michael back.

But Michael barely noticed and continued to push forward.

"Stop it," Dreamy Girl yelled.

But the woman waved for him to come forward, and he pushed at all the people in front of him until they cleared a path, until he stood before the table. Tears filled his eyes as he gazed upon *him*. Holding a pen, surrounded by stacks of books, there he sat. Around his head glowed a halo of golden curls, and his heavenly blue eyes gazed up at Michael serenely.

"Hello, Michael," he said.

The thrill of hearing him speak his name left Michael weak in the knees and he stumbled forward. A din of excited voices blended all around him. Still, it was separate from them, from himself and the divine being before him, who stared into his eyes with complete understanding and acceptance. And then he remembered why he had come. He held out his worn copy of *The Monster* and began to speak. "I . . . I did it—"

The hit came from behind, and before he realized what was happening, several men had knocked him to the floor and pinned him down. The book had flown out of his hands, and he tried to look up to see where it landed. But someone slammed his head back down and ordered him not to move.

"But I did it!" Michael screamed and struggled against the

knees that dug into his back. "I have to tell him!" As hard as he struggled, he couldn't lift his face from the floor. There was a rush of feet and excited voices as people fled the store. Everything was chaos. And Michael was terrified.

He could hear a woman shouting, "Don't let him up!"

Someone announced that the police were on the way.

Someone pleaded, "Don't hurt him!"

And Michael knew instantly who had spoken. "Patrick Denny!" he shrieked.

"Patrick, we need to leave," the woman's voice demanded.

"No! Don't leave me!"

"It's okay, Michael. I'm here." The voice was calm and close to his ear. "Stop struggling. If you stop struggling, they won't hurt you."

Michael obeyed and relaxed his body.

"Good. Now, these nice gentlemen are going to ease up a bit." After a few seconds, Michael could feel the pressure on his back lessen. "Okay, now let's all stay calm."

He heard sirens in the distance.

"Michael, what do you need to tell me?"

He tried to lift his face, but the pressure on his head increased, his cheek pushed into the filthy carpet. Slurring his words, he managed to answer, "I did it. I did it just like you told me to."

"Patrick?" The woman's voice was agitated.

"What did I tell you to do?"

"You know."

The sirens grew louder.

"I want to hear you say it."

"I trapped the monster."

At that moment, there was a screech of tires outside. He could hear men shouting to clear the area.

"That's it, Patrick, we're out of here!" the woman demanded.

"Wait. Just wait! I need to ask him some more questions."

Boots stomped across the carpeted floor toward them.

"Clear the area!" a gruff voice ordered.

"Patrick! Now!"

"Michael, what monster? Wait! I need to ask—"

Michael could hear a struggle happening above him. Someone was trying to pull Patrick Denny away, and he couldn't bear the thought. With all his strength, he heaved himself and his captors up and over. Several people were knocked to the ground, and for a brief second, Michael was able to look up. To his horror, he saw Patrick Denny fall back, hitting his head against the signing table, which tipped over, sending stacks of *The Monster* crashing down on top of him.

Before the cry of grief could escape his throat, Michael was tackled to the floor again.

. . .

Patrick pushed Helen's hands away.

"You need to at least put ice on it," she said testily.

"I need to get to the hospital," he said, standing up. His head ached and it took a moment to get his balance.

"I agree," Helen said. "Let me get the car and I'll take you to Memorial." But Patrick turned to her and patted the pockets of her blazer. "Hey!"

"I need the keys," he said as he fished them from her pocket.

"I'll drive you!" she said, exasperated.

"I'm not going to Memorial. I'm going to Everston. That's where they're taking Michael." Before Helen could protest, Patrick rushed out of the store, trying to remember where they had parked the car and trying not to let the nausea overcome him. He squinted in the bright daylight.

"You've got to be kidding!" Helen was suddenly beside him. "He's not your responsibility."

Patrick just shook his head and kept searching for the car.

"He's a loon. We're just lucky I had extra security on hand." She waited for Patrick to show her some appreciation, but he continued to shake his head.

"This didn't need to get so out of hand. He just wanted to talk to me. Where the hell did we park?"

"Are you blaming me for this?"

He repeatedly pushed the car clicker until the beeping led him around the corner to the store parking lot. A crowd of fans stood waiting by his car, chatting until they noticed Patrick step into view.

"Hey, look. There he is!"

Helen was at his heels and unwilling to let the matter drop. "I did everything I could to keep you safe."

"I don't need you to keep me safe. I've been waiting for Michael to approach me since I got his first letter."

A crowd of excited and concerned people coalesced around them as they headed toward the car.

"Are you okay, Mr. Denny?"

"It's Dr. Denny," a young woman corrected.

"That was unbelievable, dude. Does that happen to you a lot?"

Helen fumed into his ear as quietly as her anger would allow. "I give up. You've lost your mind."

The crowd pushed in around them, and Patrick felt the world begin to spin. He stumbled a little, and an elderly man reached out a steadying hand. "Thank you," he said to the man. "Do you know how to get to Everston Psychiatric Hospital?"

The man hesitated and thought for a moment. "I think so. It's just off route twenty-eight—"

"Good," Patrick said, turning to the others in the surrounding crowd. "I'm sorry that the signing got interrupted. If you follow this nice lady back to the store, she'll make sure you all get free signed copies of my book."

Helen glared at him.

He turned back to the elderly man and handed him his car keys. "Okay, let's go."

. . .

Patrick rushed into the hospital lobby, skidding across the immaculate tile floor. Lester, the front desk security guard, greeted him. "Hey, Dr. Denny. You okay?"

Patrick ignored the question. The old man had driven like an old man, and it had taken far too long for them to arrive. "Did an emergency intake come through here?"

Lester nodded. "Yeah, about thirty minutes ago. Boy, he was a fighter. Screaming and crying . . ."

Patrick didn't wait to hear anymore. He rushed past the

guard and the elevators and pushed through a door that led to the stairwell. Despite the throbbing in his head, he bounded down the steps two at a time and slammed through a security door at the bottom, tearing into the emergency intake ward.

It seemed deserted. "Dammit," he said to himself. He looked down the corridor to the reception desk. There was no one there. Racing around the corner to the examination rooms, he tossed back the privacy curtains. No one. But then he heard the ding of the elevator and muffled voices. When he made it back to the corridor, his heart sank.

Michael lay motionless on the gurney, his arms, legs, and chest in restraints. But Patrick knew he no longer needed to be restrained, clearly drugged and oblivious to everything.

Dilby stood by him, scribbling notes on a clipboard. He peered over his glasses at Patrick. "Dr. Denny. Glad to see you're not seriously injured."

"I need to talk with Michael."

Dilby shook his head and went back to writing. "I'm afraid Mr. McKay here will be unable to speak with anyone for some time. He has had a psychotic break and will need heavy sedation."

Patrick glared at Dilby. "How long do you plan on keeping him like this?"

"Hard to say."

"I need to talk to him."

Dilby didn't bother to look up. "As his treating physician, *I* will determine when he is ready to be awakened and receive visitors. For the time being, he will remain sedated." The elevator doors opened, and the orderly pushed the gurney inside, with Dilby close behind. "Perhaps you can take the matter up with

The Monster

the director. You and he seem to have a special relationship. Though I doubt this particular patient will be reassigned to you."

Patrick watched as the elevator doors closed, and Michael was transported to the third floor—the lockdown ward for the most violent and disturbed patients. A sudden wave of nausea came over him, and he collapsed onto the bench by the elevator, laying his head down on the cushioned seat. The world spun in a chaotic blur before the feeling subsided, leaving him to reflect bitterly on his defeat at Dilby's hands once again. He pushed himself upright, cradling his throbbing head.

"Having a shitty day, huh?"

Patrick gazed up, bleary-eyed, and found Detective Hugo Foret standing over him, offering a cup of coffee from the lobby vending machine. With a gracious nod, Patrick accepted the warm paper cup and stared into the swirl of curdled creamer.

Foret helped himself to a seat next to Patrick. "Trouble seems to follow you everywhere, Doc."

Patrick chuckled half-heartedly. "Demoted to public disturbance calls, Hugo?"

The detective gave him a wry smile and shook his head. "Heard the call come over the wire and wanted to make sure Waylingbrooke's biggest celebrity psychologist was still in one piece."

"Biggest celebrity *psychiatrist*," Patrick corrected. "I'm touched by your concern, Hugo." He took a sip of the questionable coffee and grimaced. "What do you really want?"

The detective scrutinized Patrick with his dark, probing eyes. "It must be hard having such devoted fans. Heard this one tried to kill you."

"Michael is harmless. Everyone overreacted, and now that bastard Dilby—" Patrick stopped himself from finishing, knowing that Foret was fishing.

The detective laughed, drawing attention to his slightly lopsided mouth and the subtle asymmetry of his other features. "You really hate the guy," he said. "What is it with the two of you?"

The latent writer in Patrick always found the detective's face appealing in a rugged, unpolished sort of way. It was the kind of face he could write about—that is, if he had ever intended to write again. "Let's just say that Dilby and I see the world differently."

Foret pushed further, keeping up the same congenial tone. "Is it professional competitiveness, or just that he spoke to me about Samantha Perez's case?"

Patrick clicked his tongue and forced a grin. "Well, thank you for whatever this is," he said, handing back the cup and standing to go. "Have a good day, Hugo."

"I mean . . . I get it, Doc," Foret said, standing up as well. He leaned toward Patrick and said in a low, conspiratorial voice, "She's a nice piece of ass. And you wouldn't be the first guy to fall for that vulnerable damsel in distress routine."

Quelling the urge to punch the face he had been admiring only moments earlier, Patrick walked away.

"You can't protect her forever, you know," Foret exclaimed, dropping the chummy façade. "The truth is going to come out!"

Patrick stopped and clenched his fists, white-hot rage burning through him as he turned back on the detective. Maintaining a tenuous calm in his voice, he said, "I like you, Hugo. I do.

But maybe the question you should be asking yourself is why you're so obsessed with Samantha Perez and the death of her parents. You seem to have taken her case very personally. Perhaps some transference or deflection is going on that needs some professional attention. I can try to squeeze you in for a session."

Foret shook his head, his cool demeanor slipping. "You know she killed her parents." A flicker of something flashed in the detective's eyes. *Was it anger? Pain? Or maybe guilt?* He quickly regained his composure, but Patrick sensed he'd struck a nerve. The detective's obsession with the death of Sam's parents clearly ran deeper than mere investigative curiosity. But he didn't have the time or energy to dig into the psyche of Detective Hugo Foret.

"Your investigation was pretty conclusive that there was no evidence she did anything to her parents except dutifully care for them as any loving daughter would."

"The forensics were inconclusive. Her mother had fibers in her lungs."

"A single fiber of unknown origin, if I remember the report correctly?"

"Dilby told me—"

"What Dilby told you," Patrick hissed through gritted teeth, "were the ramblings of an over-medicated, traumatized teenager who was grieving the loss of her parents. The parents that *you* had just dug up from their graves and had butchered for no reason! Forget the fact that Dilby broke doctor-patient confidentiality. That narcissistic bastard was just trying to get back at me for taking over her case after he nearly killed her with his so-called treatment. Let me give you an important piece of advice, Detective Foret. Don't trust Clifton Dilby. He's dangerous and way more intelligent than you are. And he will play you all the way to the end of your career." With that, Patrick spun around and stormed down the corridor, trying hard not to let the excruciating pounding in his head overwhelm him before he made it to the exit.

Foret's frustration boiled over and he hurled the flimsy cup against the wall with explosive force. He yelled after Patrick, "We'll need a statement about what happened at the bookstore! I hear your biggest fan might have confessed to kidnapping someone!"

Patrick slammed through the exit door, the impact of Foret's words hitting him hard. Since Michael's first letter and their subsequent inauspicious meeting at the bookstore only an hour before, the growing unease gnawing at his gut had become almost intolerable. Now his mind had room for only one thought: *What had Michael done?*

• • •

The room was cold. Michael tried to open his eyes, but his heavy lids refused to obey his wishes. He felt pressure all over his body, holding him down. He couldn't speak, he couldn't move, he couldn't do anything about the growing terror that filled his chest. He heard footsteps approaching in the distance, an even, rhythmic sound. He knew those footsteps. But this was impossible. He had done what Patrick Denny had instructed. He'd put an end to the nightmare, but somehow, he had been plunged right back into it.

The Monster

A door opened with an ominous creak, and Michael tried to cry out but couldn't. The footsteps were upon him. The monster had found him again. He felt the buttons of his shirt being undone and cold hands slip the dead weight of his arms out of the sleeves. Then the zipper of his pants was drawn down.

No! he protested in his mind. *Please stop!*

His pants were tugged down over his bare feet and the shock of cold air made his body tremble. He couldn't bear it. Not again. And as he had done many times before, he willed himself unconscious.

CHAPTER FIVE

He was sitting. As darkness gave way to the light of consciousness, Michael felt the chair beneath him. He breathed in the cool, antiseptic air and became keenly aware of the sounds of life around him. Dishes clinking and rubber-soled shoes squeaking across the floor. People talking about changing sheets and administering meds and restraining Mr. Lupis again because he had pissed all over Mr. Antoine. An animated game of checkers between some guys named Martin and Ned. And then there was the moaning—an awful, never-ending moaning that underlay all the other noises and conversations. To Michael, it seemed to hold them together like the basso continuo of a symphony of the insane.

He blinked the rest of the darkness away and tried to bring the room into focus. There was a dullness in his brain that he recognized. A medication hangover. An uncomfortable reminder of how he'd spent his high school days. His mouth tasted sour, and he scraped his tongue against his front teeth.

"Would you like some water?"

The voice was unfamiliar. Michael lifted his chin from his chest and looked up at the man sitting across from him.

"Water?"

Michael's head lolled up and down.

"Nurse, please give Mr. McKay a sip of water."

A hand appeared from behind Michael's head, holding a small plastic cup, and pressed it to his lips. He slurped the tepid water, dribbling some down his chin. The hand with the cup disappeared and reappeared with a napkin to wipe his face.

"Is that better?" the man asked.

Michael lolled his head again.

"Michael, may I call you Michael?" The man did not wait for a response. "Do you know where you are?"

Michael didn't know. Not where, not how, not why he had come to be sitting across from this pudgy little man with the funny accent, white beard, and silly tie with a bunch of tiny Santas dancing up and down its length.

"Michael, can you speak?"

He wasn't sure. It seemed a long time since he'd used his voice, though he could be wrong since he was oblivious to how long he'd been asleep. He licked his lips in preparation. "Where am I?" he croaked.

The man peered at him over his glasses, his expression unreadable. "You are at Everston Psychiatric Hospital. You were brought here several weeks ago. I've been treating you. I am Dr. Dilby."

Michael tried to focus on what the man—on what Dr. Dilby—was saying to him. *Psychiatric hospital? Several weeks?*

The Monster

His mind reeled. What had he done this time? He tried to push through the medication fog, but he couldn't seem to pin down what had happened.

"What . . . what did I do?" he stammered.

The doctor regarded him with detached interest. "You have no memory of what occurred?" He stroked his beard and offered no more.

Michael squeezed his brain, trying to remember, terrified that he had done something really horrible this time. "I . . . I . . ."

The doctor looked to the anonymous nurse behind Michael and nodded. The hand appeared again, this time brandishing a syringe, which it deftly plunged into Michael's upper arm.

"Hey . . ." he protested feebly, but his lack of motor control left him unable to resist. He watched the syringe empty into his flesh and immediately felt the sting of whatever substance was now entering his bloodstream.

"Stay calm, Michael. It will help to clear your mind. You want to remember, don't you? And I want to help you."

He searched the doctor's watery blue eyes for the reassurance his words promised but saw nothing except cold indifference.

"Now, Michael, can you tell me what happened at the bookstore?"

"Bookstore?"

The doctor waited as Michael searched his memory, wading through his muddled mind. Whatever he had done, it had apparently occurred at a bookstore. He couldn't recall buying or reading any new books. Lately, he'd spent all his time rereading the messages sent to him through *The Monster* . . .

His eyes went wide, and his slumped body sat at attention

as it all flooded back. The book. The basement. Standing before Patrick Denny. Patrick Denny smiling at him, recognizing him, saying his name. A surge of exhilaration spread through him. The doctor's expression remained neutral as he observed the transformation. But the next memory sent Michael pitching forward out of his chair, only to be dragged back by the omnipresent hands. Stricken with terror and guilt, Michael whispered hoarsely, "Did I hurt him?"

Dr. Dilby regarded the question carefully. "Do you remember hurting him?"

Michael's mind ran through the events at the bookstore again. A desperate need to explain what happened gripped him, and he leaned forward toward the doctor, who promptly pushed himself backward in his chair and shot a look over Michael's shoulder. Once again, the hands pulled him back.

"I didn't mean to. I was just there to tell him I got the messages and did what he told me to do. And he recognized me! And said my name!" Michael paused a moment to relive that feeling of complete joy. "He knew me."

"Who recognized you, Michael?" the doctor asked.

"Him!" Michael looked at the doctor for some indication of understanding, but found none. "Don't you know?" he asked, suddenly suspicious.

"I want to make sure you know," Dr. Dilby replied evenly.

"Patrick Denny," Michael said with an incredulous tone. "He's a doctor like you."

Dr. Dilby adjusted the glasses on his nose, his blank expression momentarily betrayed by a grotesque facial tick that came and went in an instant. "I know Dr. Denny. He's . . . a colleague."

"Well, I went to see him to tell him—" Michael could feel the doctor's full attention bearing on him now, waiting for him to say something, to reveal his secrets. "Um . . . to get my book signed. Yes. Because he was there to sign books."

"You were there for the book signing?"

"Yes. And I was excited to see him and somehow I tripped and knocked him over."

"Michael, you were tackled by three security guards who held you to the ground. Dr. Denny was knocked over because you were struggling to get free."

"It was a mistake!" Michael protested. "He recognized me and I got excited. That's all. Just a big misunderstanding." His eyes dropped in despair, and his voice grew low. "Did I hurt him?"

"The head injury wasn't too severe. I don't think he'll press charges."

The thought of Patrick Denny somehow being angry with him made Michael feel sick. "No, no, he wouldn't do that to me. He understands. He helps me," he insisted.

Dr. Dilby's eyes narrowed, "How does he help you, Michael? Does it have something to do with the messages?"

Michael felt his stomach clench. He shouldn't have told him that. Alarms started going off in his head. He fidgeted in his chair. "What messages?" he said, trying to appear confused.

"You said before that you wanted to tell Dr. Denny that you had done what he asked you to do—"

"No, I didn't."

"Yes, Michael, you did."

"Well . . . then I was just confused. What meds do you have me on? Sometimes haloperidol makes me hallucinate and I say things I don't mean," Michael rambled, trying to explain away his words. He'd said too much. This was a trap. Dr. Dilby was one of *them*.

Michael's eyes darted around the space. They were in what seemed to be a communal dayroom, the feel of which was almost medieval with its high-timbered ceiling and large slab marble floor. Three gigantic arched windows looked out over a courtyard hemmed in by tall stone walls. It was a gloomy day, and artificial light flooded the room harshly from above, revealing the emaciated creatures in johnnies and slippers mindlessly shuffling past and sitting at tables and mumbling in corners.

The duo playing checkers was, in reality, only one man who was spinning the board around and alternating between the Martin and Ned personas. At a table near the windows, a nurse was trying to spoon-feed pudding into the mouth of what seemed to be a corpse. And then, in the middle of the room, Michael located the source of the ever-present moaning. Strapped into his seat, the bloated, pale creature searched the room with tortured eyes, his tongue protruding perversely from his mouth, his moaning rising in pitch as people came near and lowering when they moved away.

Michael knew that a similar fate awaited him if he didn't find a way to escape.

Dr. Dilby watched as Michael surveyed the room. "What did Dr. Denny tell you to do?"

Michael looked back at the doctor, now certain that he was part of the evil conspiracy.

The Monster

"How does he communicate with you?"

"I want to see Patrick Denny."

Dr. Dilby shook his head. "That isn't possible."

"Why?" Michael said suspiciously. "I thought you said you know him."

"Michael, you are a very sick young man in need of help."

"Patrick Denny helps me!"

Dr. Dilby regarded him coolly. "I think perhaps that Dr. Denny has made things worse."

Michael forced himself to remain calm. This was the game that evil played—trying to undermine his faith. But he would have none of it. "I don't want you to be my doctor anymore."

"That's not up to you," Dr. Dilby informed him flatly.

Michael checked his growing hysteria and said nothing.

"Do you understand?"

"Yes."

"Good. Now tell me—"

"It dwells among the living and in the light."

"Excuse me?"

"It pretends to be a creature of God, but it is an abomination. Those who see its true nature are instantly driven mad. Only children, young and innocent, untainted by the corruption of adult thoughts and desires, can withstand the knowledge of its true essence and survive. That is why it takes them, to feed off their vibrancy and strength and destroy the good that resides within them."

The doctor sat back and removed his glasses. He was about to speak, but Michael cut him off and continued his recitation.

"For centuries, it has fled unhindered, tasting the sweet

blood of wide-eyed innocence without anyone to challenge it. That is, until it came upon a boy—a seemingly ordinary boy like so many others, full of spirit and joy. But *Michael* was no ordinary boy, a fact that would soon become painfully clear to the monster."

Dr. Dilby remained silent.

Michael could see he'd gotten to him and sat back triumphantly, confident that he'd struck a moral blow against the enemy. He was about to continue, but a commotion outside the dayroom distracted the doctor. They both looked out at the corridor and saw that a male staff member was arguing with someone who was adamant about entering.

Dr. Dilby shot to his feet. "Nurse, please take Mr. McKay back to his room."

The nurse stepped into Michael's full view for the first time and smiled at him kindly. "Okay, Mr. McKay, let us get up your feet and we go for a fun, little ride," said the surprisingly pleasant, plump young woman with an accent that was even stranger than Dr. Dilby's.

But Michael barely registered her existence, his only concern to see who was being prevented from entering the dayroom. The voices outside the door had risen to shouting, and Dr. Dilby hurried toward them, barking at the nurse, "Take him out of here now!"

The nurse fumbled with the footrests on the wheelchair as Michael stood up. "Please, sit!" she cried. But he heard a familiar voice declaring that Dr. Dilby had no right to keep him out.

Letting out a desperate cry of joy, Michael stumbled over the crouching nurse, knocking her to the floor. Dr. Dilby spun around to see Michael staggering toward him, his legs unsteady after so many weeks of disuse.

"Someone restrain Mr. McKay!" he shouted.

"Patrick Denny!" Michael shrieked as two orderlies came at him from either side and dragged him back to his wheelchair. But Michael refused to let them stop him again. With surprising strength, he shook the two men off and rushed forward. "Patrick Denny!" he wailed. Dr. Dilby, with a quick sidestep, held out his foot and brought Michael down face-first to the floor. A sickening crack was immediately followed by searing pain that radiated through his nose and across his cheeks. With a whimper, Michael curled up on the floor and rocked back and forth.

"Get the sedative!" Dr. Dilby shouted at the nurse.

"It's okay. He doesn't need that," Michael heard Patrick Denny say and then felt his strong, gentle hands take him by the shoulders.

"Don't tell me what he needs," Dr. Dilby snapped. "This is your doing."

"I've got you," Patrick Denny said as he rolled Michael over and cradled him against his chest.

"It hurts," Michael sputtered through his broken front teeth.

"I know. But it's okay. It's all going to be okay."

And without a bit of doubt, Michael believed him. He buried his face in the man's chest and held on as tightly as he could.

"Don't!" he heard Patrick Denny exclaim, but the cold metal of the needle still bit into his arm, and within moments, the blackness had consumed him once again.

Why Did God Make the Tree?

• • •

"You are a menace," Dilby stated as he stood in front of the door outside the isolation room.

Patrick struggled to control his own anger toward the condescending man. He dabbed at his blood-soaked silk shirt, futilely attempting to blot up the stain. "I only wanted to speak to him. He was trying to tell me something important at the bookstore."

"The director gave you express orders not to interfere with Mr. McKay's treatment." Dilby shook his head in exasperation. "Today was a crucial day. I wanted to acclimate him to his surroundings and determine his state of mind."

"Why would you do that in the dayroom?" Patrick glared down at him. "You've had him doped up for weeks, and when you finally let him wake up, you do it around other patients? Why would you do that?"

"Mr. McKay needs to know that he is a sick man. This isn't a spa. It's a mental institution. He needs to understand that and accept his circumstances."

"Accept his circumstances? What circumstances? We don't know enough about his condition to judge what he needs."

Turning to peer through the observation window, Dilby quietly remarked, "Michael is a very disturbed man."

Patrick followed his gaze, squinting into the bright fluorescent light that spilled out into the dimly lit hallway. Michael lay on the bed unconscious, his wrists and ankles strapped down tightly. The emergency doctor and nurses had been called in to tend to his injuries and busily cleaned up his battered face. The stark sterility of the room was unsettling, and he worried about its potential impact on Michael's fragile state of mind once he was allowed to regain consciousness.

"You broke his face," Patrick said with disgust.

Dilby nodded. "He's a very violent man, as well. I should have kept him in restraints. I won't make that mistake again."

"You don't know that he's violent."

"He broke two of Nurse Delacroix's ribs."

"She said he tripped over her. He didn't mean to hurt her. He's just excitable. If you had just let me talk to him—"

"No," Dilby stated flatly and set off down the corridor.

Patrick called after him, "Are you really going to let petty jealousy keep me from helping him?"

The other man spun around, his face more expressive than Patrick had ever seen it, the look of complete contempt unmistakable.

"Doctor Denny," he said through clenched teeth, "I can assure you that I harbor no jealousy towards you, only professional disdain. You are irresponsible with the your patients, and your methods are based on nothing but pop psychology and hunches. I'm not sure what your motivations are, whether your sudden return to psychiatry is some publicity stunt to boost slumping book sales or you're just bored with your shallow life of luxury. But it is clear to everyone at this hospital that you are only here because of your celebrity and not your professional competence."

Despite a twinge of self-doubt, Patrick passionately defended his position. "Really? Your disdain has nothing to do with the fact that my methods have helped to cure at least a half dozen of your patients?"

Shaking his head in exasperation, Dilby responded, "There is no cure for what these patients have. You've convinced everyone that there is nothing wrong with them and sent them back out into the world, where eventually they will relapse, probably in destructive ways."

"Are you hoping for that?" Patrick asked bitterly.

"It has nothing to do with hope. It is an inevitable fact."

Though tempted to launch into a scathing critique of Dilby's professional competence, Patrick restrained himself, realizing that cooperating with this intolerable man was the only way to help Michael. Pinching the bridge of his nose, he tried to make his tone as conciliatory as possible. "Dilby . . . Dr. Dilby . . . I can help Michael if you let me. I know I can. Please let me."

Dilby regarded him for a moment before responding, "You know he's developed a fixation on you. He believes you've been communicating with him directly through your novels." He paused, then continued, "He can recite *The Monster* word for word. And he's convinced you named the main character after him."

Suppressing the impish urge to comment on Dilby's obvious familiarity with one of his novels, Patrick instead suggested with all the sincerity he could muster, "Maybe we can use that to understand what's fueling his psychosis and find a way to help him cope with it."

With a scowl, Dilby responded, "The source of his psychosis is not in question. The man is a paranoid schizophrenic. And a violent one at that. There is no cure. What he needs are the proper medications and quite possibly to be institutionalized for the rest of his life."

"Maybe," Patrick reluctantly conceded through gritted teeth. "But I've found that—"

"I'm curious," Dilby interrupted. "Have you *cured* Amelia Dearborne yet?"

Patrick flinched. "No. She has a very complicated case."

"Yes . . . yes, she does." With that, Dilby headed back down the corridor, a definite spring in his step.

Patrick bristled at the mention of Amelia Dearborne, a painful reminder of his repeated failures to help her. Dilby's jab, while infuriating, held a kernel of truth that Patrick could not simply ignore. But dwelling on these failures would do nothing to help Michael, and he forced himself to focus on the immediate problem.

"Dr. Denny?"

Patrick turned toward the voice that addressed him and saw a prim, elderly woman quickly approaching. She was petite and well-groomed, with an impeccably fitted wool skirt suit, leather gloves, and a stylish cloche hat placed precisely on her head.

"Yes," he said, his charming smile returning to him without effort. "Can I help you?"

"I am Patricia Huntsman. I am Michael's great aunt and his legal guardian."

A surge of hope filled Patrick's chest. If Dilby wouldn't budge, maybe—

"Stay away from my nephew." Her words were curt and definite, and she gave Patrick no chance to speak. "I do not believe in your brand of psychiatry, and I do not want you involved with my nephew's case in any way. Now, I've already spoken to his doctor and Director Anderson. They are both quite clear about my wishes. If you make any further attempts to contact my nephew, I will take legal action against both you and this facility. Do I make myself clear?"

Patrick sighed, resigning himself to the situation. "Perfectly."

Without another word, Patricia Huntsman turned and walked away, her pace as clipped and sharp as her words.

Patrick peered through the observation window at the sedated man, who, barely out of his twenties, had already lost most of his hair. Short, chubby, and ruddy-skinned, Michael was strapped down and swaddled in blankets like an oversized infant, drool running down his chin. His nose had been bandaged, and his head now rested to the side as if he were looking out at Patrick, as if, despite his unconscious state, he were begging to be rescued.

CHAPTER SIX

"Good afternoon, Estelle. Just need a quick word with him," Patrick said to Director Anderson's assistant. Striding past her desk toward the inner office, he noted the unhappy-faced woman neither moved to stop him nor protested, but merely watched him push through the door. "Anderson—"

Patrick stopped dead.

"You said you locked the door!" Helen hissed as she pushed Anderson off her and pulled her blouse shut.

He watched silently as she scrambled to tug her skirt back down over her thighs. Anderson, on the other hand, calmly did up his pants and tucked in his shirt.

"Patrick! Get out!" Helen screamed.

But Patrick didn't budge. "I think it's too late for modesty," he said bitterly, but despite his anger, he couldn't help but make the detached observation that Helen had a predilection for seducing men on top of their desks.

As the two fumbled with buttons and zippers and shoes,

Patrick averted his eyes, moving his gaze toward the large window behind Anderson's desk. They were on the top floor in the south tower of the old mansion turned mental hospital. Anderson's office looked out over the front lawns. The grass was neat but yellowing under an early winter frost. A copse of trees hid the winding driveway that led up the steep hill to the hospital. He let his gaze continue to wander over the landscape. Beyond another line of trees, he could see the steeple of St. Michael's and, just beyond that, the tower looming over the cemetery.

"Is there something I can do for you, Dr. Denny?" Anderson asked as he took his seat, obvious amusement at the uncomfortable situation playing across his face.

Patrick looked from Anderson to Helen. He was angry and, to his surprise, heartbroken. He could feel the rage red on his face. But he also knew there was no point in making a scene. Helen was doing what Helen always did, ensuring that she wouldn't be left out of Patrick's dealings.

She had finished putting herself back together and, smoothing her long blonde hair, glared at Patrick with a confused mix of anger and guilt. He knew that she desperately wanted him to react with jealous rage. Indeed, he would have loved to grab Anderson by the neck and bash his face into the desk again and again.

But he needed Anderson, and Helen could take care of herself. With his decision made, he calmly took a seat in front of the desk. "If you're not too busy, I have a request concerning a patient."

"Of course," Anderson responded genially. "Ms. Olssen, I hope you don't mind, but Dr. Denny and I have some hospital business to discuss. Please shut the door on your way out."

Patrick didn't need to see Helen's face to feel the fury radiating from it. But with a poise that challenged both men, she responded cordially. "Very good. So you and I will iron out the details of our arrangement at dinner tonight."

"I look forward to it," Anderson replied.

"Oh," she said, almost as an afterthought. "You boys might want to make sure this door is locked before you start *your* negotiations." With that, she slammed the door behind her, the sound of her defiant high-heeled footsteps receding away until they could no longer be heard.

Patrick remained silent as Anderson chuckled and straightened the disheveled papers on his desk. "She's a very . . . determined woman."

Patrick relaxed into the leather chair, his elbows resting on the arms, and steepled his hands beneath his chin. "Screwing my girlfriend was not part of the arrangement," he said matter-of-factly.

Anderson ran his fingers through his dark, tousled hair. "Ms. Olssen and I have been negotiating our own arrangement. Seems somehow she got wind that I'm writing a book."

Patrick nodded, "Yes, she can scent a good author from miles away. I wonder what other perks she'd be willing to throw into your deal if she knew you had, say . . . two books in you?"

Anderson leaned forward and smiled greedily. "I can only imagine. What do you want?"

"I think you know."

Anderson sat back, slightly deflated. "Can't do it."

"I thought you ruled over this place," Patrick goaded.

The director stretched his long arms and placed his hands behind his head. "Even though I delight in being the most powerful person in the building, there's always a higher power running the show. You know that."

Patrick pressed him. "You have the board by the balls. You know all their dirty little secrets and—"

"I'm sure you know that Patricia Huntsman is a very influential woman. All she has to do is twitch her stuck-up little nose and the board members shit their pants. If I cross her—"

"No one would have to know. I can slip in during the night and—"

Anderson shook his head. "Maybe I could have managed something before you pulled your little stunt today, but now the entire hospital knows about it. There's no way it wouldn't somehow get back to that old bitch. And I'm not ready to give up this job just yet. Maybe after realizing the benefits of our arrangement, I can afford to take such a risk. But right now, I have a family to support." He nodded to the framed photo on his desk that had evidently toppled over during his vigorous negotiations with Helen.

Patrick snatched it up and examined the image of the perfect family: Anderson, tall and tan and ironed and coiffed; his buxom wife with the raven hair, manicured and made up and vacantly smiling; and his three teenage boys, all perfect facsimiles of their father, right down to the arrogant glint in their conceited eyes.

"I'm sure they are all very proud of you," Patrick said dryly, placing the photo back on the desk.

"Yes, we're the fucking Cleavers. The point is that this job isn't enough for me anymore, and I'm looking forward to eventually telling the board to go to hell. But you haven't come through with your side yet, and I'm not willing to go out on a limb for you until you do."

"I told you that you'll have it by the summer."

"Well, then we can revisit this conversation at that time."

"It'll be too late by then!"

A predatory glow lit up Anderson's eyes. "Too late for what?"

Patrick blinked, realizing his outburst had betrayed his urgency. He knew it would be a mistake to confide in Anderson his suspicions about what Michael might have done. The more he learned about Michael's obsession with him and his books, the more he feared the man's delusions had blurred the lines between story and reality, taking the plot of *The Monster,* in particular, too literally. "I just don't want to see Dilby do any permanent damage."

Anderson studied him for a moment. "Dilby is getting old. He won't be here forever. And I'll need a suitable replacement."

Patrick sighed. "I don't want his job. I just want to see this one patient."

"Let me consider our options and I'll get back to you," Anderson said, leaning back in his chair once again.

"Don't take too long," Patrick warned as he stood, trying to keep the desperation out of his voice.

"Denny." Anderson rose from his seat, his full stature partially blocking the window behind him. He glared at Patrick with deadly intensity. "I'm not screwing around with you when I say stay away from Michael McKay until I say otherwise. Even though I would hate to ruin our arrangement, I will bury you if you fuck with me."

"Understood," Patrick replied, but his mind was already racing with thoughts of defiance despite the clear warning. As he turned to leave, he paused, his attention captured by two large paintings flanking the door.

"Remarkable, aren't they?" Anderson said, his expression shifting with disturbing ease from anger to enthusiasm. "They're Goyas. Reproductions, of course, but exquisitely done, don't you think?"

"Yes," Patrick said absently as he examined one of the grotesque paintings more closely. Of course, he had immediately recognized it, the naked lunatics praying, fighting, languishing in their prison of shadow and light. "*Manicomio*—The Madhouse."

Anderson rounded his desk and pointed to the other painting. "This one here in the courtyard . . . I find this one even more appealing. Look at the faces, the eyes, the mouths. Can you feel the pain, the malice?"

Indeed, the images exuded a chilling despair, horror, and malevolence that was both fascinating and repulsive. But what affected Patrick the most was the wild glint in Anderson's eyes, the perverse pleasure in his voice. "They're incredible. But don't you think these particular works are a questionable subject matter? I mean, this is the office of the head administrator of a psychiatric hospital."

Anderson's enthusiasm cooled at the criticism. "They were a gift. And I think they are quite suitable for this environment. They're a reminder of how much more humane psychiatric institutions have become. We no longer throw the mentally ill together into dungeons and then forget about them."

"Right," Patrick scoffed. "Now we just drug them, tie them

down, and then forget about them."

Anderson's cheek twitched. "I think we're done here," he dismissed Patrick with a wave and returned to his desk.

Patrick shut the door behind him.

Estelle greeted him with her customary scowl and shook her head. In a rare moment of communicativeness, she admonished, "When you dance with the devil . . ."

". . . you get burned," he finished for her.

• • •

Patrick jogged down the stone steps at the back of the building. A shock of cold air blasted his face, still burning with the anger and humiliation of being cuckolded. He noted with clinical detachment how strongly his subconscious angst manifested itself in his physiological responses. It was just further evidence for his belief that most illnesses, whether mental or physical, were at their root manifestations of psychic trauma.

He knew he would eventually have to deal with the Helen situation before he ended up with a brain tumor, but for the moment, it would have to wait until the more pressing matter concerning Michael was resolved. Not at all dissuaded by Anderson's threat, Patrick was concerned that Dilby would more doggedly block his efforts.

He stopped, gazing back at the hospital and contemplating his next move. The once stately manor, modeled after a medieval French chateau, stood in stark relief against the gray winter sky. With its towers, parapets, and crenelated walls, the late-nineteenth-century building had been christened "the castle" by the locals of Waylingbrooke early in its history. Over time, many fantastic stories attached themselves to the property as it passed from owner to owner: the debauchery of the predatory headmaster during its stint as an all-boys preparatory school; the ghostly wanderings of the self-murdered monk from the days when the Catholic Church had bought up all the properties in the area; and most recently, the tale of the Witch of Waylingbrooke currently locked up behind the castle walls. Patrick winced at the thought and silently vowed that Michael would not become another one of those lost to the morbid legends of this place.

Determined to take action, Patrick started on his way again, patting all his pockets in search of his phone. "Dammit," he swore under his breath, wondering where he had left it this time. He needed Archie Philbin's help, even though his friend was consumed with the opening of Halcyon House.

Pride and envy mingled as Patrick thought of Archie's accomplishment, overseeing a new hospice dedicated to Alzheimer's patients and built in his mother's memory. Although he hated to burden Archie at such a crucial time, he felt he had no choice. His immediate focus was Michael.

As he pondered his next move, he glanced up. Gray clouds swept across the sky and a front of darker and more ominous ones moved in. Little pellets of ice stung his cheeks, and he hastened his pace. He needed to get back to his office in town and call Archie. Then he planned to revisit *The Monster*. He hadn't read it in years despite the recent reissue Helen had orchestrated with his publisher behind his back. That novel in particular had always struck too close to home, making him ashamed to have profited from the tragic circumstances of his childhood. It was a fact that Helen exploited in her marketing campaign, touting the novel as a thinly veiled autobiography. Patrick resented how Helen had pushed for the reissue without his consent. But that was Helen, always working an angle.

Down a second set of steps, Patrick rounded a corner into the staff parking lot, intrigued by the uncanny concurrence of thought and reality as the subject of his abstract musings appeared immediately and concretely in front of him. Helen leaned against the hood of his car, and when she saw him, she dropped her cigarette to the ground and stamped it out with her signature Louboutin. Her expression was neutral, but Patrick knew that there was about to be a scene.

"I guess you caught me again," she snapped, grinding the cigarette into the pavement with her red-bottomed shoe.

Patrick pressed the clicker to unlock his car and tried to keep his voice neutral. "I don't care if you smoke or not, Helen. But you should get to your car. There's a storm coming."

"You left me no choice," she said, ignoring his warning. "How could you do that to me?"

He opened his car door. "I believe Anderson was the one doing *that* to you."

Shoving him aside, she slammed the door shut with both hands. "I'm your agent. You left me out of the whole thing. You have no right to negotiate deals without me!" Her eyes smoldered. But behind the fury, Patrick could see pain and fear driving her.

Conflicted by a desire to console her, to assure her that a single act of infidelity could not sever their bond, he hesitated. But he was still too angry and hurt to be the one to take the high road. He stormed to the other side of the car. "Keep your voice down," he hushed her, glancing around to make sure they were alone. "What goes on between Anderson and me is none of your business. You're not my agent anymore. You're my girlfriend."

The sky darkened around them and sleet bounced off the tops of the cars. Helen followed him around and held the passenger door shut. "None of my business? Excuse me, but we still have a contract," she said, her voice rising. "And if you try to publish anything without my representation, you are breaking that contract."

"I'm not publishing anything," he hissed.

"But you're writing. Writing for that bastard," she yelled, pointing back at the building.

"You just screwed that bastard!" he exclaimed, the ferocity in his voice surprising even himself.

But undaunted, Helen struck back, "You have no right to give your writing away like this. I've worked too hard to make you a successful writer. Without me, you would never have been published and no one would know your name!"

He rushed back around to the driver's side of the car and opened the door quickly enough to wedge his body in before she could stop him.

"Do you know how hard it was to get your stuff published? No one wanted to even look at it. I worked my ass off to get you every one of those book deals."

Patrick slipped into his seat and pulled out his keys. He tried to shut his door, but Helen used her body to hold it open.

"And now you're just throwing it all away—all the money, the parties, the traveling—for what? So you can pretend to be some sort of Albert Schweitzer! Christ, Patrick," she sneered.

The Monster

"Anderson didn't even hire you because you're a good doctor. He hired you because he thinks you're some literary genius who can help him break into publishing. He hired you because I convinced the world that you're an amazing writer and not some talentless hack."

"That's enough," Patrick warned her. "Stop talking before you take this too far."

But she wouldn't relent, her voice approaching a hysterical pitch as the storm whipped up around her. "Tell me, Patrick, without me, do you think anything you write can get published? Without the name that I created for you, it's worthless."

He knew she didn't mean it, that she was lashing out because of her own insecurities about their relationship, that she was terrified she'd finally pushed him away like all the other men in her life. But Helen possessed a ruthless ability to identify and target the weaknesses of others, exploiting them mercilessly when she felt vulnerable. With Patrick, she wielded the intimate knowledge of his insecurities like a weapon, aiming for the most sensitive areas to inflict the deepest wounds.

"Don't worry, Helen," he retorted, unable to stop himself from striking back. "I'm sure Anderson will happily let you whore yourself out to continue to sell my books."

"Finally!" she exclaimed. "We're finally getting to it. You think I'm a whore?"

He shook his head, immediately regretting his spiteful words. "No, I didn't . . . I did not mean that." He knew they were letting it go too far. They both needed time to cool off. "Helen, let's just stop this right now before we both say more things we don't mean."

"Come on, Patrick. Let me have it. I'm a whore. I was a whore when we met. And I'm still a whore even after the great Patrick Denny lowered himself to be with me. The high and mighty Dr. Patrick Denny on his great mission to help the sick and weak." She laughed, a throaty, semi-hysterical laugh, and looked at him with pain and disgust. "If only the world knew how screwed up you really are! Crying out for your mommy and daddy in the middle of the night—"

Helen's voice faltered, her abrupt silence a sign that she knew she'd gone too far.

Patrick couldn't meet her eyes. The sleet had turned to an icy rain that pounded on the metal roof above his head. He turned the key in the ignition and the car rumbled to life.

"Wait," Helen said, her voice barely audible over the sound of the storm. She reached into her bag and pulled out a book and a ring of keys. "Here," she said, thrusting the objects toward him, the keys jingling in her trembling hand. "I found these at the bookstore the day Michael attacked you."

Patrick took the book and the keys, shaking his head in disbelief. "You've had these for almost a month?"

"Yes," was her only response.

"Do you ever think about anyone but yourself?"

Helen remained silent. The relentless downpour had soaked her through, and she stood dripping and shaking uncontrollably.

Patrick placed Michael's well-worn copy of *The Monster* on the passenger seat and slipped the heavy set of keys into his jacket pocket. "I'll be out of the apartment by tonight," he said flatly.

She stumbled back from the car. Clutching her bag to her chest protectively, she made way for Patrick to leave her.

The Monster

Still unable to look her in the eye, Patrick shut the door, put the car in gear, and sped away from the parking lot, his tires screeching against the wet pavement. As he drove on, Helen's figure blurred in the rearview mirror, her drenched, diminished form fading into the curtain of rain until she disappeared from sight.

CHAPTER SEVEN

When Patrick arrived at his office, he found Father Owen leaning against his door, taking an impromptu nap. Their appointment had slipped from Patrick's mind after the day's tumultuous events, and he had a desperate urge to back away quietly before the elderly man caught sight of him. But just as Patrick was about to flee, the priest opened his eyes and said, "I thought you might have forgotten me."

"I did," Patrick admitted and shook the man's hand. "Sorry, Father. It's been one of those days," he said, unlocking the door and showing the priest inside.

"Yes," Father Owen agreed. "I'm very familiar with that look. I hope it isn't concerning Amelia."

Dropping his overnight bag by the door, Patrick gestured to the priest to take a seat and tried to ignore the question.

"Bit chilly," the old man commented, rubbing his hands.

Patrick went to the radiator and felt the top. The metal was cold. He sighed. The proprietor of his office building liked to turn the furnace down on Friday afternoons, incorrectly assuming the building would be unoccupied over the weekend. He'd forgotten this when he'd decided to spend the next several nights sleeping in his office. "To be honest," Patrick said as he sat behind his desk, "I haven't been to see Amelia for a few days."

The priest's brow creased. "Oh. Is it the McKay boy?"

"Partly. I still haven't been allowed to speak with him," he said bitterly.

Father Owen nodded and examined Patrick with cloudy brown eyes. "What's the other part?"

"Girlfriend trouble."

"Serious?"

Patrick shrugged. "Typical relationship issues—spite, jealousy, betrayal."

"Ah . . . *in flagrante delicto.*"

Patrick chuckled.

"How is Michael doing?" the priest asked, mercifully changing the subject.

"I wish I could say. His aunt has forbidden me from seeing him."

Father Owen's lips tightened, and leaning in with a grave expression, he cautioned, "You must tread carefully with Patricia Huntsman. She's . . ." He grappled for the right word, and just as Patrick was poised to offer his own colorful suggestion, declared, "unforgiving."

Patrick smirked at the priest's understated description of the formidable woman. "Tell me more about the family," he said, already knowing that Michael had been separated from his parents at an early age and that Patricia and her husband Phineas

The Monster

were distant relatives who had become his guardians. However, these fragments were the extent of the information he could dig up about them.

"Well, they're rich and very influential," Father Owen began. "They're on the boards of most of the important municipal and charitable institutions in the area. They have no children of their own. Patricia comes from money." He paused, considering. "I'm not sure about Phineas's background, but I think he took more interest in the boy than she did. He seemed to be the one who directed his education and such. But Michael was always a troubled young man," the priest continued. "As a teenager, he was in and out of institutions. From what I know of him, though, he was never dangerous or violent, just emotionally troubled. A few years ago, Patricia got him a job as a caretaker at the organ hall. We're both on the board of trustees there. She said that Michael is very knowledgeable about music. I've only met him a few times, but as far as I know, there hadn't been any recent incidents with him until your encounter."

Patrick sat back in his chair and thought about Michael's life. Losing his mother and father. Living with relatives he hardly knew. He visualized a little boy, deposited with strangers who didn't know or love him. A sharp pain stabbed at his heart. How lonely and frightening it had been . . .

The priest cleared his throat.

"Um, yes," Patrick stammered, shaken from his reverie. "It's strange that he should suddenly become so unstable. Something must have happened."

"Come to think of it," Father Owen said, "I believe Phineas has recently taken ill. He hasn't been attending any social events in the past few months that I'm aware of. It's hard to say what's happening in that family. They are very private people. Some would say they're a bit paranoid about their privacy and—" The priest shook his head, amused at himself. "Listen to me. I'm becoming a gossip."

Patrick grinned. "An affliction hard to avoid in a small town."

Father Owen nodded. "Well, perhaps we should get to what I came for. Amelia. Do you see any hope for the poor woman?"

Of all the patients Patrick had treated in the two years since he started his practice and began working at Everston, Amelia was the only one he was tempted to give up on. He shook his head. "I wish I could tell you I knew what to do, but . . ."

"Please don't give up on her yet," the old man pleaded. "Hope is all her parents have at the moment. And your involvement is the only hope they've had for so long. The way you helped Samantha—"

"How is Samantha?" Patrick interrupted, desperate to steer Father Owen away from the subject of Amelia's case.

The priest's face brightened. "She just finished her freshman year at Oak Ridge. She's decided to sell the house. And I think she has a boyfriend, but she's only hinted at that. She doesn't want me to know she's living in sin," he chuckled.

Patrick could tell from the priest's delighted face that, premarital excursions aside, he was genuinely thrilled at Sam's progress. He, too, was delighted to hear that Sam was thriving and moving forward with her life after the tragedy and trauma she had suffered. Though he felt a strong connection to all his patients, Samantha Perez held a special place for him above all the others, and he, too, couldn't help but smile at the news of her happiness.

"You saved her," the priest said earnestly. "I know you can help Amelia as well."

Patrick nodded, his momentary pleasure buried under the priest's pleading words. "I'll keep trying," he promised and felt the weight on his shoulders grow a little heavier.

. . .

Curled up on the undersized sofa, Patrick tried to cover himself with a small wool blanket that barely reached to his feet. It was almost ten when Father Owen had left for the parish house, and Patrick was exhausted, his body and mind completely worn out. But lying on the hard, little sofa, with the moon lighting up his office and the air so cold he could see his breath, he was sure sleep wouldn't come easily.

He couldn't remember the last time he had slept without Helen by his side and wondered how she would fare all alone. *That is, if she is alone*, he thought bitterly, and he couldn't stop himself from visualizing Anderson's gigantic naked body stretched out on their king-size bed next to her. He wasn't sure what made him angrier—her cheating on him with that bastard, bringing up his dead mother and father, or keeping Michael's stuff from him.

She'd known how urgent Michael's case was. Yet she'd held on to the book and keys—possible clues—without a word. And Patrick knew why. Leverage. She was always scheming, always trying to keep the upper hand.

"Conniving bitch," he muttered out loud. But even as he said it, a pang of guilt, a small, familiar seed of shame, gnawed at him. He knew why Helen did the things she did, her traumatic past resurfacing and compelling her to retreat into old defensive patterns. And he knew that his sudden career change must have seemed a betrayal.

"Dammit!" he growled, wrestling the blanket off as he sat up. "Stop making excuses for her!"

Giving up on sleep, he reached into his overnight bag and rummaged through it until he found Michael's keys and copy of *The Monster*. He set the book on the sofa and examined the keys. He'd already identified the ones to Michael's one-room apartment, and upon investigation, had found it ruthlessly cleaned and stripped of all personal items. Worn down and oddly shaped, the remaining keys had been a mystery to him, that is, until his conversation with Father Owen. First thing in the morning, he would visit the Great Organ Hall.

He tossed the keys into his bag and picked up the book. Turning *The Monster* over in his hands, he tried to remember the person he was when he'd written it almost fifteen years before. He flipped to the inside of the back cover and stared at the younger version of himself, the intense pose, a pretentious air of intellectual self-importance in his eyes.

"Arrogant prick," he muttered.

He hesitated before opening to the first page. The story—born from the depths of his childhood pain—was the darkest of his tales of horror. But instead of providing the catharsis he had hoped for, writing about his trauma had plunged him back into the nightmare, consuming him and nearly destroying his sanity.

The Monster

Desperate to suss out any clues Michael might have left, Patrick began flipping through the pages, he found no notes, no markings, or anything that might help him understand what Michael was trying to tell him at the bookstore. He placed the book on his lap, letting it fall open to a random page. "The neighborhood was quiet," he read, and with those four words, he shut his eyes and the entirety of the story unfolded in his mind, transporting him into the world of his own creation . . .

Clouds, wispy and white, floated lazily through the vast blue sky above, their shadows rolling over Michael's body as he lay on his belly in the grass. The boy kicked up his bare feet behind him, letting the chilly spring air move through his toes while the sun warmed his soles.

As soon as he was sure he'd escaped the view from the kitchen window, he'd kicked his sneakers into the air, peeled off his sweat-soaked socks, and cooled his feet in the damp grass. He and the neighbor boy, Kevin, had spent the morning racing their bikes from one end of the street to the other. Kevin was younger, and Michael beat him repeatedly until his small opponent broke into tears of frustration and stormed home.

Crybaby, Michael thought to himself as he studied the damp grass in front of him, wondering at the way the individual blades seemed to grow before his eyes.

"Michael!" his mother called from the porch.

He groaned and rolled over onto his back, shielding his eyes from the noonday sun. "What!" he hollered.

"I hope you didn't take those shoes off!" she called back. "It's still too cold to be running around half-naked! You'll catch your death!"

"Don't worry about it!" he screamed with impatience.

"You watch that tone, young man!" she screamed back.

Michael let out a frustrated howl and then, "Sorry!"

He heard the back door slam shut. "Good, go back in the house, you old bitch," he mumbled as he opened and closed his fingers, trying to get a glimpse of the sun without burning his eyeballs. He'd only recently discovered the thrill of cursing and practiced his technique whenever possible. The night before, when his father had ordered him to put the comic books away and go to sleep, he'd whispered a string of obscenities that made even his own ears ring.

His eyes were beginning to burn, so he sat up, blinking away tears, and scanned the tree line that cordoned off the backyard. To the right, he could just make out Kevin's house through the trees. He wondered if Kevin had gotten over his humiliating defeat. *I'll have to let him win a couple next time*, Michael thought sourly as he contemplated his friendship with the younger boy. Michael was ten, almost eleven, and Kevin had just turned nine. He'd never really noticed the age difference until recently. But more and more, he found himself thinking of Kevin as a baby. He already had to put up with Annie, his annoying baby sister. Did he really need to be hanging around with a crybaby like Kevin? Confused by the strange mixture of annoyance and guilt, Michael shrugged it off and turned his attention to the trees behind his house.

There lay the forbidden forest. Stories of old cemeteries, abandoned wells, and vicious wild animals had at one time been sufficiently terrifying to keep a scared little boy from entering. But now, to the imagination of a budding young man, it was almost irresistible. Michael stared into its mysterious depths. *Soon*, he thought, the yearning for adventure tingling through his extremities. Soon, he would break his childhood promises to his parents never to venture there. Soon, he would work up the nerve.

But not today. Today, there was ice cream. Dad had promised to take them when he got home from his Saturday morning job. His mother complained that it was too soon in the season to go for ice cream, but he and Annie had pleaded, whined, and shrieked in protest until she finally relented. Michael breathed in the crisp air and sighed contentedly, relaxing on the grass.

Tires crunched on the gravel driveway and Michael sat up at attention. "Dad's home!" he yelped and rushed to pull on his sneakers, abandoning the socks in the grass. He bounded up the slope of the backyard toward the house, his untied laces flying. A car door slammed and he quickened his pace. Rounding the house, he skidded to a stop.

Instead of the silver family sedan, a strange black car was parked in his father's spot. Michael didn't know much about cars, but he could tell this one was pretty old. He circled it curiously, peering through the dust-covered windows into the backseat. Telephone books and yellowed newspapers were strewn haphazardly across the seat. He walked around to the front passenger side. Squinting through the dirty glass, Michael could see a mountain of clothes, children's clothes by the looks of them, patterned with an array of tiny animals and shapes and colorful designs.

"Shit," he said, disgusted. His mother hadn't mentioned his sister had a playdate. "More frigging little kids." He trudged back around the house and took the porch steps two at a time, crashing through the back door into the kitchen.

"Ma!" he yelled, temporarily blinded by the sudden transition from bright daylight into the dimness inside. "Ma!"

He kicked his sneakers off against the wall and headed to the refrigerator. Rummaging through the freezer, he searched for a popsicle. "Goddammit," he grumbled. "No grape." He made a mental note to torture Annie later for eating all the grape and settled for cherry. He ripped off the paper wrapper and tossed it toward the counter, watching it flutter to the floor. "MA! Whose car is in the driveway?" Slamming the freezer door, he made his way toward the dining room.

It was Saturday afternoon—cleaning day. Mom didn't usually make playdates on cleaning day. There was no one in the dining room. "MAA!" he wailed and started sucking on his popsicle. He paused in the foyer. The front door had been left open. He stepped outside onto the landing and looked around the front yard. It was quiet.

Backing into the house, Michael shut and locked the door. Something was off. He stood in the middle of the foyer, his dirty bare feet pressed against the cold tile. Nervously, he sucked on his popsicle and glanced into the living room. His mother had opened the front windows to air out the room, and the long, sheer curtains were billowing up and down, reaching toward the middle of the room, toward the fireplace, like ghostly arms. Something about the fireplace bothered him. He sucked more vigorously and glanced back at the front door.

Then, above his head, the ceiling shook with an explosive boom. Instinctively, he fell into a crouch, his cherry popsicle splattering on the white tile. Before he could recover from the shock, another boom, then another and another, traveling along the ceiling above into the living room.

Michael looked up and whimpered. Whatever it was, it was now in his sister's bedroom. Another. And another. It moved back the other way, over his head again in the foyer.

He crawled into the living room and scurried around the couch, his eyes locked on the ceiling and avoiding the fireplace.

Another boom, then silence.

He trembled and hugged his legs against his chest, cowering between the couch and the fireplace. Wet warmth spread over his thighs. Annie would make fun of him for peeing himself. He needed to change before she found out.

More silence.

He stared at the ceiling, trying not to look at the fireplace. But he could smell her next to him. Every memory of his childhood was forever entwined with the scent of that lavender perfume.

The clock above the mantel ticked louder and louder as Michael waited for some sign of movement from above. He glanced over at it. Two twenty-two. His dad should be home anytime now. But sometimes he'd stop by the market to pick up stuff for Mom. He'd always get the wrong stuff and Mom would always complain. And Michael would wonder why she kept asking him to pick things up if he kept getting it wrong. She could be such a bitch, he thought, trying to dislike his mother, trying to act as if he could do without her. But tears began to trickle down his cheeks and he could no longer stop himself from looking into the fireplace.

Her body had been shoved inside like a ball of rolled-up trash, a ball of arms and legs and head. Her feet pressed against the colorless skin of her face, her eyes glazed over like a dead fish, her mouth gaping as if she were gasping for one last breath.

"Mommy," he whispered, barely vocalizing the word.

He reached out to touch her hair, but a house-jarring crash from above made him recoil into his huddle. He whimpered softly and waited for more.

But nothing happened.

The clock kept ticking.

After a while, a familiar sound came from outside that both thrilled and horrified him. A car was pulling into the driveway. Furtively, he glanced at his mother's corpse. *Daddy is stronger*, he tried to convince himself. The driver's side door squeaked open and then banged shut.

He knew he should warn him, but he couldn't move. He heard his father's footsteps crunching across the gravel. Michael pictured him examining the strange car in the driveway, just as he had done himself a short time before.

He willed himself to say something, to shout out "Help!" or "Run!" But he could only rock back and forth, and the sound of the footsteps disappeared onto the front lawn.

"Daddy," Michael whispered. Keys jingled, and with a click of the lock and then the creak of the door, his father entered the house.

It seemed to Michael that someone had gasped, and then the floor shook, bone snapped, and his father's body flew over the couch, over his head, hitting the mantel and flopping down between him and his mother.

The Monster

The front door slammed shut. A moment later, a car engine roared and tires crunched out of the driveway.

Michael's body convulsed with silent sobs, and he waited, listening for whomever or whatever it was to come back and get him. The living room grew darker and darker. He was alone. All alone. They were supposed to be getting ice cream. Daddy had promised. Michael wanted peppermint swirl. He loved peppermint swirl. Daddy would get coffee with nuts and sprinkles. Mommy got hers in a cup because she said the cone was too messy, but she always tried a different flavor. Annie was the most boring. She only wanted vanilla. Michael had teased her so ruthlessly about it the last time they'd gone that his father had gotten angry. He pulled him aside and chastised him for tormenting his sister. It was his responsibility as Annie's older brother to watch out for her and protect her. Michael promised his father he would.

Where was Annie? He hadn't heard a sound since the strange car had driven away. Maybe she was hiding somewhere in the house. Cautiously, he pushed himself into a crouch and peered over the sofa. Apart from his father's briefcase spilled over onto the floor and the melted remains of his popsicle, the foyer was empty. He glanced back at his parents' bodies and shivered.

"Annie!" he called out, the sound of his voice excruciatingly loud. He made his way to the staircase and looked up to the second-floor landing. "Annie! Are you up there?" He started up the stairs, glancing around, anticipating his sister's appearance with each step. The air around him was still and murky in the late afternoon light. "Annie! It's okay to come out now. I think it's gone."

The upstairs doors were all closed. "Annie! Come on out. I told you it's gone." He waited.

"It's gone," he reminded himself as he approached his sister's room. He turned the doorknob and pushed. It was stuck. He examined the casing around the door, which had been slammed hard enough to crack the frame and wedge it in.

"Annie, the door is stuck. I'm going to have to break it in. Stand back." He waited a moment for his sister's response, but none came. Taking a step back, he prepared for the impact and hurled himself at it. With the crack of splintering wood, the door gave and Michael fell into the room, sliding across the blood-soaked carpet.

Frantically, he tried to stand, slipping and sliding on the slick surface. The room—usually a nauseating rainbow of frilly pinks and purples—was splattered from floor to ceiling with dark red. His eyes darted from the dripping walls to the smeared ceiling to the shredded canopy over the bed to the eviscerated stuffed animals scattered across the room, their white cotton innards saturated in blood.

"ANNIE!" he shrieked. But Annie wasn't there.

He crawled into the hallway, trailing a crimson path across the plush beige carpet. The stench of urine and sickly sweet blood made him vomit so violently that he nearly choked. When the retching had subsided, he ripped off his shirt and pants and stumbled into the bathroom. He had to wash it all off. He twisted the shower on and jumped in. Unfazed by the freezing water, he rubbed at his arms and legs until they were raw and the remnants of his sister's life swirled down the drain.

He stood there until the water flowed warm, then hot, then

icy cold again, until he was so numb that none of the events that had just transpired seemed to matter.

Pajamas, he thought. All he wanted was to put on his pajamas, crawl into bed, and then wake up in the morning and tell his mom and dad all about the horrible nightmare he had. He stepped out of the shower and left the bathroom, dripping across the carpet into his bedroom.

A pile of clean clothes lay neatly folded on his bed. The faint hint of his mother's perfume lingered in the air. He rummaged through the pile and pulled out his Superman pajama bottoms. Mom was supposed to have gotten rid of them. Michael had told her they were for babies, but she said she wasn't ready for him to be done with them just yet.

His hands shook as he tried to pull them over his wet legs. Struggling to yank them up, he realized he'd showered in his underwear. Wet and cold, they now stuck uncomfortably to him. He kicked the pajamas off to the side and rolled the wet briefs down over his legs. After grabbing a dry pair from the bed and pulling them on, he reached for the pajama bottoms again. But then he froze.

Something was behind him.

CHAPTER EIGHT

"It was a man. But not a man. It stood in the doorway, tall, slender, and wearing a dark suit. Black eyes, bottomless holes in the pasty, white face, scrutinized the boy. It hung there for a moment, seemingly uncertain about its next move. Then, with frightening speed, it crossed the distance from the door to the bed, stopping mere inches from the terrified boy. Crouching down, it lowered its face to Michael's, its breath reeking of urine and rotting flesh. It sniffed down my neck to my navel to my crotch and lingered there. I looked down at the top of its head, at the wispy white hair that barely covered the translucent skin of its skull. With a snort of derision, it suddenly stood up. Towering over me, it seemed to be contemplating something. And I wondered which fate awaited me, the quick death of my parents or the brutal end with which my sister had met."

Dr. Dilby cleared his throat. "Michael, you've slipped back into first person again."

Michael blinked at the man, confused and slightly annoyed

at the interruption. "I . . . I did? Sorry. I'll start again. It pretends to be a creature of God, but it is an abomination. Those that see its true nature—"

The doctor held up his hands. "No, Michael, you don't have to start again. I only wanted to ask you why you keep switching the perspective. Why do you keep making the story about yourself?"

Michael's brain was slow. He could barely keep his eyes open, but Dr. Dilby wouldn't let him go back to bed. He fidgeted against the restraints that bound him to his chair. "Should I go on?" he asked drowsily.

Adjusting his glasses, the doctor nodded. "Yes, please continue."

"Those that see its true nature are instantly driven mad—"

"No! Start after it sniffs the boy."

"Oh . . . okay . . . *towering* over Michael, it seemed to be contemplating something. And he wondered which fate awaited him, the quick death of his parents or the brutal end with which his sister had met. Michael held his breath and waited. Both of them started when suddenly, from somewhere in the house, the shrill ring of the telephone pierced the silence. Michael waited as the second ring came, then the third and fourth, and finally, the beep of the answering machine. After a moment, Kevin's high-pitched voice echoed, 'Hey Mikey, my dad said we can set up the Atari if you wanna come over to play. This is Kevin. Call me back, okay?' Michael's eyes widened in terror as the man, the monster, grinned with evil delight, its teeth yellow, pointed, and dripping with slime. Suddenly, it took off out of the room, down the stairs, and through the front door. 'Kevin!' Michael cried

The Monster

and raced after it, down the steps and out onto the lawn. The creature had already made it to its car. The engine roared to life and the car jerked forward. Instinctively, Michael scooped up his mother's favorite garden gnome off the lawn and ran to the end of the driveway. The car barreled toward him, but Michael, barely five feet tall and one hundred pounds, wearing nothing but his underwear, stood his ground until the car was mere yards from him. Then, with all his strength, he hurled the gnome at the windshield. The glass exploded inward, sending the car and the monster off into the embankment between the driveway and the tree line. Michael ran to the edge and stood triumphant as he looked down at the car, tipped on its side, the tires still spinning."

Michael stopped to take a breath, and a proud smile broke across his face.

Dr. Dilby scrutinized him. "You like that part of the story," the man observed.

Nodding enthusiastically, Michael kept smiling. "Oh, yes. The boy was so brave. He was trying to protect his friend."

The doctor wrote something on his notepad and spoke without looking up at Michael. "But the boy doesn't save his friend, does he?"

Michael fidgeted in his chair. "We haven't gotten to that part yet."

"Skip to it."

Michael shook his head. "We shouldn't skip. We shouldn't leave anything out."

"It's okay, Michael. Dr. Denny told me it was okay."

Michael's eyes lit up. "You talked to him?"

"Yes, and he said it was okay to skip some parts. So the

monster gets out of the car and runs into the woods towards Kevin's house, but Kevin shows up in Michael's driveway on his bike—"

"Kevin skidded to a stop next to Michael and looked down at the overturned car. 'Hey, Mikey, what happened? Whose car is that and why are you in your underwear?' Without a word, Michael grabbed the bewildered little boy by the hand and pulled him from the bike—"

"Yes," Dr. Dilby said with exasperation, "and they run off into the woods together until they come upon the old cemetery . . ." He paused and indicated that Michael should pick up the story from there.

Michael squirmed, still uncomfortable with omitting any part of the story, but skipped ahead to the part the doctor wanted. "Unable to run any farther, the exhausted boys searched for a hiding place. Most of the headstones were crumbling, broken and sunken into the mossy earth. 'We have to keep running. There's no place to hide here!' Michael exclaimed. 'I can't run anymore!' Kevin cried out. Michael spun around on him, his eyes desperate and terrified. 'It's gonna get you!' he shrieked. Kevin's eyes opened wide. 'What's gonna get me? Mikey?' Michael rubbed his bare arms and stared at his friend. 'We have to run,' he insisted, a touch of hysteria punctuating his statement. 'It's coming and it wants you.' Kevin began to whimper and a darkness spread across the front of his pants. Michael peered into the woods, sure the creature was about to spring forth. 'Stop crying, you little fucking baby! That's why it wants you . . . because you're such a little baby. That's why it killed Annie! Because she was a big crybaby like you! We have to run!' Kevin cried harder. Michael

The Monster

stepped forward, angry, frustrated, and terrified out of his mind. He raised his hand to hit Kevin, but the boy didn't move. 'Fine, stay here, you stupid baby.' Michael spun around and started to run. He pushed through the vine-strangled hedges and slid down a small embankment, landing hard against a mossy stone slab. After a moment, he realized he was standing on top of a structure. He peeked over the edge. There was a door. He turned to yell back to Kevin that he had found a place to hide, but the boy was already emerging through the branches. 'What is this place?' Kevin asked as they pried the heavy metal door open. Michael responded, 'It's a mausoleum—a place where they keep dead people who don't want to be buried in the ground.' Kevin peered into the darkness. 'Dead people?'"

Michael's narration was abruptly cut short by the impatient sound of someone clearing their throat behind him. He looked to Dr. Dilby, who shifted in his chair and, with uncharacteristic urgency, once again pressed Michael to skip ahead. "What happened in the mausoleum?"

Michael attempted to turn around to see who was standing behind him and directing the session, but the doctor lurched forward and grabbed his face roughly.

"Focus! What happened in the mausoleum?"

Michael stared into the man's insistent eyes. "Okay," he mumbled through his squished cheeks, and the doctor released his face, sitting back in his chair and picking up his notepad. "Um . . . Kevin stood at the door at the back of the mausoleum, ready to flee at the first sight of the mysterious thing that evidently wanted to harm him. The door was open just enough for him to slip out when the time came. And Michael hid outside the other door at the front, ready to slam it shut the moment the monster entered. 'Remember,' Michael had instructed Kevin, 'Shut the door and put the pipe through the handles. Then run. Don't wait for me.' Kevin nodded in terrified agreement. Now, as Michael waited for the monster's inevitable arrival, he started to doubt the plan. What if Kevin wasn't fast enough? What if it immediately broke out of their trap? And was it right to use Kevin as bait? Michael shook off the doubts. They couldn't keep running from it. They had to stop it. They waited. Michael could hear Kevin pacing and occasionally whimpering. He surveyed the forest from his hiding spot. Everything was still, so still he felt as if he were gazing at a painting in one of those boring museums his mom used to drag them all to. He turned back to look at Kevin and gasped. The monster had the boy suspended by the hair, its spindly fingers entwined in his sandy brown locks. Kevin's little legs kicked at the air. Michael jumped out and stood in the doorway. The monster glanced over and gave him a tilt of its head in appreciation for the gift. 'Mikey!' Kevin shrieked. Michael started forward but stopped. He knew Kevin didn't have a chance. He spun around, ignoring Kevin's terrified pleading. 'Mikey, don't leave me!' He heaved the door shut and wedged the metal bar through the handles. Satisfied that the door was secured, he raced around the outside of the mausoleum. Kevin's shrill cries had died away, replaced by a succession of dull, pounding thuds. At the back door, Michael couldn't stop himself from peeking inside, an urge he would regret for the rest of his life. What had once been his best friend was now nothing more than a skin sack filled with broken bones, the tiny body stripped naked and pummeled against the stone floor like wet laundry.

With a sickening crack, the monster unhinged its lower jaw and began to feed the dead boy into its gaping mouth. Unable to watch any longer, I slammed the door shut and padlocked it. Then I heard a little voice calling my name. I turned around. It was Shelly."

"Wait," Dr. Dilby interrupted, sitting up at attention. "Who's Shelly?"

"Huh?"

"Who's Shelly?"

Michael was confused. "His sister?"

"The sister's name is Annie."

"Annie's dead."

"Yes, Annie dies in the story. But you said Shelly. Who is Shelly?"

Michael tried to push through the mental fog and answer the insistent man. "I told you, the sister, the sister that gets killed by the monster and then Michael saves her and they trap it in the basement."

"Basement?" the doctor pulled a paperback book from the inside pocket of his blazer and flipped through the pages. "You just told me that Michael trapped the monster in the mausoleum."

"Yeah, Michael traps the monster and is the hero because he saves all the children from the monster. He saves Shelly, and she gets to go away and be happy."

Dr. Dilby shook his head in confusion. "There is no Shelly. And he doesn't save Kevin. Here it is." He read: "Michael crouched beside the rotting log, hidden from view. Motionless, he ignored the attack on his bare arms, legs, and chest as the mosquitoes swarmed him like vultures over a corpse. Only a few short yards from the mausoleum, from where his friend had met his terrifying and gruesome death, Michael waited for the monster to break free from its stone prison. His heart pounded so loud that he was sure others would be able to hear it. That is, if he wasn't already completely alone."

Michael blinked at him, unsure what to think. The words sounded right, but that's not how he remembered it. There was a staircase leading down into darkness. And voices. Yes, the voices of children. And Shelly. They all sang out to him as he followed the monster down.

"Michael!" Dr. Dilby snapped his fingers inches from Michael's face. "Who is Shelly?"

He tried to focus, but his mind was slow and mired in tangled memories. "Shelly?" The name conjured up an image of a girl, a tiny wisp with golden curls and red cheeks. He tried to wipe the tears that trickled down his face, but he couldn't lift his hands from the arms of the chair.

"What's wrong with my arms?"

"We've had to use restraints, Michael."

"Why?"

"So you won't hurt anyone else."

He blinked at the doctor. "Who did I hurt?"

"Try to focus. Tell me who Shelly is."

"Shelly," he repeated absently, her delicate image fluttering in and out of his mind's eye. "She's an angel." His voice trailed off and he shut his eyes. He could see her. She was flying away. He wanted her to stay, but he knew she had to leave, to escape.

He opened his eyes. The doctor was looking past him as if he were communicating with someone standing behind him.

The Monster

With a slight nod, the man stared into Michael's eyes. "Michael. Listen." Dr. Dilby's usual monotonous voice was now stern and insistent. "There is no Shelly. She doesn't exist."

"She exists," he protested feebly.

"No, Michael. She is a creation of your illness."

Michael shook his head. Some of his grogginess had faded, and he felt more certain.

"None of what you have told me is real. You are a very sick man. You have confused this cheap fiction . . ." He held up the book in front of Michael's face, "and your delusions for reality."

Michael struggled against the restraints, his agitation growing. "No, it's real. You have to let me go!"

"The only way you are going to get better is if you accept that you are a very sick man."

"I trapped the monster," Michael exclaimed. His chair rocked back and forth as he tried to stand.

"That's enough," a woman's voice, somehow familiar to Michael, ordered from behind him.

Dr. Dilby jumped up, his face draining of color and his hands shaking. "I can try something else," he protested. But two orderlies had already entered the room.

"It's real! The monster is real! Shelly gets to leave, but Michael has to stay and guard the monster because it never dies, so he has to make sure that he never gets out. He can't ever get out!" Michael cried, his eyes wide with desperation.

They held Michael's arms steady as the nurse injected the sedative.

"You have to let me out of here! I have to get back before he gets out!"

"Keep him at the same dosage as before," the doctor muttered to the nurse as he hurried from the room.

"Let me out! Let me out!"

• • •

"Hello?" Patrick called, his ear pressed against the door in the basement of the organ hall, his worst fears now confirmed.

"Let me out," the child's voice pleaded.

Patrick's mind reeled. *What had Michael done?*

"It's going to be okay. I'm going to get you out!" he promised as he examined the door. It was a heavy wooden door with a padlock. He tried every one of Michael's keys, but none belonged to the lock. He pulled on it with all his strength, but it wouldn't give.

"I need something to pry it off." He searched all around, but there was nothing. "Hello, in there? I have to go to my car to get something to open this door. I'll be right back." He listened for a response.

"Please," the little voice begged after several long seconds, "I'm dying."

Patrick bounded up the staircase, his bare foot slapping against each step. Near the top, he found his shoe and scooped it up, stopping only once he got to the front doors to put it back on. He pushed the doors open and burst out into the ice storm. The sky was dark and the wind viciously whipped the sleet against his body. He rounded the brick building to the deserted parking lot, sliding to a stop in front of the trunk of his car, sure he could somehow use the tire jack to get the padlocked door open.

"Dammit," he shouted as he patted his pockets. He'd lost his car keys, probably in his fall down the stairs. He went around to the driver's side and yanked at the door. It was locked, and when he peered through the window, he saw his phone on the passenger seat. "Shit!"

Only a mile from the center of town, Patrick considered running to get help. But with the blinding storm that raged around him, it might as well have been a hundred miles. There had to be something in the derelict old building that he could use to pry open the door, he thought as he raced back through the storm toward the organ hall.

Hours seemed to have passed as he burst into the vestibule and skidded to a stop. He frowned. The hall was all lit up. He stepped beneath the grand art déco lamps suspended from the ceiling by heavy bronze chains. An ethereal blue glow was cast over the storm-drenched floor.

"Hello!" he called out. Wind billowed in through the open doors and the organ pipes moaned. "Is someone here?" he called out as he proceeded up the center aisle, now illuminated by the tall floor sconces that stood guard along both walls every five or so feet. "If there's somebody here, I could use your help. There's a child trapped in the basement."

He waited.

No answer.

His mind went through the possibilities. Could the storm have somehow turned the lights on? Not likely. Maybe one of the board members had decided to check the building. Again, unlikely. They were all elderly, and the bad weather would keep them away. Besides, there wasn't another car in the lot or at the front of the building. *Or was there?* He had been running around in such a panic and the storm had become so blinding that he might have missed someone else pulling in. The only other possibility was the most disturbing.

"Michael?"

He glanced around. It was absurd to think that Michael could have escaped Everston. He was drugged, restrained, and locked behind a security door. Yet Patrick couldn't shake the creeping suspicion that whoever had locked that poor child in the basement was now present and ready to stop him from releasing their prisoner.

Patrick reached the open basement door and peered down the stairwell. There was light at the bottom. He descended. "Michael, if you're down there, I'd like to talk to you. I've been waiting a long time to talk to you." He paused halfway down and listened.

Still no answer.

He continued his descent, taking each step deliberately this time. "Whatever has happened, whatever you've done, we can fix it together."

Before he reached the bottom, Patrick could see that the padlocked door had been opened. A small, bare-bulb light fixture swung in front of the door, casting just enough light into the dark space to allow him to see the silhouette of a person standing a few feet inside, its features obscured by the shadows.

"Help!" the child's voice shrieked from somewhere in the darkness.

The figure raised its arm as if to strike a blow, and Patrick rushed forward.

"No!" a woman's voice cried out as Patrick wrenched a heavy brick from her hand and pulled her into the light. "He deserves to die for what he's done!" Patricia Huntsman struggled against Patrick's grip, her eyes wild and desperate. "All those poor boys!"

"Mrs. Huntsman, please stop. I don't want to hurt you," Patrick implored. But she fought with all her strength, flailing and kicking and howling with rage until her body went limp in Patrick's arms. "I'm going to let go," he said calmly into her ear and released her.

She staggered to the staircase and slumped onto the bottom step, the once proud woman now slouching like a scolded child.

He watched her for a few moments. Her eyes, which had flashed with confidence and defiance when he had first encountered her outside Michael's hospital room, now stared off into some distant personal hell where she was no longer in control.

Certain she no longer posed a threat, Patrick tossed the brick into a corner and reentered the darkness. The reek of urine, feces, and filth filled his nostrils. "It's okay. You can come out now. It's safe," he said, choking on the fetid air.

"She's going to kill me," the little voice cried.

Patrick fumbled in his pocket for his flashlight. "No, she can't hurt you anymore. Come on out." He clicked the light on and pointed it toward the voice. But all he saw was an empty corner. "I promise you, you're safe now."

"Where's Michael?" the voice asked, now from behind him.

Patrick turned quickly, trying to capture the child within the beam of his light, but again, he saw nothing but empty space. "Michael's in the hospital. He can't hurt you either."

Why Did God Make the Tree?

"They locked him up again?"

Something brushed past Patrick's leg and he spun around again. This time, he caught the child in his light. It crawled on all fours into a corner, emaciated and filthy, its ragged clothes hanging off a skeletal frame.

"And she'll be locked up too?"

Patrick glanced over to the staircase where he had left Patricia Huntsman. She was gone. "I'm sure she will. If she helped Michael to keep you locked up down here—"

A dry, unnatural whimper issued from the shadowy corner where the child crouched. Patrick was gripped by an odd, sick feeling. The child began to straighten up, and the wrongness of the situation became chillingly apparent as the length of its body unfolded to stand at least six feet tall. He moved his light up the willowy legs and over the cadaverous torso. Continuing upward to the sunken eyes, mere holes in the pale, gaunt face, Patrick nearly dropped the flashlight.

"Too bright," hissed the old man with the childlike voice and shielded his face behind gnarled, claw-like hands.

"Who . . . who are you?"

But the man didn't respond. Instead, he seemed to be sobbing into his hands, his head bobbing up and down, a few wispy strands of white topping his otherwise bald skull.

"It's . . . okay. You're free now," Patrick said, trying to pity the creature before him. But as hard as he tried, he couldn't suppress that sick feeling in his gut. And then the awful realization became clear. The sound wasn't sobbing but peals of throaty, delighted, and slightly deranged laughter. "Who are you?" Patrick demanded.

The Monster

The old man dropped his hands and fixed soulless eyes upon Patrick. "I am Phineas Huntsman," said Michael's uncle, and he staggered forward with an outstretched hand.

Patrick pushed past his revulsion and thrust his sock-bandaged hand forward. "Patrick Denny."

The old man scoffed, his overgrown nails biting into Patrick's skin. "I know who you are. My crazy nephew reads your books."

Patrick stared into his soulless eyes. "Yes. And I know who you are. You're Michael's monster."

. . .

Michael gazed sleepily at the clouds. The morning was a blur of activity. First waking to Dr. Dilby's inquisition, only to be told he was crazy and once again sedated. Then to be awakened shortly after by Aunt Patricia and Nurse Delacroix, who rushed to dress him and wheel him out into the storm, where he was transferred to a long gray limo. He shivered at the memory of the wind and ice whipping at his uncovered head. Such a contrast to the warm, safe feeling he was now experiencing as they rose above the storm into the heavens.

"Aunt Patricia," he said dreamily as the sun warmed his face through the small oval window.

"Yes, Michael," his aunt responded from across the table, having just settled down. She'd spent the beginning of their trip on the phone transferring money, arranging accommodations, and a long list of other things Michael only vaguely registered.

"Can I have a hot cocoa?"

"Of course you can, my dear. Elise, get my nephew cocoa."

The young attendant replied, "Oui," and went off to the back of the cabin.

"I always asked Mommy to give me hot cocoa when it snowed."

"Did you, dear?" his aunt said as she stared out the window.

His whole body tingled with happiness. The burden was gone. As soon as Aunt Patricia had told him that the monster was no longer his responsibility, that Patrick Denny would now watch over him, Michael felt free.

They ascended over the clouds and floated in the blue sky.

"Aunt Patricia, are we gonna be with Shelly?"

"Yes, Michael, we're going to be with Shelly."

He sighed happily.

Part Three

The Tree

CHAPTER NINE

The eyes of the forest peered out from the darkness, tiny blinking stars of light embedded in the canopy of the dense foliage. Her footsteps were silent, absorbed by the damp, spongy earth beneath her feet. She was alone, yet everything around her, even the very air, felt alive, aware of all her movements—every step, every quiet breath, every thought that inhabited her troubled mind. She held the lantern high. The flame flickered through the scratched and pitted glass of the globe, casting long, grotesque shadows against the tangled wall of branches and leaves. As she struggled over forest debris, the shadows pranced before her with devilish delight, gleefully leading her on her dark journey.

The meeting place had been agreed upon weeks before, and the terms of the contract were explicitly laid out. She waited for the appointed time, going about her mundane life and trying not to ponder the coming event. But as hard as she tried to put the matter out of her mind, she was still plagued by bouts of uncontrollable tremors that had become increasingly more difficult to hide from those around her. And now, as she approached the clearing within the oak grove, these physical manifestations of doubt took hold of her body, and her initial resolve waned. Once she crossed this boundary, there would be no return.

The clearing was empty. At its center, she came upon a shallow pit filled with kindling. She squinted out into the wood and turned slowly, holding out her lantern and scrutinizing the large twisted trunks of the ancient oaks. The others had yet to arrive. And once she had completed her revolution, she realized there was still time to flee.

But, as if in answer to her thoughts, the heavy, gnarled branches above creaked and groaned, mimicking his cruel laughter. She peered up into the dark blue sky, the moon a waxing crescent among the twinkle of stars. In her mind's eye, she saw him—his sadistic smile and the cruelty in his eyes. She felt the heat return to her face, the burning rage, the bottomless well of hatred that had compelled her to seek out this unusual form of retribution.

The first figure emerged from between the trees, clothed in a white hooded robe and carrying a flaming torch. She turned to the approaching apparition, resigned to her chosen fate. One by one, dozens of them appeared, all silent, all made anonymous by their overhanging hoods. When the last figure emerged and joined the others, the clearing was alight with the fire of their torches. The scent of burning pine hung in the hazy air. They stood motionless and silent around her.

She waited for it to begin, only the crackle of flames disturbing the stillness.

"Welcome," a deep voice intoned from the throng, and one figure stepped forward. He stood taller than the others, and the confident manner of his gait made plain his position as leader. She recognized this one as the man with whom she had bargained. He stopped before her and tossed his torch into the pit. "It is time," he stated as he removed his hood.

She nodded, transfixed by his wild eyes. He took the lantern from her and gave it to one of the others. With a wave of his hand, he motioned her to kneel, and she obeyed. Exhilaration and terror surged through her, paralyzing her with tiny convulsions. Chanting words she did not understand, he produced three sprigs of mistletoe from under his robe and pushed them into her hair, scraping across her scalp. But even as the blood trickled down her forehead, she did not cry out, knowing the time for doubts and tears had long since passed.

The chanting stopped and she trembled with anticipation. He gripped her face and spoke. "Do you come here willingly?"

"I do."

"Do you accept what we have to give?"

"I do."

"Do you agree to the price?"

She hesitated, and his grip tightened. "I do," she cried out.

He released her and motioned to the others. One by one, they dropped their torches into the pit, and the newly lit bonfire roared up to the sky, its red and yellow light rising and falling. Then they came for her, a train of faces alternately illuminated and once again plunged into shadow by the dance of the flames. She glimpsed the mark of expectation gleaming on each visage as they descended upon her, taking her by the arms and the legs, lifting her from the ground, and carrying her into the dark woods. She fought the fear, the hysteria that welled up inside her. She would do this for him. She would make this sacrifice. It was worth it if it made him pay.

※

PATRICK FOLLOWED THE DIRECTION of her gaze up along the slender trunks of the birch trees. The catkins dangled and swayed in the summer breeze, and the morning sun shone through the feathery green leaves, its dappled golden light falling upon their upturned faces like warm raindrops.

"What do you see? Can you tell me?" he asked softly and watched her face, but it remained unresponsive. Her long hair was pulled back into a neat, tight braid draped over one shoulder. The collar of her pink nightgown framed her porcelain face, her glassy green eyes staring up into nowhere. He had propped her up on the bench, her hands placed in her lap, her slippered feet dangling just above the ground. If it weren't for the wisps of white that streaked her dark hair and the deepening creases around her mouth and eyes, an unknowing passerby might have mistaken her for an oversized china doll.

"Would you like to hold Mr. Bear?" He placed the love-worn stuffed animal between the dead weight of her hands and waited, searching for the slightest movement. But there was none. "I have something else of yours," he said, pressing on, aware of the futility of the exercise. "Your dad gave it to me. He said it was your favorite book when you were a little girl. Do you remember this?" He held the little picture book in front of her. "It's called

The Tree. Do you remember?" He scrutinized her closely, but as he had anticipated, there was still no response.

"That's okay. Maybe if I read it to you, you'll remember." He held the fragile book on his lap and examined it. The cloth binding was fraying, and the cardboard covers were bent and split at the corners. He traced his finger over the faded image of a tree. Its swirling branches possessively curled around the title and author's name. "*The Tree* by Rebecca Hadaway," he read.

He gazed at his patient again, at her lifeless hands resting on the bear, at her eyes staring unfocused up into the branches. He watched for any signs of cognizance, but she remained just a doll holding a doll. Patrick turned his attention back to the book, a quiet desperation settling over him as his hope that the story might somehow reach her began to fade. Yet, he pushed on, opening to the first page with its simple black-line drawings, and read:

"'Why did God make the tree?' the boy asked his mother. 'So we would have shade for our picnic,' his mother answered.

'Why did God make the tree?' the boy asked his father.

'So we would have wood to build our house,' his father answered."

Pausing before turning to the next page, Patrick scrutinized his patient for any flicker of recognition in her eyes. But her gaze remained fixed on the swaying branches above. He rested the book on his lap and rubbed his forehead, trying to quell the sense of pointlessness that threatened to overcome him. "Just read," he whispered to himself and continued:

"'Why did God make the tree?' the boy asked his friend.

'So we would have something to climb,' his friend answered.

Why Did God Make the Tree?

'Why did God make the tree?' the boy asked the bird on his windowsill.

'So I could build my nest high up off the ground,' the bird answered.

'Why did God make the tree?' the boy asked the squirrel hanging from the branch.

'So I would have nuts to eat,' the squirrel answered.

'Why did God make the tree?' the boy asked his teacher.

'So we would have fresh air to breathe,' his teacher answered.

'Why did God make the tree?' the boy asked his minister.

'So His son could save us with His sacrifice,' the minister answered.

'Why did God make you?' the boy asked the tree.

'So I could look out over all His creation,' the tree answered and scooped him up high into its branches and showed him the magnificence of the world."

Patrick smiled faintly as he finished reading and stared at the picture of the boy in the tree, who looked out over the world with a glimmer of wonder in his eyes. *Had she lit up like that when her parents read the story to her?* He tried to imagine the dead eyes before him coming alive, seeing the new world around her and dreaming of the future. But they remained frozen, just like her life. Frozen for nearly two decades with no promise of change.

The doctor leaned back and let the sun warm the top of his head. Distant birds warbled and shrieked and fluttered from somewhere above. Nothing was working and he was exhausted. They sat there in silence for close to an hour until Patrick could no longer stand to look at her.

The Tree

"Okay, my friend. Time to head back." He slipped the book into his pocket and then scooped up her limp, almost weightless body, placing it into the wheelchair. Her head dropped forward and her hands fell to her sides. Mr. Bear landed on the grass. Patrick snatched up the toy, tucked it beside her, and, with a weary sigh, wheeled her toward the hospital.

. . .

The elevator doors opened. Down the hallway, Patrick could see Mr. and Mrs. Dearborne waiting outside their daughter's room. Forcing a smile, he pushed his patient toward them. "Look, Amelia, your mum and dad are here."

"Anything?" Amelia's elderly father asked, the desperate hope apparent in his eyes, even behind his Coke-bottle thick glasses.

"We had a nice rest outside under the trees," Patrick said, forcing a smile.

Mrs. Dearborne nodded with understanding and busied herself with her daughter's appearance. "Oh, Melly, I think we need to wash this hair. It's getting so unruly," she fussed and undid the perfect braid. Patrick watched as the hunched woman worked her arthritic fingers through Amelia's hair.

"We had a nice time reading this," he said, handing the picture book to Amelia's father.

"It's always been her favorite," the old man mumbled.

The doctor studied Amelia's parents, as frozen as their daughter, stuck between acceptance and hope. Mrs. Dearborne worked on her daughter's hair. Mr. Dearborne stood watching, clutching his daughter's favorite book. And Patrick could feel himself being sucked into their hellish existence. "Why don't we let Nurse Liebman take Amelia to her room and get her settled," he said, trying to hide the note of agitation in his voice. "I'd like to talk to the two of you alone. Let's take a walk."

"Okay," Mrs. Dearborne said, smoothing the collar of her daughter's nightgown, unwilling to let the nurse take her away.

"Come on, Mary," Mr. Dearborne prompted, taking his wife by the shoulders. "Let's go with Dr. Denny."

The three exited the building out a side door, and Patrick led them down one of the many circuitous pathways that wound throughout the vast hospital grounds. "We tried the smell thing last night," Mr. Dearborne said. "The popcorn was fresh out of the microwave. Lots of butter, just the way she liked it. I held it under her nose for the longest time. But it didn't work," he said, his disappointment palpable. "We had such a good time that day at the carnival. I won her Mr. Bear and then we got popcorn. I was sure it would bring back a good memory for her." The disappointed man limped alongside Patrick, his thumbs hitched through the belt loops of his jeans.

"Maybe it wasn't a recent enough memory," Mrs. Dearborne called back from ahead of them. She shuffled up the tree-lined path, unhindered by her warping spine and swollen ankles, her faded cotton sundress hanging unevenly from her crooked body. "She was a little girl when we took her to that carnival. We should try to get her to remember something from when she was a teenager, don't you think, Dr. Denny?"

They were relentless, Patrick thought as he steeled himself for the coming confrontation. When he had suggested attempting to reach her through sensory therapy, the willing couple had become quite excited by the prospect. "Dr. Dilby never suggested that before," Mr. Dearborne had exclaimed. "Will it work?" Trying to make them understand that her heavy sedation was an enormous obstacle, Patrick had said, "Maybe, but let's not get too optimistic just yet." But the desperate parents took on the endeavor with complete commitment. They showed up at the hospital day after day with a car full of Amelia's childhood possessions. They sang to her, brought her favorite foods, and played her favorite games. They hurled themselves at the problem over and over again, only to crash into the unbreakable brick wall of her catatonic state every time. Now, after three months of watching them fail, Patrick could no longer bear it.

"Oh, Mary, we should have brought the photo album," Mr. Dearborne called to his wife.

"Yes, that's right. She was putting it together when . . . when she got sick." Mrs. Dearborne's pace slowed, and she and her husband fell silent. They emerged from the pathway out into an open area.

The large hilltop terrace looked out over the town of Waylingbrooke, held back by a wooden railing that formed a semi-circle around a flat, elevated green. The old outside theater-in-the-round was a remnant of Everston's previous life as an all-boy preparatory school. With a clear night sky unobstructed by artificial light and the thick pine forest as a backdrop, Patrick couldn't imagine a more fitting place for adolescent Pucks and Prosperos to work their magic under the moonlight and stars. It would have been spectacular, he thought, as he watched two young Weimaraners gambol across the grassy circle, their long, gangly legs twisting around each other as they wrestled and rolled. No more performances were held here, though. Now it was just a place where the locals let their dogs off-leash to run, play, and poop.

The doctor directed the Dearbornes to a bench by the railing, and after assisting his wife, Mr. Dearborne eased himself down beside her. Patrick leaned against the railing and looked out over Waylingbrooke, unable to face them.

They waited for him to speak.

"It isn't working."

Mrs. Dearborne's face fell in disappointment.

"I was sure I saw her respond a few weeks back," Mr. Dearborne protested. "You remember, Mary. When we played the Christmas song for her—"

"'Holy Night,'" Mrs. Dearborne provided without emotion.

"Yeah, I was sure I saw something in her eyes." He let the statement hang for a moment, then, "So what next?"

Out in the distance, Patrick could see the tower. It seemed so quaint. A charming, innocuous feature embedded in the landscape of the picturesque town of Waylingbrooke. The perfect place to live, or so he had once thought. But now he hated it. The tower, the town, his job, his life. He hated it all. "I'm taking her off all the medications," he announced.

Mrs. Dearborne gasped. "That would be a very bad idea," she exclaimed. "Very, very bad."

Patrick turned to face them now.

Mr. Dearborne's usual stoic demeanor had visibly changed to one of agitation. "Not all her medication!" he cried out.

"Very bad," Mrs. Dearborne repeated and broke into tears.

"Dr. Dilby said she could never come off."

"Dr. Dilby isn't her doctor anymore," Patrick snapped at Mr. Dearborne, immediately regretting the defensiveness in his voice. "I understand your fears," he said, trying to soften his tone. "But the meds are keeping her from responding."

"They're keeping her from going crazy," Mr. Dearborne shouted as he pushed himself up to stand. "You don't understand. You weren't there when she . . ." The old man pressed his lips together and his face tightened with anguish.

"Ran around the neighborhood naked," Mrs. Dearborne said, picking up her husband's sentence, her voice hushed to a whisper. "Screaming. Oh, the screaming that never ended. And then attacking people."

"Attacking the cat!" Mr. Dearborne added.

"What she did to that poor cat!" Mrs. Dearborne reached into her pocket and pulled out a tissue. Her hands shook as she wiped her nose. She glanced up at Patrick with cloudy brown eyes. "Relieving herself in the middle of the room, throwing her poop at us."

"Like an animal," Mr. Dearborne said as he lowered himself back onto the bench and took his wife's hands, calming her with his touch. "We'll just keep doing the sensory thing. I'm sure I saw her respond to the song," said the old man defiantly.

"She didn't respond, Mr. Dearborne," Patrick stated bluntly. "You saw what you wanted to see. As long as we keep her drugged, she is nothing more than a vegetable. A brain-dead zombie . . ."

Mrs. Dearborne moaned.

"She will never look at you . . ."

Mr. Dearborne began to cry.

"She will never speak to you . . ."

"Ohhhh," Mrs. Dearborne sobbed.

"She will never know that you're there . . ."

"Please," Mr. Dearborne begged.

"And when you pass away, she won't even know that you're gone." Patrick felt sick with himself as the Dearbornes held each other and sobbed. He looked away from them and back out toward the beauty of Waylingbrooke, hating it even more than before.

. . .

Having finished up with the rest of his patients, Patrick sat at the nurses' station, finalizing his orders for the overnight staff. Exhaustion bore down on him. The Dearbornes had relented and turned over all decisions concerning Amelia to him. After a tearful goodbye, the couple went home, sent away by Patrick, who thought it best they not witness their daughter's awakening. He assured them that he knew what he was doing. But as he wrote the orders for her drop in medication and handed Amelia's chart to Nurse Liebman, he wavered.

"Dr. Denny?" the nurse questioned as she tried to take the binder from his unyielding grip.

"Um . . . I'm just wondering if I'm dropping her dosage too fast," Patrick explained. He pulled the binder back and opened it to his orders. He wasn't sure. Mrs. Dearborne's words—*very, very bad*—still echoed in his brain.

"I'm on the night shift all week," Nurse Liebman assured him. "If there are any problems, I'll contact you immediately."

Patrick still hesitated. He usually leapt right in and dealt with the consequences later. Unaccustomed to being so consumed by self-doubt, he was frustrated by his indecision.

"Dr. Denny . . . are you okay?" the nurse asked. "You don't seem yourself lately."

Patrick liked Nurse Liebman. An attractive thirty-something woman, she had a confident, maternal quality about her that he found comforting. She was an excellent nurse and, as far as he could tell, a kind person. He was sure that her inquiry was one of genuine concern, but in his present mood, he found it intrusive, almost intolerably so.

He handed the binder to her brusquely. "I'm fine. Please make sure that these orders are followed precisely."

"Yes, Doctor."

. . .

Patrick stood, waiting for the service elevator doors to slide open. Too tired to walk down the two flights of stairs as was his custom, he climbed into the cramped elevator, pushed the button for the lobby, and watched the doors slide shut, sealing him into the moving coffin.

The rest of his workday still stretched before him. He had three more sessions back at his office in town, and he was considering rescheduling for the first time since he'd begun his three-year-old practice. All he wanted was to return to his spartan, one-room apartment, flop into bed, clothes and all, and sleep until the next morning. But he'd promised Mrs. Zacharovitch that he'd go with her to the cemetery to visit with her husband for the first time since his death. And he had a new patient to evaluate. That could take a few hours. And Mr. Scarlatti would probably already be waiting for him, eager to discuss his impending death that had been fast approaching for the last sixty-six years.

The elevator jerked to an abrupt stop on the next floor, and the doors inched open with a high-pitched squeal. On the other side, Archie Philbin's surprised face greeted him. "Doctor . . . Patrick . . . Dr. Denny," he stammered awkwardly, uncertain how to address his estranged friend and colleague.

Not offering a greeting in return, Patrick stepped forward, blocked Archie's way, and pushed the button to close the doors.

"Um . . . I'm going down," Archie said, dancing toward him. But Patrick continued to block him until the doors squealed shut. "Oh . . . okay. I can wait for the next . . ." With a thud, Archie's words were cut off, and the elevator resumed its descent to the lobby, where it jolted to a stop.

"Shit," Patrick breathed. For as the doors parted, he was met by Alexander Anderson's scowling face.

"Denny!" the six-foot-six giant growled and quickly advanced, stepping into the elevator and forcing Patrick to retreat. "We need to have a word."

"Anderson, I have patients waiting at my office."

"They can wait." The doors closed, and the director stabbed the button for the third floor. Patrick gritted his teeth, clenched his fists, and did all he could not to throw himself upon the loathsome man. The two stood side by side as the elevator once again stopped at the second floor, where Archie still waited.

"Oh," the nervous man exclaimed, startled by the expressions on their faces. "I . . . I'll take the stairs."

The Tree

Anderson and Patrick rode up to the third floor in silence, then climbed two flights up the south tower staircase. When they walked into the director's suite of offices, Patrick noticed that Anderson's assistant Estelle was not in her usual spot behind her desk. Anderson shut the inner office door behind them and attacked. "Where the fuck is my book!" he demanded without any preamble.

Patrick took a seat in front of the desk. "I'm close to being finished," he said casually, crossing his legs and trying to appear confident.

Anderson placed both hands on his desk—*the desk on which he had screwed Patrick's girlfriend*—and leaned forward. "Really? You were close to being finished three months ago."

"I've been busy with patients."

"I don't care what you've been busy with. You said the beginning of June. It's the beginning of June. I'm sick of being jerked around. I want that book. I need that book," he stated, his words precise and staccato.

A smile tugged at the corner of Patrick's mouth. "Yes, I heard you were having a bit of financial trouble. Messy divorce?"

"When will I get my book?"

Patrick pressed his lips together and stared at the ceiling, calculating how long it would take to stretch the three pages he had jotted down into a complete manuscript. "End of August."

Anderson pounded the desk. "You haven't even started yet, have you? Helen told me that you were washed up and had nothing left. Is that why you wanted this job so badly? Why you wanted to handpick your patients?" He scoffed and sunk back into his chair, his rage giving way to bitter self-regret. "You were just trying to make yourself feel important again, weren't you? It's really quite pathetic. Coming to me with this scheme so you could pretend you gave up fame and fortune to return to your first noble calling. Goddammit, what a sucker I was to believe your pitch. I should fire you right now."

Patrick shot to his feet, the mention of Helen igniting a smoldering fury that had lain hidden just below a fragile façade of calm for months. He ripped open the office door, letting it crash into the wall, nearly knocking down one of Anderson's prize faux Goyas. "You'll have your goddamned book by the end of August!" he shouted over his shoulder as he stormed past Estelle's desk. "And don't worry. I know what Helen likes. It will be a bestseller."

Estelle, now seated behind her desk, stared at him wide-eyed. "Dr. Denny," she called after him.

"What!" he shouted.

"Your nose is bleeding," she informed him, pulling three tissues from the box on her desk in quick succession.

He snatched the tissues and held them to his nose. "Thank you," he said gruffly and continued on his way.

• • •

"Son of a bitch!" Patrick raged as he sped down the drive away from Everston. He was so angry at so many different things all at once that he could barely focus on the road. "What did she tell him?" he sputtered. He slammed on his brakes, nearly running the stop sign. He imagined them in bed, imagined them laughing about all the insecurities that had taken him years to confide in her. He screeched around the corner and headed for the center of town. How much did Anderson know about the breakdown? And what had she told him about his career-ending writer's block?

"Bitch!" He slammed the steering wheel with the palm of his hand. His nose had stopped bleeding, but his fury still flowed, not yet running its full course. The truth was that he'd barely been able to write those opening pages of Anderson's book. He'd been trying for a year now but couldn't get past the beginning, knowing that once it was completed, he would have to turn it over to the two of them. He blew through another intersection, this time narrowly missing a car crossing in front of him.

"Maniac!" someone on the sidewalk screamed.

The world around him seemed unreal, removed from his immediate perception of existence, a black-and-white backdrop to the bright red rage radiating from his chest. He spun the wheel and skidded onto Hideaway Lane. "They'll get their fucking book," he vowed as he pulled into the parking lot without braking and hit the speed bump. The car bounced up into the air and slammed back onto the pavement, momentarily jostling the steering wheel from his grasp. Ignoring the bystanders who shouted and pointed, he regained his grip and screeched into a space under the shadow of Tower Hill. "They'll get their book, and then they'll both pay."

. . .

Loosening his tie, Patrick climbed the steps to his second-floor office in the Old Meeting Hall building. After reassuring the people in the parking lot that he wasn't drunk, that he'd just taken the turn too fast, his rage had sputtered out, and all that was left was exhaustion and shame. He would cancel all his afternoon appointments, he decided as he searched for the key to his office door. If he were quick enough, he could catch Mr. Scarlatti before he left his apartment. But the lonely man would be disappointed, Patrick knew. So lonely and afraid, sure that at any moment, the reaper would come for him and no one in the world would know. He'd even given Patrick a key to his place just in case. "If I don't show up for one of my sessions, you have my permission to go into my apartment to find my dead body. I don't want to rot there until the neighbors smell me," Mr. Scarlatti had said.

Patrick sighed and rested his head against the office door. Maybe he could meet with Mr. Scarlatti and cancel the other two appointments, he thought.

"Are we interrupting a nap?"

Patrick recognized the voice immediately, but when he looked up, he wasn't sure he recognized its owner.

"Samantha?"

"It's her," Father Owen confirmed from beside her. "I told you she was doing well."

Samantha smiled at Patrick, and he took in the sight of her. She seemed to stand taller than he remembered. Her big brown eyes appeared wider and more alive, and her complexion had the healthy glow of someone who was spending time out in the sunshine and fresh air.

"You look wonderful," Patrick exclaimed.

She smiled wider, but the smile quickly changed to a frown.

"You don't," she said, stepping forward to get a good look at his haggard face.

Father Owen nodded in agreement. "Are you ill?" the elderly man asked, not the picture of health himself. He seemed to move with increasing difficulty and was sporting a new cane that Patrick hadn't seen him with before.

"Oh, I'm just a little overworked. Don't worry. Well, what are we standing out here for? Come on in." He let them into his office and motioned for them to sit. "This is such a pleasant surprise. I wish you had let me know you were coming. I would have cleared my schedule and taken you both to lunch."

"Oh, this was just a spur-of-the-moment visit. I've been helping Father Owen with some of his errands, and he suggested we drop in."

Patrick couldn't get over Sam's transformation. When he'd first met her, she was so miserable, so vulnerable. But now . . .

"Sam is back to get the house ready for sale," Father Owen chimed in.

A shadow of sadness crossed her face at the mention of her house, and Patrick imagined that the decision to sell her childhood home wasn't an easy one to make. "I think it's a good decision," he said. "You have a whole new life ahead of you."

Sam nodded. "I know, and I'm excited about it. I'm pretty sure Mom and Dad would be happy that I'm finally getting on with things."

"Yes, they would," Father Owen agreed. Then, eyeing Patrick with a nervous sidelong glance, he said, "Now, to some unpleasant business."

"Owen," Patrick warned, knowing exactly what the priest

was about to say. "I told you I'm done with the matter."

But Father Owen proceeded. "Phineas Huntsman has asked to see you again."

"I have nothing to say to the man."

"He's desperate to speak to you. He says he needs to tell you something very important."

Sensing the tension between the two men, Sam stood up and went to the window to let them hash the matter out on their own.

Patrick followed her with his eyes. *Had it really been almost three years since she'd first stood there looking out at the tower?* He turned back to the priest and made no attempt to hide his animosity. "If he needs to confess something, I'm sure you'll handle it fine. Or he could call the police. I'm sure Detective Foret would be very interested to know what a pervert he is."

Sam glanced over her shoulder with a knowing lift of the eyebrows.

"Patrick!"

"Don't Patrick me. He's made his bed. And his nephew's. There's nothing I can or would do for the man."

"I understand how you feel. But he insists you are the only one who can help him."

"Help him with what? The man should be in jail, not living in the best eldercare facility in the state, being catered to by people who have no idea what he truly is. I still can't believe Archie admitted him to Halcyon House," Patrick said with disgust.

"He is still a human being!"

"He's a monster!"

The Tree

"Okay, time out, truce!" Sam exclaimed, deciding it was time to step in and break things up. "Now, children, play nice."

The priest blew out his cheeks. "Sorry, Samantha."

"Sorry," Patrick blurted.

"Good," she said. "Now, let's talk about something else."

But before they could move on to a more pleasant topic, a tap on the door made the three start.

"Just a moment," Patrick called out.

"Well, we should get out of your way," Father Owen said, rising from his seat with a bit of difficulty. Sam stooped to help him. "Will we be seeing you this weekend at the reopening of the organ hall?" the priest asked sheepishly.

"That's this weekend?" Patrick said, feigning ignorance. He never had any intention of attending the grand reopening of the Great Organ Hall, a place he would have rather seen razed than rehabilitated.

"Refreshments start at six-thirty, and the concert is at seven-fifteen," Sam informed him with an expectant tone.

"Are you going to be there?"

She nodded, "Yep, I'm manning the refreshment stand. So you'd better be there, too. Besides Father Owen, you're the only other person I'll know."

"I'll try," Patrick said as he opened the door for them.

"Am I early?" a fidgety man on the other side asked.

"No, Mr. Scarlatti. I'm running late."

"Sorry," Sam said as she walked past. "Our fault."

"Oh, it's no problem—no problem at all—I just hope I didn't interrupt by knocking—I'm usually Dr. Denny's first afternoon appointment—I didn't mean to interrupt or rush you—I can wait longer if you need more time—I've got nowhere else to be—"

Patrick put his arm around Ray Scarlatti and gently ushered the anxious man into the office. "That's okay, Mr. Scarlatti, we're all done. No worries."

"We'll see you Saturday night," Sam called back as she and Father Owen made their way down the hall.

"What's Saturday night?" Mr. Scarlatti asked.

Patrick rubbed his forehead and shut the door. "Do you like organ music?"

CHAPTER TEN

Resting her hands on her swollen belly, she waited for them once again. Six months had passed, and as instructed, she returned to the clearing in the oak grove. Sunlight filtered through the bare branches and fell upon the fire pit, now cold and covered with fallen leaves. She paced back and forth, afraid of what new tribulation approached. The autumn wind whistled between the trunks of the great oaks and stirred up the dead, dry leaves in the pit. And for a moment, she was once again staring at the roaring flames, hearing the sparks and sputters of the bonfire as she was carried off into the woods to be ravaged.

"Yer early," a gravelly voice shouted from some hidden place in the forest.

As the young woman spun around to see who had interrupted her ruminations, an old woman, filthy and sporting a ragged sackcloth shawl, hobbled out of the woods toward her.

"I . . . I'm early?" she stuttered, repulsed by the ugliness of the creature that approached.

Why Did God Make the Tree?

"Yes," said the crone, who stopped just a few feet away to rest on a roughly hewn cane. "I was supposed to be here first, to wait fer ya. But yer already here, so ya must be early." She hacked and spat on the ground.

"Maybe you're just late," the young woman laughed.

But the crone was not amused. She scurried forward until her bloated face was inches away. "I'm never late! Ya, foul mouth, little bitch! Yer early!" And she punctuated her assertion with a sharp slap across the startled woman's face.

Shaking off the blow, she turned on the old woman and screeched, "I'm pregnant! You could hurt my baby!"

"Yer baby?" the crone cackled, revealing yellow, misshapen teeth, and shot her hands forward to feel the bulge of her belly. "Don't worry. Ah, yes, she's a'coming along nicely."

"Don't!" the pregnant woman protested and pushed the gnarled, groping hands away.

The crone stepped back and inspected her with cataracted eyes. "Don't worry, whore. I'd never harm this child. We'll take good care a' her."

"Where are the others? They said to meet them here."

The old woman started back toward the tree line, her tattered shawl dragging on the ground behind her. "Their job's done," she grunted. "Now come along. It's a long walk."

"But . . . I don't understand. Why did I have to come now? And where are we going?"

The crone turned on her with such ferocity that the frightened young woman cried out. After three more painful slaps, the beastly creature growled, "You'll soon learn to keep yer mouth shut, ya little slut. Now follow me."

The Tree

Stunned by the strength and viciousness of the ancient woman, she could only obey and follow her into the trees. They walked for hours, the crone showing surprising endurance.

Unaccustomed to the extra weight, the mother-to-be needed to rest but didn't dare ask for a break. And when she walked too slowly, the old woman turned and poked her chest with the pointy end of her cane.

"Keep up, cow!"

When they finally arrived at the crumbling stone cottage deep within the forest, she was ready to collapse. She followed the old woman through a vine-covered gate to the stoop at the front door and took a moment to inspect the structure. In a past life, the little cottage was probably very homey, with clinging ivy growing up the walls and around the door and windows, the gentle slope of the moss-covered slate roof culminating in a crooked chimney from which wisps of blue smoke swirled, all under the protective reach of a great arched willow.

But once through the front door, the impression of quaint comfort disappeared like the smoke from the chimney. The interior of the cottage was dark, damp, and stuffy, the air so thick with foul, pungent smells she could barely breathe. The crone lit a lantern that sat on a lopsided wooden table, revealing the clutter and filth that crammed the room from floor to ceiling. Jars filled with all manner of plant, animal, and fungal remains crowded the table. Baskets and rolled-up rugs and broken furniture were stacked against every wall, obstructing any light that may have had a chance to penetrate the dirt-covered windows. Except for a narrow path from the door to the table and from the table to the staircase by the smoldering hearth, the floor was piled three feet high with a calamity of bric-a-brac that teetered on near disaster.

"I need water," she said as the cramped room began to close around her.

The crone ignored her and busied herself at the table, searching through the collection of jars, bottles, and flasks. "Not that one . . . oh yes, this one . . . no, no, too soon," she muttered.

"Please, I can't breathe." The young woman wavered as spots floated before her eyes.

"Maybe . . . no, a'course not, that will be in a few weeks . . . oooh, this one."

She could hear the clinking of glass and the shuffle of the crone's feet as the room began to swirl and undulate. She reached out, trying to find something to hold onto. "I'm . . . going to . . . pass out," she panted.

"That's it! Heehee. I got it now," the crone sang out, declaring her success to her new charge, just as the young woman crumbled onto a pile of junk with a violent crash. "I knew I'd remember."

The old woman's delight echoed in the black void of the young woman's consciousness until the shock of the icy water made her gasp and open her bleary eyes. "What happened? Where am I?" she cried out.

The crone stood over her with a metal pail. "Get up!" she ordered and hit her with another splash of water.

"Stop it!" she choked and sat up on the cot.

"Breakfast. Time fer the trough, ya ugly horse," the crone announced and waddled down the staircase.

Wiping the water from her eyes with her sleeve and raking her fingers through her tangled, wet hair, the young woman sat on the edge of the cot, trying to get her bearings. The tiny room had slanted walls that met in a peak over a small oval window. She peered out the cloudy glass and down at the front gate. The morning was gray, and she shivered at the cold draft that seeped through the crevices around the window.

"Get yer fat arse down here!" the crone shouted up to her.

Her cheeks still ached from the violence of the day before. Afraid of incurring the crone's wrath once again, she didn't linger, wondering how the old woman had managed to get her up to the second floor. She made her way down the narrow, twisting staircase and returned to the chaotic room with the wooden table. The fire in the hearth was now stoked and blazing, the warmth providing a small bit of comfort amidst the disorder.

"Sit!" the crone ordered as she fussed over a bowl atop the table.

The young woman obeyed, balancing herself on a rickety stool. With a clatter, the bowl was deposited in front of her. She cringed at the mound of brown mushrooms, still covered with clumps of moist dirt and emitting an earthy, rotting odor.

"Eat."

Swallowing back her disgust, she whispered, "I can't . . ."

Slap!

"They might be poisonous," she protested with a whimper.

Slap!

"But the baby . . ."

"I told ya I wouldn't hurt the child. Now eat!" The crone wound up to strike again, but the young woman snatched a mushroom from the bowl and shoved it into her mouth before the punishment could be inflicted again. She chewed the spongy flesh and forced herself to swallow. "More!" the old woman ordered as she leaned on her cane and watched her from across the table.

Gagging, she took another.

"Ignorant girl. Don't even know which ones are poisonous and which ones ain't," the crone scoffed. "Do ya!"

The young woman shook her head and took another.

"Ignorant little nit. Bet ya don't even know that without mushrooms there'd be no forest, no trees. Eh. Those white-robed fools don't understand it, either," the crone grumbled and shifted her weight on the cane. "Now, mind ya, the forest is powerful. I pay it no disrespect." She tapped her cane on the floor three times and glanced up at the ceiling. "But without those beauties," she said, gesturing toward the bowl, "it'd die."

The young woman nodded dumbly as she filled her mouth with chewy stems and pulpy caps, growing accustomed to the taste of dirt and the fleshy texture against her tongue.

"The roots a' the trees only reach out so far. They use up all the food in the soil around 'em, suck it dry. As powerful as they are, left on their own, they'd starve. But under us, under the people and animals and everything else that shits upon the earth, there's an invisible being that makes all the life around us possible. It creeps out through the soil fer acres and acres, a ghostly web, a'pushing and a'probing and a'gathering." Her voice softened, and her coal-black eyes took on a whimsical shine. "It reaches out to where the soil is just teemin' with the nourishment of Mother Earth and feeds it to the roots of the trees, sucklin'em, so they grow bigger and stronger, 'til they reach their powerful branches up high into the sky, into the air and sunlight."

She stopped chewing for a moment and watched the crone,

whose sagging breasts heaved with exhilaration.

"Eat!" she snapped, suddenly aware that she was now the one being watched.

Obediently, the young woman crammed the mushrooms into her mouth, smearing her lips and chin with the creamy brown flesh.

"But it's not one-sided," the crone continued less whimsically. "The trees give succor a' their own, a sweet nectar that helps this gossamer web grow larger, vaster, more productive. And when the time is right, when all the elements join together to make just the best conditions, when the soil is warm and moist and ready, this being changes its gauzy self into solid flesh and penetrates up through the soil into our world . . ." She paused and inspected the bowl. It was almost empty. She grinned. "To spread its spore."

The young woman jammed the last cap and stem into her mouth, down her throat, nearly gagging herself. And when the bowl was empty, she looked frantically around the room and shrieked, "More!"

☙

THE SHRIEK OF THE TELEPHONE startled him awake.

"Dr. Denny, you need to get here quickly," Nurse Liebman informed him, the urgency in her voice spurring Patrick out of bed and into his clothes. He flew down the narrow staircase of his apartment building half-dressed, zipping and buttoning himself up as he drove through the deserted streets of Waylingbrooke.

His plan to reschedule the rest of his afternoon appointments and retire to bed early was never realized. After meeting with

Mr. Scarlatti and Mrs. Zacharovitch and finally his new patient, the young Mr. Tomás Torrente, a rather talkative adolescent with a mysterious case of extreme paranoia, Patrick was too wired to fall asleep straightaway. Now past midnight, he raced toward Everston, sleep-deprived, his body trembling with adrenaline.

Amelia was awake. That's what the nurse had said. Patrick hadn't gotten any more out of the conversation with the commotion going on in the background—the ceaseless shrieking, which he could only assume was Amelia Dearborne's first communication with the world outside her mind in almost two decades. He had to hurry. He'd given the staff orders not to sedate her without his approval. But Dilby was there. At least, he thought the nurse had said something about him being there.

Patrick's car peeled up the winding drive and rounded the hospital into the parking lot. As he hurried up the stone steps, the building loomed before him, the entire row of second-floor windows ablaze with light. Amelia's awakening had caused quite an uproar.

"Damn you, Dilby!" he seethed as he took the steps two at a time. Dilby would sedate her against his orders. He had no doubt about that. After Patrick had accused him of complicity with Patricia Huntsman in first drugging her nephew and then disappearing with him, all pretense of professional disagreement had been replaced with open hostilities. Anderson's brief investigation was a farce. But even though Dilby was exonerated, his reputation in the eyes of his colleagues and the staff was tarnished. And the affronted man now walked the halls of Everston in search of ways to settle the score, his mission to discredit Dr. Patrick Denny.

The Tree

Patrick could hear her as soon as he entered the building. The inhuman sound grew more terrible the closer he got to her floor, her wing, her room. Nurse Liebman met him in the corridor. "He's going to sedate her," she exclaimed as she fell in step with him. "I told him that you left orders not to push any meds until you got here, but he won't listen."

The two flew down the corridor, and in each room they passed, staff members tried to calm the other patients churned up by the banshee wails emanating from Amelia's room.

"Don't let it get me!" someone pleaded.

"Make it stop!" another demanded.

"It's a witch! A witch!" a petrified man hissed.

"No, no, no, no . . ." Amelia's roommate muttered outside the door to their room as she was led away.

Patrick's heart raced and he quickened his step. He and Nurse Liebman burst through the doorway to find Dilby, syringe in hand, and two male staffers dancing back and forth as if trying to corner a wild animal.

"What the hell are you doing?" Patrick shouted at the three determined men. He pushed past Dilby.

Cornered between her bed and a pair of tall barred windows, Amelia paced, crying out in a shrill, pain-filled voice. "Amelia," Patrick called, trying to get the tormented woman's attention. He stepped toward her and she lashed out at him, her long hair hanging wild and tangled in front of her face. He jumped back and crashed into one of Dilby's cohorts, an overly muscular young man whose neck was as wide as his head.

"Careful, Doc, the bitch tried to scratch my eyes out," he warned.

"Get out!" Patrick ordered them all.

But Dilby advanced, wielding the syringe in one hand while protectively holding his other, bandaged and bleeding, against his chest. "You lunatic!" the squat, aging doctor yelled. "You took her off the meds!"

"Get out," Patrick repeated, this time directly at Dilby.

Dilby didn't move, and for an agonizing moment, Nurse Liebman stood wringing her hands. The two staffers looked at each other nervously as the standoff between the two doctors dragged out. All the while, Amelia continued to shriek.

"She's my patient," Patrick stated.

"You're endangering your patient and everyone around her."

"Get out!"

"I'm going to the director," Dilby growled and stormed out of the room.

"Good luck finding him," Patrick shouted after him. "You can leave, too," he said to the two men awaiting orders, and they quickly followed Dilby out.

Nurse Liebman waited by the door, her face exhausted yet determined. "What now?" she asked over Amelia's cries.

"Get two milligrams of lorazepam ready. And shut the door behind you."

The nurse nodded and hurried away.

Patrick turned his attention back to his patient, pulling back his tousled hair, unsure of what to do next. Amelia traveled back and forth between the bed and the windows, her screaming becoming even more unbearable. "Amelia, I'm going to be just over here," he called to her as he backed himself up against the door. "Give you a little space so you can calm down."

He watched and waited in silence, but her tirade continued unabated, her stamina almost inhuman. At a loss for what to do and unable to fight his exhaustion, Patrick slid to the floor and leaned his aching head against the door. He closed his eyes and listened. After a while, he began to detect a pattern in her howling, a regular rise and drop in pitch with which he unconsciously synced his breath. His thoughts drifted, and he no longer felt the hard floor beneath him. He was floating on the waves of the rhythm, away from the hospital, away from Waylingbrooke . . .

"It's stopping," someone whispered loudly from the other side of the door. Patrick's eyes snapped open. Amelia's pacing had slowed to a shuffle, and she roamed the entire room now, her arms dangling at her sides, an occasional moan of despair escaping her throat.

Patrick pushed himself up to his feet and peered at her. Through the tangled mass of hair, he could see her lips moving. He strained to hear, but people were arguing in hushed tones in the corridor.

"Should we go in?"

"No, he'll tell us when to go in."

Patrick stepped closer to Amelia and cocked his head. He could hear it, the susurrations of a small voice—one side of a conversation. Though he couldn't make out the words, it seemed she was trying to explain something to someone, her tone almost singsong and childlike. Her wandering stopped suddenly, and she came to rest a few feet from Patrick and stared down at her feet. Gesturing with her hands, she chatted on. He took another tentative step toward her. He could just make out some of the words, almost able to grasp a tiny fragment of a sentence . . .

A crash and a series of clangs from outside the door stopped Amelia's rambling dead and her head snapped up. Patrick flinched, his breath catching in his throat. Her eyes were wide, focused, and locked on him with such violent hatred that he stumbled back in fear. The pale skin of her face was pulled taut, her jaw clenched, her brows furrowed. He had no doubt that she saw him and wanted to harm him. He fought the urge to flee, preparing himself for the imminent attack. But as suddenly as she had looked up and caught him in her murderous gaze, the muscles of her face relaxed and her head dropped back down. Once again, she shuffled aimlessly around the room until she climbed into bed, curled up under the blankets, and fell into a deep sleep.

Patrick exhaled but remained motionless, watching until he was certain she was actually asleep. After a few moments, he moved slowly, dimming the lights and quietly opening the door. Nurse Liebman stood vigil just outside. He held out his hand and she gave him the syringe. He mouthed a thank you and shut the door. Amelia didn't stir as he administered the mild sedative. He left her sleeping soundly, her breathing even, resuming her unresponsive state—the china doll once again.

"How did you get her to stop screaming?" Nurse Liebman asked as Patrick shut the door behind him.

"I just waited until she stopped," he said while he read over Amelia's chart.

"Well?" The nurse waited for more information about the encounter. "What happened? Did she say anything?"

Patrick concealed his unease, unwilling to admit to the

inquisitive nurse that his patient had spooked him. "Just mumbling, nothing coherent. What happened before I got here?"

The nurse shook her head. "I'd just finished my midnight check of the rooms when she started screaming. I rushed in to see what was happening and found her hiding in the corner. I guess Dr. Dilby was already here for another patient, and someone called him. He told me to get the sedative. I tried to tell him about your orders, but . . ." she waved her hand in exasperation. "So I ran out to the desk and called you. When I got back to the room, Dr. Dilby's hand was bleeding. She'd bitten him."

"She bit him?"

The nurse nodded and Patrick's face broke into a wide grin.

"That's very unprofessional, doctor," the nurse said, trying not to laugh. "How should we handle her if it happens again?"

"Let's keep her on the lorazepam for now." He wrote some notes on the chart. "I'll be here tomorrow afternoon."

"You mean this afternoon," she said, glancing up at the big round clock on the wall. It was already past four in the morning.

"Dammit," he said, slumping over the desk at the nurses' station. "I'll be lucky to get a couple hours of sleep. I'm going to see her parents later this morning, and then I have to stop by Halcyon House." He clenched his jaw, resenting Father Owen for guilting him into visiting Phineas Huntsman.

"I guess you don't get weekends off either, do you, Dr. Denny?" she said as she tucked a stray lock of auburn hair back into the bun on the top of her head and rubbed her eyes.

Realizing that he wasn't the only one who had been up all night, he asked, "Have you been here since yesterday morning?"

"Yes. Someone called out sick."

He sighed apologetically. "You must get sick of us doctors whining all the time."

She chuckled, "It's okay. I'm used to it."

"When do you sleep?"

"I'm off in a couple hours, and I'll sleep most of the day until my next shift. Oh, and don't worry, I'll make sure the day shift knows what to do for Amelia."

He stared at her for a moment, amazed at her energy. He wasn't much older than she was, yet she seemed to handle the stress of the job and crazy hours with much more stamina and grace. Though clearly tired, her hazel eyes were alert and her cheeks round and rosy with health. Unlike Patrick, who was slumped over the desk, she stood erect in her loose-fitting pink scrubs and white sneakers. She held herself with a natural ease that Patrick suddenly found thoroughly appealing.

"It's Susan, right?"

"Yes."

"Susan, thank you for your help tonight . . . today, I mean."

"Just doing my job, Doctor," she said with a smile.

"Well, you do it very well. Will you be here tonight?"

"Tonight and tomorrow night."

"Good," Patrick said. "I'm glad you'll be here."

She blushed and busied herself at the desk.

"I mean, I know you'll take good care of her while I'm gone," he said, over-explaining himself. "I have to go to that damned reopening ceremony for the organ hall tomorrow . . . I mean tonight. I promised a friend."

"Oh, a hot date?" she asked, studying a blank chart on the desk.

"No, no, nothing like that." He stood quickly, nearly knocking the telephone off the desk. "Just a friend, really an acquaintance, not . . . not a date."

"Okay."

The two stood there in awkward silence for a moment.

"Okay." Patrick pushed back from the desk. "Call me. I mean, if anything comes up with Amelia."

"I will," she called after him as he hurried toward the elevators.

. . .

Patrick exited the building just as the sun rose above the horizon, troubled by the events of the evening. He cringed, still embarrassed by his awkward attempt to compliment Nurse Liebman. He'd always been able to charm the ladies. When had he turned into such a blabbering idiot? And what was he to do with Amelia Dearborne? What had happened all those years ago to turn a happy, normal fifteen-year-old girl into the frightening beast that Patrick had momentarily glimpsed up in that hospital room? He sat in his car and closed his eyes, replaying the disturbing episode in his mind. There was something in all that incoherent mumbling. He could almost grab onto it, a fragment of a sentence, a few essential words, but then the commotion in the corridor, the inhuman eyes that locked upon him . . .

With a shiver, he sat up and looked across the parking lot. Cars pulled out of the lot as others pulled in. The night shift made way for the day shift. It was almost time to face Amelia's parents.

"She was such a happy little girl," Mrs. Dearborne said as she handed Patrick a glass of freshly squeezed orange juice. "She never had any problems until . . ."

Patrick accepted the glass and took a sip. It was sweet and cold, just the pickup he needed at that moment.

"What Mary is saying is that nothing like that happened. All the people around her were good, decent people and would never do what you are suggesting," Mr. Dearborne declared.

Patrick placed the glass on the table and glanced around the modest kitchen. "I'm sorry to ask these questions again. I need to make sure I know as much as possible about what might have happened to her before she started to get sick."

Mr. Dearborne nodded, his expression more heartsick than angry now.

"Has anything happened yet?" Mrs. Dearborne asked, clearly afraid to hear his answer.

Patrick nodded. "She was up last night," he said quickly and took another sip of juice.

"Did she . . . what did she do?"

Patrick responded, unable to look directly at the apprehensive woman. "She was frightened. She cried. Wandered around the room. Then went to sleep."

Mrs. Dearborne blinked. "That's all?"

Patrick swigged down the rest of his juice, knowing the anxious mother could tell he was leaving out the worst of it.

"Did she say anything? Did she ask for us?" Mr. Dearborne asked, reaching for his wife's hand.

Patrick shook his head. "Nothing coherent. It was like she was mumbling in her sleep."

"But it's still a good sign!"

"Well, I should get these breakfast dishes cleaned before the egg gets too hard," Mrs. Dearborne said, pulling her hand from her husband's. She went to the sink and blasted the water so she couldn't hear them speaking.

"Tell me about that summer again."

The old man sighed. "It was just like every summer. Melly finished with school. And we packed up and drove to the cottage. She was excited about some bird she was going to find."

"She did a lot of birdwatching?" Patrick asked.

"Oh, yeah. She'd take her little Nikon camera we'd gotten her for one of her birthdays out into the woods and spend all day waiting to take pictures of the different birds. I can show you that album we told you about." He stood up and waved at Patrick to follow.

Mrs. Dearborne glanced over her shoulder at them as they left the kitchen and walked down the hallway of the one-floor, ranch-style house. At the far end, Mr. Dearborne opened a door and led Patrick into a bedroom clearly once inhabited by a teenage girl. A poster of Kirk Cameron dated the décor of the room to the mid-eighties. The motif was rainbows, shooting stars, and unicorns. Patrick's gaze swept across the space, taking in the pastel hues and glittering accents that adorned every surface, from the wallpaper to the bedspread to the mobile of stars above her desk. The shelves next to her bed were crowded with soccer trophies, blue ribbons, and photos of a happy, healthy young girl barely recognizable as the woman he was currently treating.

A photo album lay open on the neatly made bed. Mr. Dearborne flipped through some of the heavy pages and pointed at the different birds Amelia had captured on film. "She liked the little yellow ones. Said they were little bursts of sunlight. These here in the album are from previous summers. She never got around to adding the pictures from that last summer at the cottage. Um, here," he handed Patrick a pile of glossy four-by-six photographs that he grabbed from the desk. "I had them developed for her. But she didn't seem interested in them anymore."

Patrick took the photos and flipped through the stack. At first, they seemed similar to her previous work. Blue jays and bright red cardinals singing, preening, and sleeping up in the trees. A group of chickadees bathing in a sandy patch on the ground. A nest of newly hatched robins screeching up to the sky for their parents to feed them.

"She was an excellent photographer," Patrick observed. "She must have been incredibly quiet to get so close."

Mr. Dearborne nodded his head proudly. "She walked like a cat and climbed like a monkey."

Patrick flipped through more of the photos, admiring Amelia's work until he came upon one that differed from the others.

"That one upset her," Mr. Dearborne said, peering over Patrick's shoulder at the photo of the dead baby bird. "Robin hatchling that fell out of its nest."

Patrick stared, transfixed by the fragile little creature, its scrawny neck twisted unnaturally so that the bulbous, oversized head faced up toward the sky with eyes that would never open.

The Tree

Its featherless wings stretched out to the sides as if it were making a pathetic attempt to fly. He could hear the buzz of the flies that swarmed over the little corpse. *Had the fall killed her?* he wondered. *Or did she suffer on the ground, blind and alone, before finally succumbing to her fate?*

"I think that's when she started to get sick. She kept going on about how the tree had shaken it out of the nest on purpose. I didn't want to tell her it was probably one of its siblings. They do that, you know, push the weaker ones out so they don't have to share the food their parents bring back to the nest."

Patrick abruptly returned the photos to Mr. Dearborne, his pained expression fleeting but not unnoticed. "Thank you for letting me see them," he mumbled. "Do you mind if I have a few moments alone in her room?"

The old man nodded, seemingly unsettled by the doctor's sudden agitation. He made to leave the room but paused just before the door. "Doctor, will I ever get my little girl back?"

Patrick wanted to lie to the man, to give him some bit of hope, but all he could say was "I don't know."

The door shut behind Mr. Dearborne, and Patrick sat on the bed. He rubbed his trembling hands together and squeezed his eyes shut. "Focus," he told himself. Amelia had been an ordinary fifteen-year-old girl when they drove up to the cabin. But by the time the new school year had started, she had transformed into a feral beast. He searched through the room, opening drawers and rifling through boxes in the closet. He was careful to put everything back as he found it, knowing Mrs. Dearborne kept the room tidy in anticipation of her daughter's eventual return.

There was nothing. Nothing to indicate any traumatic

experiences, any drug use, any boyfriends. Except for the photograph of the dead baby bird, everything in Amelia's room pointed to a happy, innocent existence. Patrick sat back down on the bed and closed his eyes again. He was tempted to lay his head on the pillow, but a tap on the door made him jump up. Mrs. Dearborne poked her anxious face in.

"Dr. Denny, John went to the post office. He'll be gone a few minutes. Can I talk to you?"

"Of course."

She scrambled into the room and shut the door. "I found something in Amelia's closet some years ago. I didn't ever tell John because I knew it would upset him." She entered the closet and pulled out a shoebox that Patrick had already rummaged through. It was just another box of memorabilia—seashells, plastic rings, and odds and ends that you'd get from a gumball machine or at a fair. Mrs. Dearborne put the box on the bed and carefully placed each object aside. With a heavy sigh, she held out a half-burned black candle and a crinkled business card.

"We disapprove of this sort of thing. Amelia knew that, but she was a teenager, and you know how rebellious they can be."

Patrick took the candle and the card, reading it out loud. "Madam Flora, Psychic and Spiritual Healer."

"I think Amelia might have gone there with some of her summer friends. You know how girls can be. Excited about silly things like getting their palms read, finding out the name of their future husbands and how many children they'll have. That sort of nonsense. Harmless fun. It's not real," she said, but a hint of uncertainty tinged her words.

"No, it's not real," Patrick assured her.

"We're good Catholics," Mrs. Dearborne insisted. "And Amelia was . . . *is* a good girl."

"I'm sure this has nothing to do with Amelia's illness."

They heard the front door close. "You can keep those," Mrs. Dearborne said, relieved to be ridding her house of even the mention of the occult. And she hurried from the room to greet her husband.

Patrick slipped the candle and card into his coat pocket and packed the rest of the memorabilia back into the box. Something happened that summer up at the cabin, and maybe Madam Flora could help shed some light on it.

• • •

"Hallo, Dr. Denny," a plump young woman greeted him as he climbed the winding staircase toward Phineas Huntsman's room.

"Hello . . ." Patrick floundered, unable to place her face.

"I work at Everston last year," she said, her European accent heavy and indistinct.

"Oh, of course, Nurse Delacroix. I didn't know you worked here now," he said, joining her on the top landing.

"Oh, ja, I left Everston last winter after incident with Dr. Dilby and Mr. McKay."

"Yes, that was all very unpleasant. I'm sorry you got dragged into the whole affair."

She shrugged, her short, blonde curls bouncing with the gesture. "Was not too bad. Mr. Anderson asked only a little questions and then he help me get job here after return from visiting with my family. I like here better. The patients here are more . . . how do you say . . . tranquil."

They both glanced down at the spacious foyer, where many of the residents of Halcyon House had settled peacefully on wing chairs and dainty sofas. Some closed their eyes, resting in the pleasant warmth of the sun shining in from the tall front windows. Others held attractive leather-bound books taken from one of the many bookshelves that lined the walls. With the tiffany-style lamps, Chippendale furniture, and freshly cut flowers, the place seemed more like an exclusive private club than a hospice for those dying from dementia.

"You are here on visit to Mr. Huntsman?"

"Yes," Patrick said, taking in the aroma of freshly made bread that hung in the air. Warm, pleasant, and welcoming, nothing about the aptly named Halcyon House felt institutional. Archie had outdone himself. But as he turned to follow Nurse Delacroix to Phineas Huntsman's private room, Patrick was haunted by the image of Michael McKay's time at Everston. Strapped to his hospital bed, under the blinding fluorescent lights of the sterile room, cold and crying, Michael had been hurt, scared, and treated worse than an animal. It just wasn't fair.

"He is very anxious to see you," the nurse chirped. "Not many visitors come and he not leave room too much, so will be good for him to have company." The door stood slightly ajar, and she opened it wider so Patrick could enter.

"Mr. Huntsman, you have visitor," she announced in a sing-song voice.

Patrick stepped into the pleasant little room. The quilt on the bed appeared to be handmade, and the furniture was in the same style as that in the foyer. Phineas sat by the window, holding back the lace curtains and looking out at the sprawling and impeccably maintained lawn in front of the old Victorian mansion. He showed no response to the announcement of a visitor.

"Go sit with him by the window," the nurse whispered.

Patrick approached the old man whom he hadn't seen since they first met. Imprisoned by his nephew in the dark dungeon of the organ hall basement, Phineas had been filthy and emaciated. Now sitting comfortably in front of the oversized window, clean and well-fed, Patrick's impression of him was the same. There was something sick about the man. Evil, twisted, and unnatural.

Nurse Delacroix left the room pulling on the door, leaving it open a crack.

Patrick took a seat next to Phineas, but before he could speak, the old man barked, "Did you catch her yet?"

Patrick glanced over at the door and then back at the belligerent old man whose toothless grimace repulsed him. "No, your wife left the country with Michael. You remember Michael, don't you?"

"You're a lying bastard. She's still here. They both are," Phineas accused. "What kind of policeman are you?"

"You know I'm not a policeman," Patrick answered, his voice raised in the hope of garnering the attention of anyone within earshot. "Let's not play this game, Mr. Huntsman. You know I'm a doctor. It's time to stop pretending that you're sick."

Phineas screwed up his face suspiciously. "You're the one playing games, *Doctor*. I know she's still here."

Patrick sat back and rolled his eyes. "Tell me, why do you think your wife is still in Waylingbrooke?"

Phineas licked his dry lips and leaned toward him. "She comes into my room at night and sits on my chest."

"Who?"

"Patricia!" he hissed. "She whispers to me."

"Really?" Patrick said skeptically. "What does she say?"

After a moment of indecision, Phineas whispered, "She says . . ." He looked around the room as if fearful they were not alone. "She says that my sins will all come back on me . . . soon."

Patrick scrutinized the man. Though his words sounded like that of a paranoid delusional, his expression appeared lucid and sincere. He leaned in even closer to the old man's face and stared into his soulless eyes. "Let's hope so."

"Ah! You're working for her, too, aren't you?" He snorted and looked out the window again, up into the giant oak that hung high above the roof. A family of blue jays cheeped excitedly, the young fledglings following their parents up and up from branch to branch until they disappeared from view.

"Noisy little bastards. Wish I had a gun," Phineas grumbled.

Patrick stared at the back of the old man's head, at the spidery veins that pulsated beneath the paper-thin skin, and he shuddered. "What do you want from me, Mr. Huntsman?"

"Get me out of here," the old man whispered, stealing a glance over at the open door.

"Why the hell would I help you get out of here?"

"She's not done with me. You know what she and that halfwit tried to do to me—locking me in the dark to die. You're a doctor. You can't let her murder me!"

Patrick did know. But no one in Waylingbrooke wanted to hear it. Not the Huntsmans' attorneys, not the doctors, and especially not the police. Not even the intrepid and obsessive Detective Foret ventured to investigate the case when Patrick laid it out for him, telling the doctor bitterly that he'd already been ordered to stand down. It seemed that Patricia Huntsman was as powerful as the rumors suggested. Even Patrick's attempt to file a report with the FBI was met with a cold dismissal. The agent he spoke with showed no interest in a case that the local and state police had already put to rest. The official story they were going with was that somehow, Phineas had locked himself in that basement. Luckily, the doddering old man had a bag full of candy with him, and a cracked water pipe had provided a slow drip of water. Otherwise, he never would have survived. Patricia Huntsman was never there. She was on her way to Europe to get treatment for her sick nephew. *But it was understandable that Dr. Denny was confused. He'd had a terrible fall down that flight of stairs.*

Pushing aside his frustration, Patrick focused on the man in front of him, folding his arms and leaning back in his chair. "Then stop pretending to be this fragile, confused old man. Go to the police. Tell them what happened. If you're so afraid that Patricia will get you, come clean about everything. I'm sure they'll put you two in separate prisons. Then you'll be safe from her."

The old man momentarily contemplated Patrick's words and then regarded him with a derisive sneer. "Do not delude yourself, *Doctor*. You are no different than I!" With startling dexterity, the old man shot out his talon-like hand and latched onto Patrick's inner thigh. "You despise me because I've had something that you've always wanted. It's what every man, every little boy wants."

Phineas's touch made Patrick recoil in disgust, and he batted the hand away. "No, Phineas," he snarled, seizing the front of the old man's shirt and pulling him so close that he could smell the stench of his sour, decaying breath. "It's not. You're disgusting and evil. And I'm going to make sure you never get out of here. You're going to sit in front of this window for the rest of your life waiting, knowing that one of these days, Patricia *is* going to get you."

His eyes growing wide with terror, Phineas grabbed at Patrick. "Please, please, don't leave me here," he begged, his voice near hysterics. "Please! They lock me in at night and the lights won't turn on. Then she comes in the dark. I . . . I don't want to be in the dark. Please! Please, don't leave me here, please!"

Revolted by his own involuntary urge to pity the man, Patrick shoved the pathetic creature back into his chair and stood up.

"Please!" Phineas pleaded, throwing himself to his knees.

But Patrick didn't look back, bolting from the room and past the hovering nurse.

"You are leaving already?" Nurse Delacroix called as she trailed Patrick down the staircase.

"Yes, I am."

"I know is hard to see him like that," she said, catching up with him in the foyer. "Their mind go and it frighten them. He do not know what he says."

"Oh, he knows exactly what he's saying," Patrick informed her as he marched past the reposing residents in the lobby, yanked open the front door, and stormed out onto the porch.

"What you mean?" she called as she hurried to keep up.

"He's faking. He's not sick."

"Dr. Philbin says he is much deluded," she countered.

"Philbin's wrong," he shouted, unable to suppress his frustration. "I know everyone wants to pretend that nothing happened, that somehow poor, confused Phineas accidentally locked himself in that basement. That he didn't molest his nephew. But I know what really happened. That man up there, that monster—"

"Dr. Denny, please," Nurse Delacroix whispered, glancing around them and pulling him away from the front door. "You must not worry. What he did, whatever his sins, his judgment will come. You can be sure of that. Everyone is judged in the end, especially monsters." She squeezed his arm, smiled an odd smile, and reentered the house.

Patrick stared after her. He lingered for a moment on the grand front porch of Halcyon House with the unsettling notion that he was sure of nothing.

CHAPTER ELEVEN

The air inside the herb shed was cold and dry, and she clutched the shawl around her as she struggled to reach a bundle of dried dandelion greens hanging high from the rafters. "Damn witch," she complained as she swatted at it until it fell to the frozen dirt floor. The morning sun shone in through the open door and she glanced out at the snow-covered glade. Spring seemed to be taking its time, she thought as she tried to bend over to pick up the bundle, but her protruding belly got in the way. "Dammit!" she grumbled, resorting to an unladylike squat. She grabbed the bundle and hoisted herself back up, tossing the crumbling greenery into a basket that hung from the crook of her arm. She'd been instructed on which herbs to collect and, in the dim light of dawn, had been sent on her way with list in hand. Never mind that her back was aching and her feet were so swollen she had to wear a pair of the crone's smelly, worn slippers.

"Ya'll work for your keep, cow. Now get yer fat arse out there and do what I told you," the withered hag had commanded, shoving her out into the frigid morning. "Don't come back unless ya have everything I need."

Casting silent curses at the intolerable old woman, she had trudged through the slushy snow toward the herb shed, a ramshackle structure a quarter mile behind the cottage. By the time she had pulled open the rickety door, her feet were wet and numb, her mood bordering on homicidal. She collected the items on the list, and as she'd done night after night while she lay on her back watching the hideous bulge in her abdomen expand, she plotted the old crone's death.

At first, her imaginings were just harmless fantasies. An accidental fall down the stairwell would do the job. Or she could mistakenly lock her out in the cold on a long winter's night. But as the pregnancy advanced and the crone's abusive treatment of her continued, the fantasies turned more violent, more sadistic, and more *possible*. It would be so easy to come up behind her while she was hunched over a pot of boiling water and shove her head in, holding it under until the crooked old body went limp. It would take even less effort to wait until the old woman busied herself inside the cottage, to block the doorways, and to set the whole structure aflame, watching it burn to the ground with the shrill cries of her tormentor dying away in the embers.

Only the night before, as she worked at the table having been ordered to cut the last of the previous season's turnips into small cubes for a stew, she gripped the knife like an assassin. She was sure she could gut the old bitch without immediately killing her, spilling her innards out onto the floor, letting her writhe in pain as the life oozed from her. *No mercy*, she thought to herself, a sadistic smile pulling at the corner of her mouth. With this image set happily in her mind, she checked the crone's list. One item remained.

"Devil's claw," she read and searched around. Hanging from the sloped rafters were rows and rows of neatly tied bundles of desiccated sage, chervil, basil, rosemary, thyme, and many other herbs that she could not identify. Baskets of all shapes and sizes sat on shelves, each filled with an assortment of bulbs, pods, roots, and barks. Devil's claw was aptly named. Just as the crone had described it, the pincer-like hooked pods were in a large basket atop a shelf. She counted out fifteen pods and dropped them into the bottom of her basket next to the licorice root and willow bark. "Done," she sighed, surveying her collection of ingredients, hoping that she'd be allowed to rest for the remainder of the day. She had no idea what concoction the crone planned to brew, nor did she care. She'd take whatever she was ordered to take, knowing she was safe as long as the child was still inside her.

"Oh!" she cried out, dropping her basket to the floor and clutching her belly. As if knowing that her thoughts had turned to its existence, the child began to flail, battering her insides. "Stop it, you little monster," she hissed. "You'll be out soon enough. And then I'll be rid of you."

The baby seemed to hear her and stopped moving.

"Good," she spat and squatted once again to retrieve the basket.

It wasn't her child and she wasn't its mother. Though the notion had seemed unnatural to her at first, over the long months of pain and humiliation, she'd learned to accept it without question and looked forward to being rid of it.

Why Did God Make the Tree?

She stood up and staggered to the side, bumping into a fan of dried purple flowers hanging against the wall. Tiny shriveled petals sprinkled the floor, filling the air with the scent of lavender. She breathed it in and a long-forgotten memory washed over her, a wave of warmth and calm, a tinkle of tiny bells, the soft caress of gentle hands, warm lips brushing the fine, wispy hair on her head, a heartbeat against her cheek as she dozed off to sleep . . .

And then it was gone. She brushed her hand over the flowers again, hoping to retrigger the memory. But it was no use. As fast as it had come, it had disappeared, leaving her with an indescribable sense of loss.

Later, she leaned against the wall by the hearth, reclining on a stack of old cushions with her swollen feet propped up in front of her. At the table, the crone worked, throwing the ingredients collected from the herb shed into a pot and mumbling to herself, every now and then casting a surreptitious look her way.

The hearth blazed with a roaring fire, casting the room in its hazy glow. She stroked her stomach and watched the crone work. The child inside her hadn't stirred since its scolding in the shed. She moved her hands over the bulge, searching for some evidence of life, wondering if she had somehow harmed it with her words. Again, the hollow sense of loss stole over her, and she willed the child to stir, to show her it was still alive.

The crone snuck another sideways glance at her and muttered. And just as her worries began to give way to outright panic, it moved. She felt the child stretch inside her as if it had just woken from a long nap. Tiny fingers rippled under her flesh and reached out to touch her hands. Her breath caught and the crone's full attention snapped to her.

"Ya need some tea," she stated, waddling over to her with a bowl of her brew. "Here, drink this."

She took it, not bothering to ask what it was, not wanting to feel the palm of the old woman's hand against her cheek. She sniffed it as she brought the edge of the bowl to her lips, the steam rising into her nostrils with a pungent sting. Sipping at the bitter concoction, she fought the urge to spit it onto the floor.

"More! Drink more!"

She obeyed, slurping it all down, then wiping her lips with her tattered sleeve. The crone took the bowl from her and refilled it with water from a pitcher on the table. "Now come and look."

She sighed, not wanting to get up, but obeyed nonetheless. The floor creaked beneath her stockinged feet as she made her way to the table.

The crone pointed at the water and commanded, "Look!"

She peered into the bowl, squinting in the dim candlelight, but saw only cloudy water. She gave the old woman a furtive glance.

"Look!" the crone repeated.

She blinked and bent closer. The candle on the table flickered, the reflection of its flame undulating on the water's surface like tiny ripples on a pond. The ripples grew larger, and the water began to heave and surge. There was something there. The surface roiled. She bent even closer. She was sure she could see it, a face, his face, and she gasped just before the crone pushed her head into the bowl.

His smile sent electricity through her naked body. His blonde hair, long and wavy, hung over his bare shoulders as he stared down at her. The pure joy of the moment blotted out all the doubt, all her misgivings. She stared up into his eyes, bluer than the ocean, and trembled with pleasure. He heaved a contented sigh and rolled off her.

She turned to look at him, no longer shy about their nakedness, willingly exposing her body and heart to someone for the first time. "I love you," she whispered as she touched his arm.

He laughed with happiness—or so she thought at first. But when he yanked his arm from her touch and stood up, she knew he was mocking her. "Okay," he sneered, pulling on his trousers. "This was fun, but I have to get to work."

She wrapped herself in her arms, her nakedness suddenly unbearable. "But . . . but we just made love."

"That's sweet," he said as he buttoned his shirt.

"You said I was special," she choked, unable to stop the tears that streamed down her cheeks.

"A thirty-year-old virgin—that's certainly special." He glanced into the mirror on the door, arranging his luxuriant hair with a self-absorbed smirk, as if she were no longer worthy of his attention.

"You said you loved me!" she cried. "And I love you!"

"Oh, sweetie," he snickered, unable to tear his attention from the mirror as he continued to preen. "There's no way I could ever love someone like you. You just don't have any of the things that I need." After a final tug to straighten the collar of his shirt, he reached for the door.

"Wait!" she shrieked and rushed him, latching onto his arm. "Please, please, tell me what you want. I'll give you anything you want!"

He shook her off. "The only thing I wanted from you, I just got." He looked her up and down and grimaced. "You've got nothing else."

The Tree

He slammed the door behind him and left her there alone. Unable to move or breathe or think, all she could do was feel. And she felt only one thing. Letting loose a terrible howl, she filled the very air around her with violence, scorching it with red-hot rage.

"It's time," the crone cackled in her ear and yanked her from the water by the hair.

She staggered back, dripping and disoriented, blinking away the confusion. Rage consumed her, and she balled up her fists and made ready to carry through with one of her murderous fantasies. But before she could attack, she doubled over, struck by an excruciating blow from within. A rush of warm liquid poured forth from between her legs, and the crone hooted with delight.

☙

A NURSE PUSHED PAST PATRICK and rushed down the corridor, her sneakers squeaking on the polished tile floor as she disappeared around a corner.

"It's coming! It's coming!" a wild-haired woman announced to Patrick as she shuffled from her room and latched onto his arm.

"What's coming, Mrs. Hamesh?"

"The angel of death, it's coming for me. Do you think I should go with it, Doctor?"

"Hello, Dr. Denny," said Ed Onyeka. The second-year resident detached the patient from Patrick's arm. "Trudy, Trudy, Trudy, my love, let's get you back to bed."

"But it's coming for me," the slight little woman protested, sheepishly gazing up.

"You go with Ed, and I'll be in to see you in a few minutes. Then we can talk about the angel."

"But Eddie, the voices told me it's coming right now," she insisted as she let him escort her away.

"Son of a bitch! He bit me!" The scream echoed from down the corridor, and Patrick rushed toward the commotion.

"Nooo! It's coming. Let me go!" squealed a young-looking man as he squirmed under the attendant's grip.

"Stop fighting, you little bastard!" the attendant shouted, pressing the patient's face against the floor and pinning him down with his knees.

"Everyone calm down," Patrick ordered, taking the syringe from the trembling nurse who stood by watching. "What is this?"

"Um . . . two milligrams of lorazepam."

Patrick popped the cap and made sure there were no air bubbles before jabbing the needle into the patient's flaccid arm.

"It might have been four milligrams," the nurse said chewing on her lip with uncertainty.

Patrick stared at her. "Which is it?"

"I . . . I don't—"

"The little animal bit me," the attendant griped.

Patrick recognized him as one of Dilby's cohorts from the night before. "Let me see your hand. He barely broke the skin," he said, dismissing it with a wave. "Go get it cleaned up and take a break."

"This place is a fucking freak show," the attendant muttered and stomped away.

"Help me get him to his room," Patrick ordered the very-young-looking nurse, whom he did not recognize.

The Tree

"Okay, one, two, three." They heaved the semi-conscience man up and shouldered him into his room and onto his bed. Patrick straightened the man's hospital gown, which had come loose during the struggle and exposed his emaciated body.

"Whose patient is this?"

"Um . . . I don't know. Maybe Dr. Denny's?"

"I'm Dr. Denny."

"Oh," she said, her face turning bright red.

The patient stirred and turned toward Patrick with heavy-lidded eyes. "Did you hear it?" he asked.

"Hear what?" Patrick asked as he took the patient's pulse.

"I heard it," was his only response and his eyes fluttered shut.

"He just jumped up and started throwing things," the nurse said, wringing her hands. "He was so quiet and then he just went crazy. I wasn't sure what to do."

Patrick was about to ask her to locate the patient's chart when the corridor once again erupted with shouting. "Watch him!" he ordered. "I think that dose might have been too high for his weight." And he rushed out of the room.

"It's my birthday!" Mr. Lupis shouted as he ran down the corridor, Susan trailing behind him. "Happy Birthday to me!"

"Mr. Lupis!" Susan pleaded as she grabbed at his arm, but the spry old man kept sprinting out of her reach. "Please, Mr. Lupis, you'll fall!"

"Hallo! Hallo!" he shouted as he passed each room, greeted by catcalls and frightened shrieks.

Patrick took up a position at the end of the corridor and waited until Mr. Lupis danced in place before him.

"It's my birthday," he informed Patrick.

"Happy birthday, Mr. Lupis. How old are you today?"

"I'm one. Time to blow out the candle." The old man hooted and yanked open his robe. Patrick jumped back, but not in time to save his six-hundred-dollar Italian leather shoes.

"Got to be quicker than that, Doc," Ed said, taking charge of Mr. Lupis, who serenaded the ward with a chorus of "Happy Birthday" all the way back to his room.

Susan tried to help wipe up the mess, but Patrick dismissed her attempts and peeled off his urine-soaked socks. "What the hell happened here?"

She shook her head. "New nurse."

"Yes, I just met her." Patrick flung his socks into the wastebasket and toweled off his feet.

"She mixed up two of the patients' meds, and one of them had a bad reaction and riled up some of the others—"

"And they went like dominoes," Patrick summed up for her.

She nodded. "Here, try these." She handed him a scuffed-up pair of walking shoes she'd scrounged from the nurses' station.

Patrick shoved a bare foot into the white faux leather shoe. "A little snug, but they'll do. Thanks. How's our patient doing?"

"I checked in on her when I got here at four, and she was sleeping." They began to walk toward Amelia's room.

"What?" Patrick asked, seeing amusement on Susan's face.

"Why, Dr. Denny, you always wear such stylish shoes, but those shoes are to die for. You'll have to tell me where you got them," she laughed.

Patrick examined the utilitarian footwear. Not one of his usual designer brands. "I guess everyone around here must think I'm pretty vain."

Susan shrugged. "There are worse things to be than well dressed. Amelia was kept on the lorazepam per your orders, and according to the day staff, she's been pretty quiet."

"Good," Patrick said, but as they turned into Amelia's room, doctor and nurse came to an abrupt halt.

For in the middle of the room, Amelia Dearborne stood naked, her rail-thin thighs streaked with blood.

"Oh!" Susan gasped.

But Patrick held her back. "Wait," he whispered as he watched Amelia's face. She looked at him, not glaring like the night before but with a vulnerable, pleading expression.

"Hello, Amelia. It's good to see you up."

She gazed at him, her sunken green eyes both suspicious and curious. She grimaced and rubbed her hands over her lower belly, trying to soothe some kind of discomfort.

"Does it hurt?" Patrick asked, taking a step forward.

She watched him, and as he got closer, she let her arms drop to her sides. The years of inactivity and harsh medications had not been kind to Amelia's body. She had the stature and bone structure to support a shapely figure, and given a healthy diet and physical activity, Patrick imagined she would have been quite attractive. But the poor creature that stood before him with slumping shoulders, deflated breasts, and sharply protruding hip bones was only a skeletal caricature of that potential other self.

"Don't be scared. You seem to have your period. That's probably why your belly hurts. Let's get you cleaned up and dressed," Patrick said and heard Susan rummaging behind him.

Amelia kept her eyes trained on him, and her lips curled into a coy smile.

Patrick returned the smile. "I'm happy to see you awake, sweetheart. Can you tell me how you feel?"

She giggled and twirled a lock of her long hair.

Appearing beside Patrick, Susan held a sponge and a basin of water. "Should I clean her up?" she whispered, and with an abrupt turn of the head, Amelia snapped her attention to the waiting nurse, the juvenile expression of delight twisting into something very different. Startled, Susan dropped the basin on the floor with a splash and a clatter.

The hair on the back of Patrick's neck stood on end. Amelia transformed before his eyes, just as she had done the previous evening. Fixing her attention on him once again, she hunched over and reached between her legs, drawing them back soaked in clotted blood. She smeared her sunken belly and drooping breasts crimson. After completing this inexplicable ritual, she stepped forward and extended her hands toward Patrick.

Susan shifted nervously, but Patrick motioned her to stay still. They watched Amelia in stunned silence until she dropped her head and let her hands fall to her sides. Patrick knew he had to act, but within less than a heartbeat, she was on him in a wild frenzy, her legs wrapped around his waist, her hands scratching at his face, pulling at his hair, as she let out a feral scream. With the crazed woman clinging to his upper body, Patrick stumbled out into the corridor, knocking Susan to the floor.

"Help us!" she shouted, scrambling to her feet and following them out of the room.

"Grab her!" someone else shouted.

Patrick heard a commotion of people rushing forward. He staggered back and forth, fighting to keep his balance, struggling to keep Amelia's hands from ripping at his eyes, holding her away as her teeth snapped at his cheeks and ears. The others tried to pry her off, but the more they pulled, the tighter her legs gripped his waist. He stumbled through the corridor with the naked, bloody beast attached to his body until his legs gave out, and he fell backward. His head bounced against the tile floor, and sparks of light exploded before his eyes.

"Get her off," Susan shouted, and a mass of hands descended upon them.

"Get that ankle!"

"I got it, now pull!"

"Go, go, yeah, pull!"

"I got her! Help me!"

"That's it! Lift her!"

Amelia howled as she was ripped away from him.

"Doctor, don't move," Susan ordered. But Patrick pushed her away and sat up to see his patient being wrestled to the floor.

"Dr. Denny, what should we give her?" someone yelled.

But Patrick couldn't answer. He didn't know what to do.

Amelia bit at her captors and continued to howl.

"Dr. Denny! What do you want us to do?" an attendant screamed.

"Doctor?" he heard Susan say from far away.

The world around him spun out of focus. He glanced down at his shirt. It was red and sticky, and he could smell Amelia still on him. Out of the corner of his eye, he could see three men rushing toward the scene.

"Nurse, get me a haloperidol-promethazine bolus!" Dilby shouted. "Now!"

Patrick didn't counter the order. He merely sat and watched as his patient was held down for the injection. She fought hard, contorted and struggling, teeth bared, grunting and shrieking. Her movements slowly weakened. Her legs stopped kicking. Her spine relaxed. Her shrieks quieted to grunts, then to mumbles. At last Amelia's body went slack, her naked chest rising and falling in a slow, heavy rhythm.

"Get a stretcher! He needs to go to emergency!" Susan called.

He watched Dilby's henchman grab Amelia under the arms and drag her back into her room, where they threw her sprawled over the edge of the bed.

"Dr. Denny, we're going to lift you onto the stretcher now."

He felt a gentle pressure under his arms and his body being lifted. "No, I'm okay," he said, pushing his helpers away and standing shakily on his own. "I just need a minute."

"Doc, you hit your head pretty hard, and your face is . . ."

"I'm fine!" Patrick snapped at Ed.

He continued to watch in disgust as the attendants flung Amelia's legs one by one up onto the bed, treating her body like the carcass of a dead animal they had just put down.

"I want her cleaned up," he said to Susan. "I don't want her left like that."

"I'll take care of her, but you should get that head checked right now," Susan pleaded.

"I'm okay."

"Denny, get to emergency," Dilby said with irritation. "Director Anderson should be informed about this," he instructed Susan.

The Tree

Leaving her naked, limp body on the bed, the attendants strolled out of Amelia's room. "This whole place has gone crazy since they woke up that friggin' witch," the one who had been bitten earlier commented with exasperation. "They should toss her in a padded cell and throw away the key."

"Shut your fucking mouth!" Patrick roared, springing at the attendant and knocking him against the wall. "Don't talk like that about her again! Ever! Do you understand me? Do you!" But before the stunned attendant could react, two steely arms wrapped themselves around Patrick's chest and lifted him away.

"Hey, Doc," Ed said calmly into his ear. "Let's cool down. We're all a little worked up today."

After a few seconds of struggling, Patrick let his body go slack. "I'm okay. It's okay," he said. Ed released him, and he staggered forward. Stunned faces gawked at him from all around. Susan seemed to want to say something but remained silent. The attendant he attacked stood frightened, his imposing bearing now somewhat diminished. Even Dilby, usually stone-faced and inscrutable, appeared unnerved.

"Please take care of her," he said to Susan and limped away, the laces of his borrowed shoes undone and flapping against the floor with each step.

• • •

"This is so exciting!" Mr. Scarlatti exclaimed, following behind Patrick as they entered the organ hall.

How different from the last time he'd been there, Patrick thought bitterly as he tried to ignore the persistent thrumming in his head. Instead of cold, dark, and silent, the air was filled with excitement, abuzz with celebratory activity. People milled around the now brightly lit hall, admiring the grand architecture, searching for the best seating, and greeting one another. The marble floor had been buffed to a mirror shine and the wooden benches gleamed in the festive lighting. The smell of pine-scented wood polish hung in the humid summer air as people fanned themselves with their programs. He walked up the center aisle with Mr. Scarlatti trailing on his heels.

"Thank you again for inviting me, Dr. Denny. You saved me tonight."

"I'm happy you could come," Patrick said as he searched for Sam and Father Owen. Up ahead, he could see that the organ console had been repaired and returned to its alcove. Its walnut housing shone, the intricate carvings polished and detailed.

"I didn't realize how big it would be," Mr. Scarlatti marveled as he took in the sight of burnished organ pipes that reached high up to the vaulted ceiling. "It's wonderful."

"Yes," Patrick muttered. "They did an excellent job covering up the mess."

"Patrick," Father Owen called from behind him.

He turned and greeted the elderly priest with an outstretched hand. "Owen, the board outdid itself here."

"Yes . . . uh, we were fortunate that Mrs. Huntsman donated the funds for the repairs. What on earth happened to your face?"

"His cat scratched him," Mr. Scarlatti answered for Patrick.

"Cat?"

"I know, it looks awful. When Dr. Denny came to pick me up, I thought he'd been mugged, and I said, 'Good God,

Dr. Denny, were you mugged?' But he said, 'No, my cat was a little cranky today,' and I said to him, 'That's why I don't have pets.' You know that if you die in your sleep and no one finds your body, your cat will eat you?"

"She just needs her nails trimmed," Patrick interrupted, ushering the two old men down the aisle. "I haven't seen Sam yet. Is she here?"

Father Owen nodded, limping up the aisle with his cane, still staring at Patrick's face. "She's downstairs manning the refreshment stand. When did you get a cat?"

"Downstairs? In the basement!" Patrick exclaimed.

"Oh, yes, didn't I mention it to you? Mrs. Huntsman was quite clear that the basement should be completely renovated. The donation was contingent upon that detail."

"Of course it was."

The priest didn't react to the bitterness in Patrick's tone, his attention now drawn to the front of the hall. "Oh, will you excuse me for a moment? No, not there," he called to the volunteer setting up a microphone in front of the organ console, and he hastened away.

"Did he say refreshment stand?"

Patrick smiled at Mr. Scarlatti and led the eager little man to the basement door. He stood at the top of the staircase and hesitated. It was unrecognizable. The creaky wooden steps he had tumbled down almost a year before were replaced by a sweeping marble staircase gleaming in the glow of the recessed lighting above. The bare stone walls were now hidden behind heavy tapestries embroidered with golden swirls and flourishes.

"Excuse me, are you going down?"

Patrick looked back to find an elderly couple, dressed in their finest summer clothes, waiting behind them to go down.

"Sorry," he said and allowed them to pass. He watched their descent to the red-carpeted floor below, the woman holding tight to the brass railing.

"Doctor," Mr. Scarlatti urged, keen on getting to the food and drink.

Patrick motioned him ahead, but still hesitated for a moment before following down. The basement had been transformed, its dirty secrets stripped away by the Huntsman wealth. Patricia wanted to make sure that there was nothing left, no evidence of her attempt to murder her husband and erase his sins. The walls and padlocked door that had held Phineas in his confinement had been torn down, and the entirety of the basement was now one large room, the dirty dark corners illuminated by the warm glow of wall sconces and recessed ceiling lights. Along the back wall where Phineas had first hidden himself from the beam of Patrick's flashlight, a concession stand had been constructed reminiscent of an old nineteen-twenties theater. People stood in line, chatting and milling around, admiring the wall tapestries and paintings that hung on the huge support pillars throughout the room. Café-style tables had been set up, and people lounged around them, talking about the amazing transformation.

"Dr. Denny!" Sam's voice called over the pleasant din. She waved at him from behind the counter.

Patrick approached the concession stand where Mr. Scarlatti had already arrived.

"Working hard?" he asked.

"As hard as anyone else who's not getting paid," Sam said,

her smile fading a bit at the sight of his battered face. But to Patrick's relief, she refrained from asking about it.

"I'll have a box of chocolate bonbons and a can of root beer," Mr. Scarlatti announced.

"Sorry, we're out of chocolate, but we still have vanilla."

"Oh, okay, yes, that's fine. I don't really care if they're vanilla or chocolate. It's no problem. I'd rather have vanilla anyway—"

"Here, you go."

Mr. Scarlatti fumbled for his wallet, but Patrick handed Sam a twenty. "I got this. You go ahead and sit. The concert is starting soon," he said, shooing the surprised man along before he could start gushing his gratitude.

Sam handed Patrick his change, which he deposited in the tip jar. "Thank you, kind sir," she said. "It was nice of you to bring him."

Patrick shrugged. "He's lonely. There's not much else I can do for him."

"Just bringing him with you is amazing," she said and glanced at the table where Mr. Scarlatti sat watching the other people and shoving bonbons into his mouth. "There aren't many doctors like you, Patrick. You're really wonderful."

The use of his first name caught Patrick off guard, and an uncomfortable silence stretched between them as he noticed the intensity of her gaze.

The lights dimmed three times. They both looked up.

"The concert's about to start," Sam observed. "The first row is reserved for board members and volunteers. You guys can sit there with us." She started to close the candy case, and people queued at the bottom of the stairs.

"Should we wait for you?" Patrick asked, still trying to process Sam's evident feelings for him.

"No, you guys go. I'll be there in a few minutes."

"This is so exciting!" exclaimed Mr. Scarlatti, suddenly at Patrick's elbow.

Up in the hall, there was a general feeling of enthusiasm despite the oppressive heat. Patrick wished he'd dressed more appropriately and pulled at his tie to loosen it. He scanned the crowd and saw that he wasn't the only man who'd made that mistake. Father Owen waved them over to the front row.

"You can sit here," the priest directed and started toward the organ platform.

"Aren't you sitting?"

"I've been asked to say a few words before the concert starts," he said, tugging at his collar while standing a bit straighter. "I'll probably sit off to the side, but I'll join you after intermission."

"Intermission? Will the refreshment stand be open for that?" Mr. Scarlatti broke in.

Father Owen nodded and made his way toward the other board members gathered around the microphone, now set up to the right of the organ console.

Intermission, Patrick groaned to himself, realizing that it was going to be a very long evening. Ushering his excited companion along the bench, he sat near the end, leaving enough room for Sam.

"This is my first organ concert," Mr. Scarlatti informed the woman sitting next to him. She smiled politely and fanned herself with her program, her forehead beaded with sweat and her black eyeliner running down her cheeks. "This is Dr. Denny.

The Tree

He's my psychiatrist."

The woman raised her penciled-in eyebrows, suddenly interested in Mr. Scarlatti's prattling. Her gaze shifted to Patrick, who greeted her with a wave and then stood to remove his jacket, draping it over the back of the bench. He glanced up at the balcony. It was bursting with people.

"No, I wouldn't say I'm mentally disturbed per se . . . No, no antipsychotics . . ."

Patrick was just about to sit down when he saw them. They were scooting along the first row of seats above. His stomach lurched.

"Committed? You mean to an asylum? Oh, no, nothing like that . . ."

Helen was wearing a sleeveless sundress, her tanned shoulders shining with perspiration. Anderson followed behind her. More casually dressed than Patrick had ever seen him, he wore a short-sleeved plaid shirt, cargo shorts, and sandals. His skin was bronze and his thick, dark hair slicked back. They could have just stepped out of an L.L. Bean catalog, Patrick thought sourly. Anderson helped Helen settle herself and sat beside her, draping his arm around her shoulders.

Patrick flung himself around into his seat, desperately hoping they hadn't see him. He slid down and hunched his shoulders.

"Dr. Denny, would you say I'm clinically depressed or suffering from generalized anxiety disorder?" Mr. Scarlatti asked with his newfound confidant leaning in to hear.

"What?"

"Anxious or depressed?" the woman chimed in.

"Um . . . both?"

"Oh, yes, I *am* both," Mr. Scarlatti agreed happily.

Patrick snatched up the program beside him on the bench and tried to read it. The first piece was by Bach. He wasn't an expert on organ music, but he knew you couldn't have an organ concert without at least one piece by Bach. *Sandals!* The thought exploded in his mind. *How could she be sleeping with someone who wears sandals?* He forced himself to concentrate on the words in front of him: "Toccata and Fugue in D Minor (BWV 538)." A bit cliché, he mused, but appropriate to his mood. He looked up and tried to imagine the sound that would shortly burst forth from the enormous organ pipes. *And what's with that hair!*

"Would you say I'm a suicide risk?" Mr. Scarlatti asked, posing the question as if they were having an academic discussion.

"What? No!" Patrick fought the urge to turn around and look up at the balcony. "You're terrified of death."

"It's true. Yes, yes, that is my greatest fear."

"Good evening, everyone," Father Owen's voice boomed. He covered the mike and spoke to someone off to the side. "A little too loud," Patrick heard him inform the volunteer.

The hall had grown quiet, and Patrick felt exposed. Sitting in the front row, he might as well have been standing at the mike. He could feel the entire balcony level staring down at him, their eyes boring through the back of his throbbing head. He would have bolted down the aisle and right through the enormous oak doors if he weren't afraid to draw more attention to himself.

"Hello." Sam slipped in beside him and looked around the hall. "Wow, this place is packed." Patrick saw her glance up at the balcony, and he couldn't stop himself from following her gaze. Helen's eyes were locked on the two of them. Sam turned back around, unaware that they were being watched. She leaned into his shoulder and passed him a cold bottle of water. "It's murder in here," she whispered in his ear.

Helen glared, her jaw rigid, and Patrick sat up straighter. "Thanks," he said, turning to the lovely young woman beside him. Sam wore no makeup. With her youthful complexion, she didn't need to. Her dark brown hair was pulled back into a knot, revealing a long tan neck. "All that money they got, and they couldn't get some air conditioning," he said, draping his arm across the back of the bench behind her, careful not to actually touch her.

Sam laughed at his joke, and Patrick glanced back up at Helen.

"I think that woman up in the balcony is staring at me," Mr. Scarlatti whispered at Patrick. "And she looks like she wants to kill me."

"Good evening," Father Owen greeted. "Oh, that's better. Thank you all for coming."

CHAPTER TWELVE

"I will kill you, you miserable old bitch!" she shrieked, stumbling back from the table, seething with rage at having to relive the humiliation and heartbreak inflicted upon her by her cruel lover. But for all her murderous intent, the quickening life within her swollen belly was determined to come forth into the world. It would not wait for her to exact her long-festering desire for revenge. Crippled by wave upon wave of crushing pain, she was brought to her hands and knees, only able to glance up to see the evil old woman gleefully gathering all the necessities needed to help birth this portentous child. As she crawled towards the door, blood streamed down her thighs, marking a crimson trail along the floor. Her desperate attempt to escape, however, had not gone unnoticed.

With sadistic delight, the old crone used a stubby, clubbed foot to give the helpless mother-to-be a shove, tipping her over onto the hard, filthy floor. "They'll be a'coming fer ya now, cow," she cackled and hobbled with an almost spritely step to the front door, flinging it open to peer out into the dark forest.

Overcome by the futility of her situation, she lay sprawled out on the floor, just able to see up through the door into the night sky above the trees. The specks of white light flickered in the midnight blue, and, for a fleeting instant, the pain inside her ebbed. They would be coming for her now . . . and the baby. The thought horrified her. With her last bit of strength, she forced herself to rise from the floor. Marshaling every bit of hatred she harbored for the cruel world that had deprived her of all hope and love, she made a savage charge at the repulsive hag and pushed her out into the freezing night, slamming the door and securing it with the heavy, wooden bar.

The door shook on its hinges as the old woman beat on it and hollered, "Ya ungrateful bitch! There's no turnin' back! Ya made your deal and now ya have to pay the devil!"

With growing hysteria, her muddled brain tried to form an escape plan. She stumbled to the table for support as another excruciating contraction hit. "Nooo! Make it stop!" she wailed and begged and prayed to whomever or whatever could relieve her from her unending suffering. Another rush of blood gushed from her, pooling at her feet. "This isn't normal," she cried out, clutching at her contracting abdomen. There was too much blood, too much pain. "What did you do to me?" she sobbed.

The clamoring from outside stopped. A muffled titter of laughter broke the brief silence. "Ya can't stop it now. Stupid, stupid woman! Don't even know what willow bark and licorice root do. Haha, and the devil's claw!"

"The tea!"

"Ya gathered the ingredients yerself, ignorant wench.

The Tree

Nothing can stop it from a'coming now."

With a defeated sob, she gazed down at the bloody floor. "Will it hurt the baby?" she cried out.

"The child is strong, conceived and nurtured by the powers of the mushrooms and the unyeildin' nature of the forest. Nothing will harm it." And with a coo of delight, the crone announced, "I see 'em. The lights. They're a'coming. *Now let me back in!*"

☙

The small lakeside town of Candlewick was a two-hour drive north of Waylingbrooke. Patrick had been playing with the idea of driving up there for weeks, but he never seemed to have enough time. However, on that early Sunday morning, as he lay staring at the yellow water stain on the ceiling above and contemplated his recent personal and professional humiliations, he determined to make the time. Despite the obscenely early hour, he had dragged himself out of bed and called Amelia's parents.

Of course they gave him permission to investigate their summer cabin on the lake. Mr. Dearborne even offered to ride up with him, but Patrick declined. As he drove down the shop-lined main road of Candlewick, he glanced at his reflection in the rearview mirror and cringed at Amelia's handiwork. The Dearbornes didn't need to see what their daughter had done to him. They'd know soon enough that Patrick had failed.

The car rolled down the street past quaint little candy shops and sidewalk art dealers. His head throbbed from the thrashing Amelia had given him the day before. He popped open a bottle of aspirin, shook a few into his mouth, and forced himself to swallow. The bitter taste lingered on his tongue, a reminder of the unpleasant task that lay ahead. The trip was an exercise in futility, he knew. Come Monday, he would have to tell Amelia's parents that he couldn't help their daughter, that Dilby might be better suited to care for her. The thought made him grimace. He wished he had stopped for a bottle of water to wash away the aftertaste, but he knew even that wouldn't be enough to rid himself of the bitter prospect of turning Amelia's case back over to Dilby.

Patrick slowed to a stop as a group of pedestrians in swimsuits and flip-flops sauntered across the road, joking and licking their ice cream cones. Waiting for them to reach the other side, he fished out Madam Flora's business card from the front pocket of his linen shirt. The card listed her former address as 16 Bayberry Street, but when he tried to call the phone number, it was out of service. A quick online search of the street address led him to a place called The Magick Shoppe, apparently a popular spot for local Wiccans to meet up and purchase supplies. However, the website made no mention of Madam Flora, leaving Patrick to wonder if she were even still alive.

He drove farther down the road until he reached a small roundabout, a bronze statue of a Revolutionary soldier on horseback at its center. Circling slowly, he read the street signs: Chestnut Street, Acorn Hill, Strawberry Lane. No Bayberry. He made another loop. Chestnut Street, Acorn Hill, Strawberry Lane. Still no Bayberry. A horn honked behind him. In his rearview mirror, he saw a minivan driven by a red-faced, middle-aged man, kids bouncing in the back and a woman in the passenger seat frowning at her impatient husband—the quintessential family on the quintessential family vacation. Patrick waved his apologies and pulled off the roundabout into a gas station on the next corner. A gigantic arrow-shaped sign flashed "McClaron's Gas." He parked in front of an ancient-looking pump and waited.

"Hello, sir. Fill'r up?" asked the young attendant, whose nametag read "Willie."

"Yes, thanks."

Willie pumped his gas and gave his windshield a complimentary squeegee.

"That'll be forty-two. Cash or credit?"

Patrick handed him a fifty, and while the young man was counting out his change, he asked, "Do you know how I get to Bayberry Street?"

Willie grinned, his metal braces glinting in the noontime sun. "You one of those witches?" he asked.

"Excuse me?"

"Well, you don't look like you're interested in getting your hair done, and the tax place went out of business last year. The only other thing on Bayberry is the devil shop."

"No, I'm not a witch," Patrick responded, showing him the business card. "A friend of mine used to know this woman. Madam Flora?"

"Never heard of her," the teenager said, scratching his head. "The place is run by some weird hippie guy who says he's a wizard." It was apparent that Willie found the whole idea enormously amusing. He leaned into the window, close enough that Patrick could smell the cigarettes on his breath. "Ya know, they dance around naked up in the forest. Me and some of my friends snuck up on them last summer and watched one of their sabbaths. They take off all their clothes and dance around the fire, chanting and singing and everything—both the guys and the ladies. And a lot of them are really old and . . . um . . . saggy," he said, grimacing.

"You're scaring me," Patrick said dryly. "Which way?"

"About a half mile up the road, that way." Willie pointed in the direction Patrick needed to go. "Bayberry's a couple of lefts up. The shop is about another mile from there."

Patrick nodded his thanks and started the car.

"Make sure you leave before sunset. I'm still having nightmares," Willie warned and walked away, chuckling to himself.

• • •

It was pretty much what Patrick expected. Wedged between Martha's Hair Emporium and the defunct Tax Hut, The Magick Shoppe's window display promised the full occult experience. The life-sized, golden statue of a horned, goat-headed figure stood prominently at the center of the display, its hairy, muscular body naked except for a black silk sash wrapped loosely around what Patrick assumed to be a very impressive representation of virility. A sign in the window read, "Open," but the lights inside were dim. Patrick squinted through the glass. The interior of the tiny store overflowed with the accouterments of those interested in exploring "the mysteries of the supernatural and forbidden," as the website claimed.

"It's okay to go in," a tiny voice informed him.

The Tree

Patrick looked down at the small boy, who was now standing by his side. "Oh, hello."

"Hi," the boy responded and shifted his broom to the other hand. "I'm Jacob."

Patrick shook the dirty little hand offered to him. "Nice to meet you, Jacob. I'm Patrick."

"Nice to meet you, Patrick. Don't be afraid to go in. Larry isn't an evil witch. He's really nice."

"Oh, that's good to hear. Are you going to fly on that thing?" he asked, pointing to Jacob's broom.

"No, silly," the boy giggled, "I'm sweeping up hair for my Aunt Martha. She gives me ice cream money if I keep the floors clean."

"Double chocolate mint?" Patrick asked, suddenly craving something cold and sweet.

Jacob shrugged his little shoulders and scrunched his nose. "Oh no, I hate mint. Double chocolate chip."

"That sounds good too."

"What happened to your face?"

Patrick touched the scratches on his forehead and cheeks. "These? Oh, I got into a fight with a werewolf."

"You're silly," the boy giggled again.

"Jacob!" a woman shouted from the door of the Hair Emporium.

The boy jumped, his aunt's summons stirring him into action. "Gotta go!"

"Good to meet you," Patrick called after him.

Just before the boy disappeared into the salon, he turned back and called out, "Hey, Patrick, you going in?"

"I guess so," Patrick answered and gave him a quick salute.

Jacob saluted back and dashed off to earn his ice cream money.

The door chimed as Patrick entered, and the stifling, pungent air that hung visibly about the place immediately accosted him. He glanced around and tried to take in the array of esoteric paraphernalia that cluttered every surface of the tiny space. Candles of all shapes and sizes and colors, books and pamphlets on subjects ranging from angels to the zodiac, statuettes of gods and goddesses, baskets full of herb sachets for spellcasting, vials of potions and elixirs, tarot cards, and scrying boards. His already-throbbing head spun as he tried to bring the place into focus.

He appeared to be alone. No one was behind the long glass counter that extended across the back of the store, and no customers were in sight. He wandered carefully between the overflowing display tables and tried not to inhale too deeply. "Hello," he called out. "Anybody here?"

On top of the counter was an old-fashioned, turn-of-the-century register, and next to it, a small altar paying homage to the spirits, complete with a pentagram and a skull of some horned animal. Candles and incense burned, and Patrick waved the acrid smoke away. Behind the counter hung a black velvet curtain.

"Hello! Larry?" He waited for someone to step from behind the curtain, but no one appeared. "Great," he sighed and occupied himself by examining the contents of the display case underneath the counter. "Ah, this is the good stuff," he said, eyeing the jewel-encrusted chalices and ceremonial daggers. He

The Tree

stooped down to read the price tag on a large egg-shaped geode, its green crystal innards glowing neon in the artificial light of the display case. He whistled with amazement. "Nine hundred and fifty dollars!"

He stood up straight and rubbed his burning eyes, ready to give up on Larry and Madam Flora and the whole pointless trip. But just as he was about to turn and leave, something in the display case caught his eye. He bent over to take a closer look. From a delicate chain hung a sterling silver sphere. The tiny pendant's elaborate filigree design was that of a tree, the canopy of leaves forming the top hemisphere and the twisting roots the bottom.

"It's the Tree of Life," a deep voice announced from behind the counter.

Patrick looked up, startled. "Where did you come from?" he asked the bald, bespectacled man, who wore a brightly colored dashiki and seemed to materialize out of nowhere.

"The realm of light and darkness," the man said, waving his tattooed arms and ringed fingers above his head.

Patrick cocked an eyebrow at him.

He dropped his hands onto the counter. "Backroom."

"Larry, I presume?"

"Yes, welcome to The Magick Shoppe."

Patrick pointed at the pendant. "Tree of life?"

"Old Celtic symbol," Larry said, opening the back of the display case and carefully separating the chain from the stand. He held it out to Patrick. "It symbolizes the interconnectedness of all things. The branches lift us up to the heavenly realm; the roots ground us to Mother Earth."

Patrick took the pendant and dangled it before his eyes.

"This one is particularly special. See, it's a sphere."

"So?" Patrick asked as he examined the intricate detail of the tiny acorns hanging from the branches and the interweaving of the complex root system.

"Oooh," Larry cooed. "Spheres are sacred space. When we do our magick, we cast a circle, but that's just a two-dimensional representation of our workspace. We stand at the center of the sphere and let our energies radiate out into the universe in every direction. *As above, so below. As within, so without.* This piece is quite powerful. You've got good intuition."

"Ah," Patrick responded. "How much?"

"Two fifty."

"I'll give you one fifty," Patrick countered.

Larry scratched at his scraggly beard. "Two."

"One seventy-five."

"Cash or credit?"

Patrick placed the necklace on the counter, pulled out his wallet, and handed Larry his credit card.

"So what brings you to Candlewick? Here with the family? Or a romantic rendezvous? We're having a two-for-one sale on all love potions. Oh, and these dragon blood candles are seventy-five percent off," he said, gesturing to the blaze of candles on the countertop altar.

Patrick wrinkled his nose at the repellant smell and held up his hands. "A bit too potent for me. Actually, I'm trying to find someone who used to run her business from this address. Madam Flora?"

Larry held up a pen, indicating it was time for Patrick to

sign the credit card slip. "Madam Flora. I haven't heard that name in a long time. She retired a few years back."

Patrick signed and handed the slip and the pen back. "Is she still in Candlewick?"

Larry nodded. "Do you need someone to do a reading because I can set you up with a great lady who—"

"No, no. I just wanted to ask her a few questions about a friend who came to see her a while back."

Larry eyed him suspiciously. "You a cop?"

"I'm a doctor. A patient of mine had some trouble, and I think she might have told Madam Flora about it. I'm trying to help her. Any information I can get might be useful."

The man hesitated for a moment, as if he were trying to peer into Patrick's soul. He seemed to decide that Patrick wasn't trying to make trouble. "I can give her a call, if you want."

"That would be great. Thank you."

He slipped his hand into one of the large square pockets of his dashiki and pulled out his iPhone. "Home," he said to the device. From somewhere above, a telephone rang. "Hey, I got someone here who would like to speak to Madam Flora . . . No . . . I'm sure." He took a moment to reappraise Patrick. "Yeah. I'm sure."

Patrick could hear the buzz of someone's voice coming from the phone but couldn't make out the words.

"Okay . . . okay . . . yes," Larry rolled his eyes at Patrick. "Yep. Okay." He touched the phone and slipped it away.

"She'll talk to you."

"Great!"

"For fifty bucks."

"Of course."

Larry pulled back the velvet curtain behind the counter and waved Patrick around. "Just up those steps," he said, pointing to an old staircase on the other side of the cluttered storage room beyond the curtain. "You can pick up your purchase on the way out."

Patrick climbed to the top landing and paused in front of the door. The stairwell reeked of fried fish and cigarettes, and he fought the urge to gag. He tapped on the door.

"Come in!"

On the other side, Patrick crossed over into a filthy, cramped space that smelled worse than the shop and the stairwell combined. Broken mini blinds hung in the windows and a game show blared from a television in another room. Sitting at a crooked kitchen table, an old woman smashed out her cigarette in an ashtray overflowing with butts and ashes.

"Come," Madam Flora said, waving him over. "Sit."

He settled himself on a rickety chair across from the self-professed psychic and took in the sight of her. Her face was shriveled like a golden raisin, and she wore a dirty house dress that reeked of sweat and beer.

"You wish to speak with Madam Flora?" she asked, leaning on the table with flabby, white arms.

"Yes," he replied.

"Fifty dollars," she said and held out her hand.

He placed a fifty-dollar bill in her palm.

"Now, let's see . . ." She pocketed the bill and grabbed his hand with her filthy, nicotine-stained fingers, tracing the scar on his palm, a souvenir from that day in the organ hall when he discovered Phineas Huntsman. "This was a deep wound. Just like the wound on your heart."

Patrick yanked his hand back and slapped down her old business card.

"Where did you get this?" she asked, snatching it up.

"A fifteen-year-old girl named Amelia came to see you about twenty years ago. I want to know what she told you."

Madam Flora broke into a toothless cackle. "Do you know how many teenage girls used to come to me for answers about what boy they're going to marry, how many babies they'll have, and—"

Patrick produced Amelia's half-burned candle from his pocket and placed it before her.

Madam Flora slammed the table, upsetting the ashtray and knocking over the candle. "That little thief. I knew she took it. She didn't have the money to pay for the prayer, so she swiped my candle instead."

"You remember this girl?"

"Yeah, I remember her. Paranoid little thing. Scared something was following her in the woods."

"What did you say to her?"

"What do you think? I told her it would get her if she didn't do something to fight it. She was petrified." The repulsive woman snickered, then started to hack, pulling up a gob of phlegm and spitting it onto the floor. "You should have seen her hands shaking. I felt bad for her." She held up the candle, waving it in front of Patrick. "So I told her I'd light a candle of protection and pray for her, calling upon my guardian angels to watch over her."

Patrick shook his head. "How much?"

Why Did God Make the Tree?

The woman thought for a moment. "She was pretty scared, so I probably asked for at least a hundred. She said she'd have to come back with it and then left. When I was closing up for the night, I noticed the candle missing and I knew she swiped it. Little thief." She spat on the floor again. "I work hard for every cent. Can't be giving my candles away. Besides, they're paying for the prayers. I always tell them the candles don't work unless they have me praying over them. I should have called the cops on her. But I'm too nice a person. Did something happened to her?"

"She's very sick."

Madam Flora grinned knowingly. "See. Threefold law."

"Excuse me?"

She scratched at the thin patch of hair on her balding head. "What you put out into the world comes back to you three times stronger. If you wrong someone, you pay for it three times over. Universal justice. She shouldn't have stolen my candle."

"Did she say what she thought was following her?"

"Um, something about the trees. She said the trees moved, that they followed her. She was probably out in the woods doing dope with her friends."

"I don't think so." He reached forward to retrieve the candle.

But Madam Flora clutched it to her sagging chest. "This was never paid for! A hundred dollars, and I'll let you have it back."

Patrick counted out the cash and traded it for the candle. "Thanks for the help," he said, not even trying to hide his disdain, and stood up.

"Wait!" She grabbed his hand and, turning it over roughly, examined it. "There's a woman. A vengeful woman. She seeks retribution. I can pray over a candle for you."

The Tree

Patrick pulled his hand away. "That's okay. I've got my own magic candle now."

• • •

The Dearbornes' lakeside vacation home was really just a dilapidated old cottage deep in the woods and too far from the lake to have a view. Before he left Waylingbrooke, Patrick had swung by the elderly couple's home to pick up the key they'd left in the mailbox for him, but he knew that he wouldn't need it the moment he pulled up the rutted dirt drive.

The front door hung precariously on its hinges, and he gave it a gentle push. With an echoing clatter, it fell into the cottage, revealing the extent of the vandalism. Mr. Dearborne had mentioned that it had been a couple of years since they had checked on the place. Patrick couldn't bear the thought of the defeated old man seeing what had been done to his family's beloved getaway. Broken furniture that had evidently been smashed against the walls lay strewn across the floor amid discarded beer bottles and cigarette butts. He picked his way through the debris, noting the inartistic graffiti along the walls, the letters "WM" prominently rendered in bright orange. Up the narrow staircase to the second floor, he found a cramped loft with several dirty cots. Burned-out candles and used condoms littered the floor. Nothing of the Dearbornes remained. All remnants of their happy family had been carried off or smashed to pieces. And with them, Patrick's last hope to help Amelia.

Outside, he walked around the cottage, curious to see if the purposeless vandalism extended to the whole exterior of the building. He pushed past the saplings that had sprung up along the foundation. He was in no hurry to go home. *Home,* he thought bitterly as he stumbled along. *As if that dismal little apartment could qualify as a home.* The back of the cottage seemed to have been spared, mostly likely because the forest had crept its way so close that there was barely enough room to shimmy along the wall. He plucked at the prickly burrs that clung to his pant legs and peered in between the thick boughs and dense foliage that walled off the house from the rest of the forest. *"Amelia liked to go off into the woods by herself,"* he remembered Mr. Dearborne saying.

"There must be some sort of trail back here," he murmured as he wrestled himself into the tangle of branches and vines that seemed unwilling to let him pass. After a few minutes of struggling, he pushed through, stumbling onto an overgrown footpath that the forest had not yet wholly reclaimed. "This is the way she went," he said, convinced he was walking in Amelia's footsteps. Around the narrow path, the trees stood densely packed and reached up high into the bright sky. He looked up and winced. His headache had slowly evolved into a rhythmic thumping, and he had to fight the dizziness and nausea that threatened to bring him to his knees. He patted his pockets, searching for his bottle of aspirin. "Damn," he exclaimed, realizing that he'd left the bottle in the car.

He looked back at the thick foliage from which he had just emerged. The gray clapboard siding of the cottage was lost behind the leaves. He decided it would be too much trouble to fight his way back just for aspirin. Besides, there wasn't enough time. It would be dark soon, and he wanted to see where Amelia's trail led. Venturing forth, compelled by an inexplicable urgency, he hurried along, following the winding path. His loafers, which were usually quite comfortable and suited for a leisurely walk, gave him no support or purchase on the rough, slippery woodland debris, and he stumbled and slid over fallen branches and mossy trunks that had been collecting on the forest floor for years. Yet he continued, a hound single-mindedly driven by instinct to follow the scent of its quarry, pushing deeper into the darkening woodland, the path growing narrower with each difficult step, the air growing mustier with each panting breath. He batted the low-hanging boughs out of his way, but it was an impossible battle, as there was always another waiting to block his progression.

He should turn back, he knew. But back toward what? What did he have to go back to? A failed relationship. Two failed careers. Loneliness. Humiliation. He wiped the sweat from his upper lip and swatted at the cloud of mosquitoes that accompanied him on his journey. The dim light around him was fading fast. His heart raced. His temples pulsated, ticking off each second, compelling him to move faster. There was no going back, only forward, forward toward Amelia's past. He swiped at the branches, ripping at the leaves as the forest swallowed him up. Staggering and tripping and recovering himself, he tried not to succumb to the forces that wanted to drag him down, to the branches that battered his face and arms, to the vines that snatched at his feet. But with one ill-placed step, he found himself falling, the trees and the sky kaleidoscoping above him as he tumbled back.

He sighed. The mossy earth beneath him was warm and

soft. Lying sprawled on his back, he gazed up at the slivers of pink and fading blue that showed through the feathery, green canopy above. *Beautiful*, he thought as he let go. His head no longer pounded out the time, and his mind drifted peacefully as he watched the forest sway in the gentle summer breeze. He opened and closed his eyes and surrendered to the pleasant numbness that washed over his exhausted body. Time no longer mattered. He wasn't even sure if it still existed. Nothing mattered. He'd found the quiet and he never wanted to leave it.

But as he floated deeper and deeper into the nothingness, something began to shake him. At first, he tried to disregard it, but it was relentless and uncomfortable and would not be ignored. He opened his eyes and gasped. The forest had been transformed, stripped of all its warmth and color. His body shivered and quaked in the frigid night air, the darkness broken only by shafts of silver light that penetrated the forest ceiling above. He pushed himself up onto his elbows and listened. Things moved around him in the shadows, chittering and squealing and murmuring. And then from amid the dissonant chorus of the unseen beasts, a voice emerged. A tiny voice whispering in the night air. Amelia's voice.

Patrick's mind was pulled back to the night of Amelia's first awakening. The quiet ramblings that had been forgotten once she had turned her terrifying gaze upon him were now remembered, now understood. *"The trees . . . the trees . . . the trees whisper,"* her childlike voice had rambled. *"Baby bird . . . kitty . . . the trees told me to hurt them . . . and Mumma . . . and Daddy."* A roar of wind thrashed the branches above his head and the swaying trunks groaned. *"She said the trees followed her,"* Madam Flora's voice joined in. Fast-moving clouds rolled over the forest, blotting out the moonlight and wrapping him in darkness. He scrambled to his feet, squinting into the inky abyss. *"And the tree scooped him up high into its branches,"* the memory of his own voice recited. Uncontrollable tremors shook his body as he waited for something to happen. *Trees . . . the trees whisper . . . the trees follow . . . the tree scooped him up.* Seized by hysteria, he plunged into the darkness, bounding blindly ahead.

Invisible monsters attacked him from all sides, clawing at his face, ripping at his clothes, forcing him to his hands and knees. But he continued forward, crawling into the unknown over the jagged, biting terrain, pushing himself to keep moving until he could go no further and collapsed face-first into the muck of the rotting earth.

He lifted his head, choking on a mouthful of woody debris, spitting out bits of leaves, twigs, and mildewed peat. The forest had grown quiet. He listened but no animals scurried or squeaked. The wind had stopped blowing and the trees had ceased their grumbling. Now deprived of both sight and sound in the black silence of the forest, he was gripped by a new wave of panic. He searched the darkness, desperate to cast his eyes upon some reassuring solid form. *Over there!* he thought. Or was it just a deception of his unreliable eyes? *No. Something is over there.* He was sure of it. It quivered in and out across the sable curtain of the night, an undulation of empty space. He rose to his hands and knees and forced his eyes wide. There, just a few feet in front of him, he saw it, a faint glimmer of iridescent green.

He focused all his attention on the ethereal flicker, and as if the mere action of gazing upon it imbued it with more life, it glowed brighter. It was a mushroom, a tiny and perfectly shaped umbrella of translucent flesh. And as he stared, transfixed by its emerald glow, another appeared beside it out of the void. And another. And another. Until he found himself at the center of a fairy circle that lit up the dark forest around him. He straightened up onto his knees, awed by the spreading bioluminescence that radiated out over the forest floor, up the craggy bark of the tree trunks, forming glowing shelves of oysters, brackets, and lichen, filling up the empty knots and rotting hollows. Above his head, tiny living jewels dangled from the arched canopy of branches like pendants from a grand chandelier. He staggered to his feet and gaped at the shimmering green sphere around him, a giant living geode in which he had somehow become encased.

Reaching up, he brushed the dainty caps with his fingertips. They quivered and brightened, jingling softly like tiny bells. He giggled, delighted by the magical little beings, relieved that the madness he had succumbed to was pleasantly benign. With the impetuous fascination of a child, he plucked a mushroom from its perch on the tree and held it up to his face. Reacting to this thoughtless act of violence committed against it, the wounded mushroom flashed angrily and began to shriek, a high-pitched siren sound that pierced Patrick's eardrums. From all around him, the others joined in, loosening shrill cries of outrage for the crime committed against their sister, radiating brighter and brighter until their light almost blinded him. Panic-stricken, he tried to fling the mushroom away, but it clung to his hand, pricking his skin, oozing its milky green sap over his fingers. Numbing cold spread over his hand, up his arm, diffusing through his whole body. He dropped to his knees. The forest pulsated angrily, closing in from every direction. Then the earth rumbled to life beneath him and he was propelled backward.

"Patrick Michael Denny! Give it back!"

Patrick blinked. He could feel the gentle thrumming of the car's engine. His mother scowled at him from the front seat. "Stop teasing your sister! You need to have a talk with him, Al. He's turning into a bit of a bully."

"Jesus, Ginny, he's just being a boy. Boys tease their little sisters," his father tried to whisper over Lilian Anne's outraged shrieking.

"And fathers punish their sons," his mother snapped.

"Okay, okay. Patty, stop teasing your sister," his father called back, winking at Patrick in the rearview mirror. "Big brothers are supposed to take care of their little sisters. Now give it back."

Patrick looked at his hand. The purple popsicle was sticky and cold and melting over his fingers. He swallowed a lump in his throat. This wasn't a dream. It felt too real. He turned to his sister. She was just as he remembered her. Her face was red and streaked with tears. He handed her the popsicle which he had stolen from her decades before. "Here Lil. Sorry."

"Thank you," Lilian Anne said, wiping her cheeks with her sleeve as she reclaimed her property.

The windshield wipers ticked back and forth, and Patrick's mother turned to him and smiled. The scent of lavender hung in the air. "Good boy," she mouthed and turned back to the front just in time to witness the impact.

Time slowed. He watched his father sail through the windshield, his body flopping against the hood of the car. The sound of twisting, scraping metal accompanied the horror of watching his mother being folded and crushed like garbage in a trash compactor until her head was turned to him, gawking at him over the back of the seat with dead eyes. The motion and noise of the accident finally ceased, and Patrick broke his eyes away from her lifeless gaze. Lilian Anne was gone. He knew she would be. Just as he knew the inevitable outcome of everything that was happening. He climbed out the shattered window into the rain, miraculously unscathed, just as he had been when the accident had actually occurred all those years ago. His body trembled as he rounded the car, its crumpled shell hugging the tree that had ended their family vacation. He tried not to look over at his sister's broken body, slumped against another tree on the other side of the road, her head unnaturally twisted up. He would not run to her, slipping through the pool of warm blood. No, this time he would go directly to the cause of the accident.

So many times in his dreams, he wanted to break the cycle of the past, to rush over to the drunk who had destroyed his family, sending them headfirst into the giant oak and prematurely ending his happy childhood. He wanted to bash the bastard's head into the pavement until he was dead. But night after night, he was trapped in the same sequence of events, unable to stop himself from going to his sister, holding her broken body, and sitting in the growing pool of warm blood until the flashing lights came and the dream ended.

But this wasn't a dream. Somehow, the magic of the forest had transported him back in time. And he was in control. He walked past his dead little sister and headed to the side of the road. In the ditch, the long black car was tipped over on its side, the tires still spinning. He knew the murderer of his family was alive and uninjured, sitting in a stupor in the driver's seat, waiting for someone to rescue him. Patrick had never gotten the chance to see his face. Never gotten the chance to confront him. But this time was different.

He was all grown up, and his rage toward this monster had grown in proportion to his size. He slid down the wet, grassy embankment. But before he could reach the car, it began to sway and rock. He watched in confusion as the front windshield exploded outward. There was a moment of eerie silence, and then something poured itself out through the opening, rolling out onto the dirt, a slithering black form that uncoiled itself into a standing position.

Patrick looked up into the hollow eyes of Phineas Huntsman, who flashed him a pointy-toothed grin and then, in a blur, flew off into the forest. Without losing a second, Patrick followed, pushing through the branches, bounding over the fallen trees and stumps. He could hear the old man ripping through the forest ahead with inhuman speed. He tried to keep up, but his legs became heavier and heavier, and his breathing harder and harder until he had to stop. Gasping for air, he bent over and wretched neon green vomit. When he had finished, he looked up through the drizzle of rain and mottled foliage and saw a flicker of light. He staggered forward into a clearing. A huge bonfire blazed at its center, crackling, sputtering, and writhing in the rain. Phineas was nowhere to be seen.

Standing at the edge of the clearing, Patrick tried to untangle his confounded mind. He knew this place, but how had he gotten here? Thunder clapped from overhead. The curtain of rain suddenly parted, and the clouds receded, revealing twinkling stars set in a clear night sky. He stepped away from the tree line and into the grassy theater-in-the-round out behind Everston.

The bonfire raged at center stage and then, with a burst of sparks, died away. Patrick watched the glowing embers fade into the darkness, and just as the last one blinked out, a moonbeam descended upon the smoking remains. A hush fell upon the clearing in anticipation of what was to come next. From behind him, the tops of the pines exploded into flames, lighting up the night like giant torches, and, from the ashes of the bonfire, sprung a tree. Its sinewy branches unfurled into the burning sky, swelling into huge leaf-covered boughs that blotted out the stars and the moon. Its trunk expanded in great undulations, growing enormous before Patrick's astounded eyes. The earth rumbled as gargantuan roots snaked beneath his feet and knocked him to the ground.

"Patrick!" Father Owen's voice called from high up in the crest of the tree.

"Owen!" Patrick shrieked at the sight of his friend. The priest moved through the air as the tree continued to grow. Impaled through the chest by a mighty bough, his arms and legs and head dangled like Christmas tree ornaments. Patrick clambered to his feet and threw himself at the tree and climbed. "I'm coming!" he shouted.

"No! Forget me! Save her! Please! Save her!"

Hugging the trunk, Patrick looked down to where the priest pointed. A hollow had opened at the base of the tree, and inside, Amelia crouched, naked and giggling. She looked up at Patrick with crazed emerald eyes and held out her hands. Little brown mushrooms began to bubble and pop out of her palms.

The Tree

"Help her!" the priest pleaded.

The tree lurched and continued its expansion. Patrick dug the fingers of his right hand into the widening ridges of bark and, with his left, reached out to Amelia. He grasped at her, but her arms were covered with a milky slime, and she slipped away. "Amelia!" he cried as mushrooms sprouted from all the orifices of her body, her mouth and nose and ears and eyes, then from between her legs, spreading over her until she was nothing but a pulpy mound of brown, quivering flesh. The hollow closed around her and Amelia was gone.

"No! I'm too late! Owen, I'm too late!"

But the branches had grown so long and so high that the priest was no longer there. Patrick clung to the massive trunk as the tree continued to grow, overtaking the forest and the terrace and pushing out into Waylingbrooke, leaving a path of destruction in every direction. The colossal roots bore through the ground, overturning pavement and foundations like a giant tiller. Electrical lines sizzled and sparked and fell. Water mains erupted. Trees, telephone poles, and entire buildings toppled, crushed to splinters and dust by the arboreal juggernaut.

Patrick squeezed his eyes shut and clutched the tree until the world stopped moving, and the apocalyptic sounds died away. He opened his eyes. The tree had grown to such size that it had almost overtaken Tower Hill Cemetery, ceasing its expansion about halfway up the hill. Headstones lay in pieces amid overturned earth, coffins, and decaying corpses.

"Please, don't eat me," a small voice pleaded from somewhere close by.

"Stop squirming!" a raspy voice hissed.

Patrick climbed down from his perch and dropped between two mountainous roots.

"Ow! That hurts!"

"It wouldn't hurt so much if you'd stay still!"

He hurried toward the voices until the roots disappeared into the earth and he found himself in an undisturbed part of the cemetery. It was the oldest part at the base of the tower, and sitting cross-legged against a crooked, yellowed headstone, Phineas Huntsman gnawed on the leg of a little boy, who grimaced and groaned with each bite.

"Hello, Patrick," Jacob said sullenly. Phineas worked along the boy's thigh as if munching on a juicy cob of corn. "This witch isn't a very nice one. Do you think you could make him stop?" the boy implored politely, his large eyes hopeful.

"Let him go!" Patrick demanded.

"You should have let me kill him," Patricia Huntsman said matter-of-factly, leaning over from behind the headstone. "Look at this mess!" She pointed to a pile of bloody little pants, shirts, and shoes. "You know, he's never going to stop."

"Of course not!" Phineas picked at a piece of Jacob's flesh caught between his pointy, serrated teeth. "Once you taste the flesh of a little boy, you can never get enough."

"You sick bastard!" Patrick growled and propelled himself at the evil man, but he was snapped back high into the air with a startling lurch. The tree had taken him, coiling a rough-barked limb around his chest and squeezing until he could barely breathe. He sailed through the chilly night over the destroyed town until he came to a stop, suspended just outside the topmost window of the tower.

The Tree

"This town is so fucked up," Detective Foret chuckled perched on the branch that held Patrick aloft. "Popcorn?" he said, leaning over and holding out a bucket of movie popcorn.

"What are you doing here? Huntsman is down there . . . he's . . . he's got a little boy," Patrick gasped as the coiled end of the branch squeezed around him tighter and tighter.

Foret laughed and then choked on a mouthful of popcorn. Clearing his throat, he explained, "After the Perez case, no one takes me seriously. The bosses say I'm too obsessed with finding the truth. Kept me from going after that rich old chick, Patricia Huntsman. Fuckers. So I'm just here to watch the show. Oh, look," he pointed to the tower window. "Something's about to happen."

"You can't save them! They all belong to us now!" a familiar voice cackled. Grinning her yellow teeth, Estelle leaned out the window, her long silver hair flapping freely in the wind. Patrick struggled to speak, but with every exhalation, the branch constricted his chest tighter and tighter. "Oh, he's coming!" she exclaimed and melted back into the darkness of the room behind her.

As if on cue, the moon broke through the clouds and lit up the inside of the tower with its ghostly light. By some preternatural force that Patrick couldn't comprehend, Anderson's office had been transported through the lunatic night and now occupied the tower's top floor. Patrick looked through the window over Anderson's desk, past the leather chairs, past the Goyas that flanked the open door, out to where Estelle sat. Milling by her desk, familiar faces queued up outside the door. One by one, they checked in with Anderson's assistant, who dutifully entered their names on her list. Susan, Ed, Archie, and the rest of Everston's staff. Mr. Lupis, Mrs. Hamesh, Ned Martin, and all the other patients who had taken up permanent residence at the hospital. Cloaked in the moon's white light, they filed into the office, expressionless apparitions that hovered around the desk and blocked Patrick's view.

"I'm sorry I'm late," Ray Scarlatti apologized as he hurried in. "It took me a while because the streets are all broken up and the electricity is out and I thought there was no way I was going to make it but I'm finally here." He took his place in the circle and waited patiently with the others.

Moments passed, and then Patrick heard it. A grunt, a moan, and then an ecstatic cry. He struggled against the force that restrained him and craned his neck to see. With a collective sigh, the crowd parted and revealed the scene playing out on top of the desk. Patrick let loose a silent cry, flailing and kicking until he had no more strength as Anderson and Helen violently fornicated before their captive audience.

"Ouch. Sorry, Doc. That's gotta sting," Foret commented, nudging Patrick's shoulder.

With a final beastly thrust and grunt, Anderson flashed his wild eyes at Patrick and tossed Helen's now lifeless body to the floor. "This one's all used up. I need a new one," he panted.

"I knew you two were up to something," Dilby's flat voice declared to Patrick as he materialized from the shadows by the window. "You made a pact with him, didn't you?" He shook his head disdainfully. "Arrogant fool."

"Bring the next one to me," Anderson growled.

"Well, time to sacrifice another." Dilby held out his hand.

From the shadows, a young woman emerged.

"Oh! I did not see that coming!" Foret exclaimed. "Finally, a little justice."

Patrick's eyes widened with horror as Sam gave Dilby her hand and let him lead her to the desk. She glanced back through the window with a sad smile. "It's okay. It's all going to be okay."

"You've done everything you can. You should go home now and rest," Father Owen said, suddenly appearing by his side, still impaled and dangling from the branch.

Patrick tried to speak, to scream, to plead with Sam to run, but he had no voice. He watched impotently as Anderson pulled her onto the desk. "It's okay," he heard her say as the crowd closed around them and again cut off his view. "I'll stay with him. You can go. You've done enough."

Patrick groaned in hopeless frustration. He couldn't save her. He couldn't save any of them. He let his body go slack and dropped his head. The pressure on his chest diminished, and the world around him melted into blackness.

"What's happening?" Sam called out from a distance.

"I think he's waking up," answered Father Owen's disembodied voice.

"Oh, thank God!" Sam cried.

Patrick strained to see through the heavy darkness. He felt the touch of warm fingers on his arm. He heard the soft hum of electronics around him. He recognized the orientation of his body now. He was lying flat on his back, a firm cushion of support beneath him. The air was cool, dry, and sterile. He tried to inhale, but something had been shoved down his throat, and he gagged on it. He started to panic and fight.

"It's okay, it's okay. You have a breathing tube," Sam's voice explained, trying to calm him.

With great effort, Patrick opened his heavy eyelids and saw Sam's exhausted but relieved face hovering over him. Father Owen stood beside her, shaking his head and holding back the tears that threatened to burst from his tired eyes.

"Hey, Doc. Welcome back," Sam said, taking his hand in hers.

...

Dr. Fujito flashed his penlight into Patrick's eyes. "Good," he said, clicking it off and slipping it into the front pocket of his crisp, white doctor's coat. "Now squeeze my hands."

Patrick did as instructed, wincing as the IV in his hand pinched.

"Excellent. Okay." Dr. Fujito scribbled something into Patrick's chart. "Everything seems good so far. We'll keep you here for a few more days to monitor the concussion and keep you on the intravenous antifungal. Make sure those lungs are clear. But if you continue to show improvement, we'll send you home to finish up the treatment with a prescription." The doctor nodded his head in complete agreement with himself. "Any questions?"

"No," Patrick croaked, his throat still raw from the breathing tube. "Thank you, doctor."

"Very good. I'll tell your family it's okay to come back in. Have a good night."

Father Owen and Sam returned to Patrick's bedside.

"So, what's the verdict?" Sam asked.

Patrick took a sip of cold water and gave her the thumbs up.

"Thank God," she said. But her smile of relief morphed into a scowl. "Don't you ever do anything like that again!" she scolded as if he were a child who'd just run out into the street without looking. "You could have died out there all alone. If it wasn't for Mr. Scarlatti, no one would have known you were missing until it was too late."

Patrick cleared his throat. "How long was I gone?" he rasped.

"Mr. Scarlatti sounded the alarm on Tuesday when you didn't show up for his appointment. He called Father Owen," she said, glancing at the old priest, who stood back staring at the floor. "And Father Owen called everyone he could think of. He finally got in touch with Mr. Dearborne, who took us up to Candlewick, where we found your car. The search team didn't find you until early Thursday morning."

"Five days?" Patrick couldn't believe that so much time had passed. It had seemed like only a few nightmarish hours.

"And then another three days here unconscious," Sam added. "You know they thought they lost you in the ambulance. You were hypothermic, and you actually stopped breathing!"

Patrick squeezed her hand. "I'm okay. I had a lot of respiratory infections when I was a kid. Makes me more susceptible. That'll take care of it," he said, glancing up at the IV bag, feeling the cold spread up his arm.

"Then you should know better than to go traipsing around the damp woods breathing in all that moldy air. Fungal pneumonia." She shook her head, her voice rising with each word. "It sounds so awful. Don't do it again!" She punctuated her final sentence by pointing an accusatory finger at him.

"Yes, ma'am. Owen, when did she get so bossy?"

But the priest continued in his silent ruminations.

"Owen?"

"This is all my fault," the priest blurted out, his face drawn with exhaustion and guilt. "I shouldn't have pressured you about Amelia. Her parents told me how hard you've been trying to help. That's why you went to the cottage and got lost."

Patrick shook his head and was about to tell him to stop beating himself up, when lightning struck his brain.

"This is not your responsibility anymore," Owen continued, oblivious to the sudden change in Patrick's demeanor. "Sometimes we have to give things up to the Lord and trust that He does things for a reason."

Patrick tried to take a deep breath, but congestion strangled his chest, just like the tree in his dream. The tree that had swallowed Amelia up after the mushrooms had consumed her. He *had* been traipsing around the damp woods, breathing in all that moldy air, the same damp woods where Amelia had spent the summer wandering before she got sick.

"When I think about what could have happened to you out there—"

"Dr. Denny? Are you okay?" Sam interrupted.

The same damp woods . . .

"Should I call the doctor?" Father Owen asked as Patrick tried to get up from the bed.

"No . . . yes! Get Dr. Fujito. I know what's wrong with Amelia."

The Tree

• • •

"I don't understand. You believe it's an infection?" Mr. Dearborne asked for the third time.

Sitting in his wheelchair outside of Amelia's hospital room, Patrick tried to explain to her parents why he had woken them in the middle of the night to sign off on Amelia's transfer to the medical facility at which he was currently being treated. "Yes. Probably something like cryptococcal meningitis. They're going to do a spinal tap. Then we'll know more."

Mrs. Dearborne gazed into the room as her daughter was being prepared for the procedure. "You mean all this time she's just had an infection? Why didn't anyone do these tests before?"

Patrick cleared his ragged throat. "She didn't present with any of the typical symptoms, and her behavior strongly suggested a mental disorder." He tried to maintain his composure, not wanting the bewildered parents to see that he, too, was upset by the thought that Amelia had possibly missed twenty years of her life because of a treatable infection.

"I'll get you some water," Mrs. Dearborne said, needing to do something with her nervous energy, and she shuffled down the corridor.

"If she does have this crypto thing, what can we do about it?" Mr. Dearborne took a breath, still reeling from the shock of the midnight call. "Will she get better?"

"She'll be treated with antifungal chemotherapy," Patrick explained. "It will be a long process, so we'll have to be patient. This infection has been hiding in her body for a very long time, and there will probably be some neurological damage." He paused, seeing the pain and hope in Mr. Dearborne's eyes, and placed a hand on his arm. "But there's a real possibility she'll recover something of her old self."

Amelia's father let the tears flow down his cheeks. "No matter what happens," he said softly, "thank you. Thank you for not giving up on my little girl."

Before Patrick could respond, Mrs. Dearborne returned with his water. She gave her husband a faint smile and wiped his cheek. The three watched as Amelia was wheeled away down the corridor for her procedure.

CHAPTER THIRTEEN

The phone call came just as Patrick had arrived home after being released from the hospital.

Phineas Huntsman was dead.

"I can't believe this is happening," Archie said to Patrick. The two men waited outside the back entrance of Halcyon House, watching the ambulance and firetruck pull away, their lights and sirens off. "This isn't happening," Archie repeated, as the coroner's wagon backed up toward the handicap ramp.

"Tell me again. How did he open the window?" Patrick asked, his eyes following the tall oak tree up to Phineas's window.

Archie glanced up involuntarily, but quickly averted his eyes. Even though the hot July morning had already risen to ninety-two degrees, a visible shiver shook the man's body. "All the windows on the second floor have keyed safety locks. Professionally installed. I made sure they were the best available. I can't believe this is happening."

Patrick wiped the sweat from his forehead. "Archie, who has

the key to the lock on Mr. Huntsman's window?"

"What . . . the key? You can't possibly think one of my staff . . . well, that's just ridiculous . . . they're all excellent . . . I hired every single one myself. You might as well accuse me!"

"Archie!" Patrick grabbed him by the shoulders. "Pull yourself together. The police are going to ask you the same questions."

At the mention of the police, the remaining color drained from Archie's face. "Right. Police. Um, okay. All the window locks have the same key, and everyone on staff has a copy of that key."

"Everyone?"

"Yes, nurses, aides, cooks, cleaners, even I have one." He held up his ring of keys and pointed to an oddly shaped orange-capped key. "The locks are to prevent accidents and to keep the patients from wandering away unnoticed. They're not for locking down the facility though. I need to make sure the staff can get the patients out if there's a fire. I don't understand how he unlocked that window, Patrick."

Archie focused on the two men climbing out of the coroner's wagon and spoke softly. "I suppose I owe you an apology. You were right. He didn't belong here. He fooled me too. I thought . . . well, I guess I thought wrong." He reached into the inside pocket of his blazer and pulled out a white, letter-sized envelope. "I was supposed to give this to you in the event of Mr. Huntsman's death."

Patrick took the envelope and turned it over in his hands. On the front, "Dr. Patrick Denny" was printed in neat black lettering. The back was sealed and signed in the spidery scrawl of

Phineas Huntsman's hand, ensuring no one else would open it. "When did he give this to you?"

"About a week ago. He threatened to have Halcyon House 'dismantled piece by piece' if I failed to follow his instructions exactly." Archie related the ominous words with a touch of embarrassed disbelief. "To be honest, he was terrifying. I really should have listened to you."

Patrick nodded and watched the coroner and his assistant round to the back of their vehicle. "Well, I was out of line. I shouldn't have accused you of being bought off by Patricia Huntsman."

"Hmm, yes, that was pretty insulting . . . and hurtful," Archie agreed, watching the coroner, a short, round man, and his tall, lanky assistant struggle to extricate the gurney from the back of the wagon. "And I guess I was out of line when I called you an overindulged pretty boy with a superiority complex."

Patrick hummed in agreement. "Yes. Pretty boy? Really?"

Archie's face relaxed. "Yes, Patrick, I find you very pretty."

"Well, just as long as you know I'm not easy."

Both men grinned, but the light-hearted moment soon evaporated when the flashing blue lights of a police patrol car appeared behind the coroner's wagon.

"Oh, I can't believe this is happening," Archie groaned as Detective Foret's vintage 1980s red Chevy Camaro pulled up beside the patrol car.

Patrick shoved the envelope into his pocket and touched Archie's shoulder. "Tell me quickly," he whispered as Detective Foret conferred with the coroner. "Who was the last person to see Phineas alive?"

"Um, Nurse Delacroix. She said everything seemed normal. Mr. Huntsman was given his evening medications and settled down for the night. But when she went to check on him . . ." Archie swallowed hard and gazed up again to where Phineas Huntsman had been hanging from the tree just outside the open window when he arrived. "The collar of his shirt somehow got tangled up in the branches. It strangled the life out of him. He . . . he was just dangling there. God, Patrick, you should have seen his face." Archie shuddered. "I'll never get the image of it out of my head."

Patrick was trying hard not to picture it himself when a young police officer approached and addressed him with the forced baritone of someone attempting to sound older.

"Mr. Philbin?"

Patrick shook his head and pointed to Archie.

"Yes, well, it's Dr. Philbin, but yes," Archie said, nodding.

"Sorry, *Doctor*. So, you found the body?"

"Um, no, it was one of the nurses."

"So, *Doctor*, were you on the premises when it happened?"

"Well, no, I got the call—"

"At ease, Gomer. I'll talk to the doctors," Detective Foret said, dismissing the officer. "Why don't you go get in touch with the fire crew that hauled the body back in through the window and find out why the hell they left so quickly after disturbing my crime scene!"

"Crime scene? This is just a horrible accident?" Archie blurted out.

Officer Gorman's shoulders slumped. "Yes, Sir." Biting his peach-fuzzed lip, he marched back toward his patrol car.

The Tree

"Dr. Philbin," Foret addressed Archie, giving Patrick a suspicious sidelong glance. "Can you show me and the coroner here the deceased?"

"Certainly . . . uh, this way." Archie flashed a worried look at Patrick and then led the officials up the ramp that wound around to the side of the house. He held the door open for the detective, the coroner, and the assistant, who wheeled the rickety gurney over the threshold and into the air-conditioned kitchen. The clinking, clanking, and casual banter of the cook staff gave way to an immediate and uncomfortable silence as all eyes fell upon the grim band of men. "Carry on, everyone," Archie urged his staff with a forced smile of reassurance and waved them back to work. "Just through here, gentlemen."

Following up the rear, Patrick tried to keep his distance as they walked through the laundry room and out toward the front of the building. Unlike on his last visit, Patrick noticed that none of the residents were sitting in the lobby, enjoying its pleasant atmosphere. No doubt Archie had his staff make sure they were all tucked away in their rooms until Phineas's body was removed from the building.

"So, Dr. Philbin, can you tell me what happened here?" Foret asked and glanced back at Patrick, most likely suspicious of the man's presence at yet another crime scene involving the Huntsmans. They paused at the bottom of the staircase.

"Well, you see—"

"Don't you have an elevator?" the coroner interrupted as he inspected the long, winding ascent before them.

"Oh, well, because our facility has only two floors, and the budget—"

"No elevator. Great," the rotund man grumbled and exchanged an annoyed look with his assistant.

"We do have this chairlift," Archie offered helpfully.

"So, you want us to plop the dead guy in the chairlift and give him a ride down?"

"No!"

"Come on, Ronny," the coroner grumbled to his assistant. Lugging the gurney between them, they followed Archie and the detective to the second floor, grunting and complaining the whole way.

Patrick lingered at the bottom of the staircase. Up above, Phineas's dead body awaited. A creeping unease sent goosebumps along his back and neck. He heard Archie tell Foret about the window locks and the excellent staff and how he couldn't understand how Mr. Huntsman had opened the window.

"So he opened it himself?" Foret asked, a hint of disbelief in his voice.

"It appears so," Archie responded with his own less-than-certain tone.

"Who was the last person to see him alive?" Patrick heard the detective ask as the two disappeared through the door to Phineas's room. He pictured them standing over the corpse.

Patrick wrestled with conflicting emotions as he waited below. On one hand, he hoped Foret's relentlessness would finally expose the Huntsmans' secrets. On the other, he worried about the toll this would take on his kindhearted friend's well-being and reputation. With growing anxiety, he listened to the muffled voices above, wondering what would happen next.

"Dr. Denny," a hushed voice called to him from the front

entrance. Patrick turned to see Nurse Delacroix peeking around the door and waving for him to follow. He glanced over his shoulder to where the coroner and his assistant had just hauled the gurney onto the top landing. Hesitating for only a moment, he turned and calmly strolled toward the entrance, trailing Nurse Delacroix out into the heat and down the porch steps. They stopped beneath the shade of a giant oak at the edge of the road.

"I'm sorry . . ." he said, sure she would need to be comforted at the loss of her patient under such horrific circumstances, but her cheerful expression stopped him in mid-sentence.

"I told you, everyone is judged in the end," she tutted. "The poor fellow. He climbed out the window, grumbling something about snapping the necks of those noisy baby birds. He must have slipped and caught the collar of his shirt on a branch. There was nothing anybody could do."

Patrick stood dumbstruck, puzzled by her words, which were no longer marked by the heavy accent and broken English. His heart pounded at the sight of the orange-capped key hanging from a chain around her neck. "Nurse Delacroix, what did you do?"

"Oh, please, call me Shelly," she said, cocking her head like a little girl, her bouncy, golden curls catching the morning sunlight. Just then, a long, gray limo pulled up to the curb, the driver's face only a shadow behind the tinted glass. "Oh, this is my ride. I'm going home to my family now."

"But the police—"

"Oh," she exclaimed, "don't worry about them. It's all been taken care of. Be well, Dr. Denny." Her disconcerting smile lingered on Patrick for a moment until she skipped away toward the waiting car. She slipped into the back seat and disappeared behind the tinted windows. As the car pulled away, Patrick was left standing alone under the tree.

When he returned to the foyer, Archie stood at the bottom of the staircase next to Officer Gorman as Foret paced back and forth, yelling into his phone. "This is bullshit!"

Archie caught sight of Patrick and gave him a bewildered shrug. But Patrick hung by the door, knowing without a doubt that Foret's investigation was being shut down at that very moment.

"So this Melissa Delacroix—I'll need a witness statement from her just to wrap things up," Officer Gorman said to Archie.

"Um, it's *Michelle*. She was very fond of the man. She spent so much time with him. She even came in on her days off to sit and chat. I try to hire dedicated people, you know." Archie shook his head and wrung his hands. "The sound she made when she found him scared the rest of the staff and residents half to death. The poor woman. I gave her a sedative as soon as I got here. She's resting in the staff lounge."

"Right. Well, the coroner is pretty sure it was just a terrible accident. When Nurse, um . . ."

"Delacroix," Archie supplied again.

"Yeah, have her give me a call at the station at her earliest convenience. That's *Sergeant Gorman*," he enunciated his name with an air of importance.

Clearly unsettled by the speed at which the morning's events were transpiring, Archie gave the young officer a nod. "Sergeant Gorman, yes."

"You should, um, you should probably write that down."

"Come on, Gomer!" Foret roared, having finished his phone call. The startled officer tried to keep up as the detective stormed across the lobby. "This town is so fucked up," the detective spat as he passed by Patrick and out the front entrance.

Archie looked back and forth between the staircase and the front door, confused and quite perturbed. Patrick rejoined him at the bottom of the staircase. "The coroner has tentatively deemed it a tragic accident, most likely caused by a defective window lock and Phineas's dementia," Archie informed him in disbelief. "We just had a state safety inspection last month?"

Distracted by his own bizarre encounter, Patrick asked, "What do you know about Nurse Delacroix?"

"Um, Michelle? Nice young woman . . . I check all the safety locks myself once a month," Archie continued, still puzzled by the suggestion of a defective lock.

"Did Phineas know her before they sent him here?"

"What? Oh. I have no idea," Archie mumbled.

"No elevator," the coroner muttered from the top of the staircase where he and his assistant had wheeled the now-occupied gurney to the edge of the landing.

"How are they going to get him down?" Archie mused, staring at up the precarious situation developing. He and Patrick watched as the coroner and his assistant collapsed the gurney to the floor and heaved it up between them. They started their descent with the assistant leading the way.

"Slow down," the coroner barked.

"Stop pushing," the assistant complained. "You're gonna knock me down."

The coroner tried to get a better grip, his face a bright red. "Hold up your side more, Ronny!"

"Maybe we should help them," Archie said, but it was too late.

"Shit!" the assistant shouted as the gurney slid under him, and he sledded down the staircase on top of the corpse of Phineas Huntsman. Still clinging to the back of the gurney, his boss bounced behind him, hitting each step like a giant beach ball, until the two men, the gurney, and the corpse lay in a heap at the bottom.

Archie and Patrick, with quick sidesteps, narrowly avoided the catastrophe. They stood frozen for a moment, eyes wide, before rushing to help.

"Sweet Jesus! Are you okay?" Archie exclaimed.

"You need a goddamned elevator!" the coroner shouted, staggering to his feet.

"Get it off me! Get it off me!" the assistant shrieked, pinned under the gurney and the corpse.

Patrick and Archie heaved the overturned gurney off the hysterical man and set it right on the floor.

"Jesus!" Patrick exclaimed.

"Christ," Archie breathed.

The black vinyl bag in which the coroner had enclosed the body had split straight down the front. Patrick looked down at the exposed corpse. Phineas Huntsman's dead eyes stared up at him, bulging as if still straining for breath. His toothless mouth gaped open in a perverse, twisted grin, his purple tongue protruding grotesquely.

"I shut the eyes myself," Archie blurted out, taking a step

back from the corpse, his hand instinctively covering his mouth.

"It happens," the coroner assured him matter-of-factly, and turned to his assistant. "Ronny, get off the floor and stop acting like a baby. We gotta get this guy to the morgue."

"Christ," Archie repeated.

"Yes," Patrick concurred. Though quite dead, Phineas Huntsman looked even more like the monster he had been in life.

...

The letter lay open on his desk. Patrick stood before the window in Sam's spot. His eyes rested a moment on the red brick of the tower, its rigid architecture softened by the hazy summer heat. Then, with a slight turn of the head, his gaze leapt many thousands of feet, traveling toward where Everston stood obscured by the dense summer foliage. The fact of its existence, however, was a clear reality to Patrick's troubled brain.

"Damn you, Phineas," he breathed, angry and unsure what to do next. The monster had confessed. By his own hand, he'd detailed his perverse crimes and motivations and unapologetically laid them out for the world to judge. However, being the conscienceless sociopath that he was, Phineas Huntsman did not make these admissions in the hope of some posthumous absolution. Rather, he sought to inflict the maximum amount of damage on as many people as possible, both the innocent and the not-so-innocent. And in his final sodomitical act, he thrust upon Patrick the responsibility of unleashing these venomous aspersions on the world.

Why Did God Make the Tree?

"Bastard!" Patrick stalked back to his desk, snatched up the letter, and read it again:

My Dear Dr. Denny,

I have been murdered. No doubt, my death has been orchestrated by my wife, Patricia Hillary Gladsworth Huntsman. Though your apparent abhorrence for me might lead some to believe that you were also a part of this conspiracy, it is my contention that you are innocent of such accusations. You have always been quite adamant that I am the key villain of the plot and should be judged by the law. However, though I do not believe that you were a part of my wife's conspiracy, let it also be on record that you, Dr. Patrick Denny, did not honor your oath as a physician to maintain the utmost respect for human life and that you callously disregarded my pleas for help, allowing my subsequent murder to occur.

That being said, I wish to make a full confession of my crimes as seen by the narrow and unsophisticated purview of our current judicial system. I have, for the entirety of my adult life, craved the touch of young boys. I make no apologies for this desire, as I firmly believe it is my inherent right to pursue my pleasures, societal norms be damned. I have always been a powerful man of means and was brought up with the understanding that whatever I desire, I have the right to attain. My wife Patricia, a frigid and utterly useless creature, gave me no children. So, without any prospect of having male progeny, and given my wife's utter failure as a woman, I took it upon myself to procure one from distant relatives.

The Tree

Michael's parents were drug addicts, the most lowly of all creatures. People who could not put up even the façade of control over their desires. They eagerly accepted when I offered to purchase Michael from them for a generous sum. I maintain that the boy was better off with me than that subhuman refuse. The only hindrance to our agreement came in the form of Michael's younger sister of whom his parents also wanted to rid themselves. Having no use for her, I dispatched her to associates of mine in Europe whose tastes were more inclined to little girls. With Patricia wanting nothing to do with my new charge, the boy was left to me entirely, and I made good use of him until his teen years, when he lost his desirability. By then, he had also started to display some rather grotesque behaviors, so I turned him over to my wife to deal with. Afraid of public embarrassment, and driven by her insatiable hunger for power and control, Patricia ensured that Michael would be kept silent. So, I found other outlets that would meet my needs. Attached, you will find a list of names and addresses. My hope in including this list is that the families of these young men will descend upon the Huntsman Estate, greedily picking it clean and leaving Patricia not only humiliated but also destitute.

As you can bear witness, sometime last summer, my imbecilic ward, Michael Ian McKay, imprisoned me in the basement of the organ hall, subjecting me to unimaginable squalor and degradation. On the pretense of winning back my affections, he lured me to the organ hall with the promise of meeting a young boy whom he had procured for my use. Needless to say, discovering that no such boy existed was immensely frustrating. It appears that even in matters of deception, Michael remains a disappointment. And once I realized that he intended to leave me there to starve to death, I began to suspect that Patricia had a hand in my confinement. With Michael being a feebleminded dolt, I couldn't imagine him contriving such a plot on his own. It is clear that at some point in our forty-eight-year marriage, Patricia, in her relentless pursuit of my downfall, concluded that my demise was the only means to achieve her twisted sense of happiness. This can be attested to by you, Dr. Denny, whose timely arrival prevented that bitch from smashing my head in with a brick.

There is no doubt that the second and obviously successful attempt on my life points to a larger conspiracy perpetrated by a number of individuals, as listed below. As I am sure you know, my faculties have never been sharper, and I only executed a ruse of mental infirmity in order to evade prosecution. This subterfuge was made quite easy by a certain Dr. Archibald Philbin, who is either the most gullible rube of a man I have ever encountered, given to stomach-turning sentimentality and softheartedness and easily swayed by my masterful deception, or, more likely, a mere puppet dancing to the tune of my wife's machinations, as are most of the important people of Waylingbrooke. Either way, with his diagnosis and the concurrence of many of my wife's other lackeys, including but not limited to Alexander Anderson, the Executive Director of Everston Psychiatric Hospital, Dr. Clifton Dilby, Chief Medical Director of Everston, Theodore Davison, Chief of the Waylingbrooke

The Tree

Police Department, and Father Owen Fielding, Pastor of St. Michael's Church, I was admitted to Halcyon House with a diagnosis of advanced dementia. I planned to bide my time here until the appropriate moment when I would make a miraculous recovery and return to my life, free from Patricia's wrath while she remained in exile. However, it became quickly apparent to me that Patricia's homicidal intentions had not died in the basement of that organ hall. I do believe that with the aid of the persons mentioned above and a certain Nurse Delacroix, whose continuous presence and incessant prattling about the importance of family seemed designed to inspire me to take my own life, my wife had me murdered.

 Well, there you have it. I have "come clean," as you so forcefully suggested on our last visit. You have my confession. Show the world what a vile creature Phineas Huntsman was. But I urge you, doctor, to act accordingly and ensure that the full weight of the law comes down upon those complicit in my demise.

Sincerely,

Phineas Huntsman

P.S.

 Many years ago, Patricia purchased a home in Brussels, undoubtedly a sanctuary from my presence. I am confident that is where she has taken Michael. Their extradition should be a straightforward affair for the authorities.

Patrick slammed the letter onto his desk, his chest heaving with a pain. He reached for his inhaler, giving his weakened lungs a blast of medicine. His mind raced with the implications of Phineas's confession. Anderson, Dilby, and the Chief of Police might have been persuaded to look the other way, but Archie and Owen were innocent, their involvement driven only by a desire to help a sick old man. Phineas had to know this. Why else would he use them as his messengers?

"Sadistic mind games!" Patrick blurted out, his voice echoing in the oppressive silence of the room. These were nothing but empty accusations designed to cast unwarranted suspicion and damage on his friends. How could he put them through that? And yet, the names of the six other victims screamed out to him for justice—innocent, damaged souls who didn't deserve to be forgotten.

There was no doubt Patricia Huntsman had arranged Phineas's murder, which Michelle Delacroix—or as he now realized, *Shelly McKay*—had actually carried out. Shouldn't they face justice for their actions? But then there was Michael . . .

"Michael," Patrick sighed. What would happen to him if this twisted confession-condemnation was revealed to the world? Patrick believed Michael to be happy and free, convinced that the tormented man had been reunited with his long-lost sister under Patricia's protective care. How could he ruin that for him after so many years of suffering?

"Damn you, Phineas. Why couldn't you have just died quietly?" The light outside the window had faded, and Patrick found himself sitting in the dark, no closer to a decision than when he had first read the letter. He took a long, painful breath and surrendered to the anguish of the situation, letting himself melt into the gloom and shadow of the room. Then, seized by

The Tree

an impulse, he spun his chair around and groped along the bookshelf in the dark until he found it. Turning back around, he clicked on the desk lamp, placed Michael's copy of *The Monster* in front of him, and read the last page:

As he had done every day, three times a day, for decades, Michael checked the chains to make sure they were secure. He listened for the familiar rustles and scratches from within. With bitter spitefulness, he banged on the old metal door. "You still in there, you sick bastard?" he laughed derisively. "You hungry? Got a nice little fresh baby out here for ya!" A weak thud against the door made Michael laugh harder. "Come on, is that all you got left? Don't you want this sweet, juicy little girl?" The door thudded more violently. "Ho, that's better." The sound of nails clawed at the door frenetically. "That's right, try to get out, try to escape, ya evil bastard." From within the stone enclosure, a cry of anger, despair, and frustration echoed out into the dense wilderness around them. Michael snickered and limped through the debris of the old cemetery, aware of the location of every broken piece of headstone, every depression in the spongy earth. "You're not going anywhere," he mumbled as he hobbled toward his home in the forest. "You're stuck here!" he shouted over his shoulder. "Just like me," he said matter-of-factly to the overhanging trees.

He settled under the makeshift lean-to that served as his house and untied his sneakers. Stretching out his arthritic toes, he examined the holes in his socks. He'd have to venture out of the forest into the real world soon for supplies, he thought unhappily. He scratched his grizzled chin. He hated leaving the forest now. He hated seeing the wider world, a world to which he didn't belong and which didn't belong to him. He hated how the clean, happy people looked at him and how the children shrunk back at his approach, disgusted and afraid. "Nope, out there, that's not for us," he spoke to the monster, as if it were sitting right beside him and not locked up in the mausoleum on the other side of the cemetery. "This is where we belong. With the dead and forgotten." He chuckled at the thought of death. What a relief it would be to be dead and free.

Patrick didn't bother to wipe the tears from his cheeks, so intent on ending this tragic story once and for all. Without another thought about what to do, he folded up the list of Phineas's other victims and tucked it into the left pocket of his shirt. He slipped the confession between the last pages of the book, shutting it with a soft thud. After addressing the large manila envelope to the Huntsman Estate, he sealed Michael's book inside, knowing it would be forwarded to Patricia, wherever she, Michael, and Shelly were in the world. Perhaps the letter would motivate her to come forward on her own and reveal the truth about Phineas's crimes, leaving the innocent untainted by her dead husband's false accusations. But at least for now, the monster was dead.

EPILOGUE

SOMETIME LATER . . .

"They stood around her, watching, waiting, a blur of faces floating above her in the smoky haze. 'No!' she screamed, and with one final excruciating push, the baby came out of her, delivered right into the hands of the crone. 'She's perfect,' the old woman cooed as she cut the cord and swaddled the bloody infant in a cloak of white. A collective gasp of pleasure preceded the dispersal of the white-hooded spectators. 'Can I see her?' the new mother begged. 'Just for a moment?' But the crone ignored her and, with the child cradled in her arms, followed the others out of the cottage. 'Wait! Please! I want to see her face!' she cried, picking herself up from the floor. 'Please! I've changed my mind. Give her back to me!' she shrieked and stumbled after them despite the pain, despite the blood that continued to pour from between her legs. Down the crumbling steps and through the gate, she chased the procession into the dark woods. 'Give me my baby!' she demanded hysterically. But she could barely keep up, growing weaker and weaker as she lost more and more blood. And then they were gone. She'd lost them somewhere in the night. 'No,' she sobbed and fell to her knees, crawling forward with her last bit of strength. But just as she was about to give up, to let herself collapse onto the frozen ground and let the forest take her, she heard it. Her child cried somewhere ahead, and she made herself continue until she pushed through a tangle of brush and out into the clearing of the oak grove. They stood in a circle around the blazing fire pit, singing their incantations, the crone holding up the screaming, naked newborn. 'I want my baby,' she cried out weakly and then collapsed against one of the giant oak trees. 'Give her to me,' she whispered. The chanting died away and the child was soothed. 'Don't worry,' the one she'd bargained with called out and ripped back his hood, revealing a head of short, wavy blonde hair and crazed blue eyes glinting in the firelight. 'We'll teach her well. And one day, she will destroy him!' Consciousness began to fade from her, and her eyes fluttered shut. The fire crackled and the forest around her rustled with movement. When she opened her eyes, she was alone. Leaning against the oak, her legs splayed out in front of her along the tree roots, she could feel the life oozing from her, seeping into the earth. And as she died, she tried to decide if the sacrifice was worth it . . . End of chapter one," Alexander Anderson finished, shutting the book and looking up at his captive audience. "You'll have to buy a copy of my book to find out what happens next."

The audience groaned, then broke into applause, hoots, and whistles. They queued up in front of the table to get their copies signed.

Patrick stood on the other side of the bookstore and watched

Epilogue

Helen as she leaned against a gigantic poster of *The Tree* that had been plastered on the wall behind Anderson. She stared blankly ahead, the spark gone from her eyes. But she'd done it. She'd found a publisher for the unknown author and secured him a sweet three-book deal that included a hefty sum for the media rights. She moved her gaze across the room and Patrick ducked behind a display case.

The plan had been to wait until the book had met with some success, until Anderson had started his publicity tour and the eyes of the public were upon him. Then he would do it. He'd destroy the bastard's reputation with one simple sentence—*I wrote it.*

He peeked over a stack of books and saw a local newspaper reporter he'd met years before chatting Helen up, getting the story on the new hometown author. *The timing couldn't be more perfect*, he thought. He examined the books in front of him. It's not how he pictured the cover of his creation. With the title spelled out in a small nondescript font, the focal point of the cover was Anderson's pretentiously oversized name. He stepped away from the display. No, his book would have had an enormous, sprawling oak tree with the title tangled in the gnarled branches and his name embedded in the roots.

But it wasn't his baby anymore. He'd given it away. He fingered the curve of the tree-of-life pendant in his pocket and watched Anderson soaking up his newfound fame. The fans fawned over him, and the reporter snapped a picture of him holding up the book. He was on his way to becoming a superstar.

"Good luck coming up with your next book," he muttered, letting the door to the bookstore slam behind him. As he walked back to his car, he unfolded the local newspaper he'd purchased from a kiosk just outside the bookstore entrance. The headline shouted in bold letters, "Local Police Detective Suspended." Sitting in his car, Patrick read the article, which hinted at Foret's increasingly erratic behavior and his refusal to let go of the Huntsman case. Patrick couldn't help but feel a twinge of sympathy for the man, recognizing in him the same dogged pursuit of truth that had always driven his own actions. But he was sure this wouldn't be the last they'd hear of Detective Hugo Foret. His story wasn't finished yet.

. . .

The day was clear, and the grounds at Everston were alive with activity. Patrick walked around the front of the building and admired the flower beds in full bloom. He'd had all his patients brought out into the sunshine for the morning. The idea had caught on, and at least a dozen other patients had been brought out onto the lawns.

"Dr. Denny!"

He turned to see Archie Philbin hurrying toward him. "Archie, my friend, how are you on this beautiful day?"

"I've got bad news. They made Dilby director."

"Yes, Susan told me."

Archie frowned. "You'd better tread lightly. He's going to try to get rid of you, you know."

"Don't worry about me."

"Really, Patrick," Archie warned. "You've got to be careful. We all do. God, I can't believe Dilby's in charge."

Epilogue

"Oh, Dr. Philbin, there's always a higher power running the show. And I'm pretty sure I'm in good with her," Patrick said, knowing there was at least one influential person somewhere in the world who owed him a big favor.

With a quizzical expression, Archie asked, "When did you become a man of faith?"

Patrick gazed over his friend's head and smiled. "Look," he said, gesturing toward where Amelia and her parents were having a picnic in the grass.

"Now that is a miracle," Archie agreed. "Is she speaking?"

"More and more every day." Patrick waved to Amelia, who giggled and waved back shyly. "Her parents are moving her to a rehabilitation facility in a few weeks."

"Good, good. She should improve more quickly there," Archie said, his voice trailing off a bit. "Um . . . so you talked to Susan this morning."

"Yep."

Archie scratched his head. "Did she . . . um . . . say anything about our date?"

Patrick nodded.

"Well?"

"Excuse me, doctors," Estelle interrupted, appearing beside the two men seemingly out of thin air.

"Jesus!" Archie started.

"How do you do that?" Patrick exclaimed.

She shrugged her hunched shoulders. "Do what?" she asked flatly, then flashed them a quick grin displaying her perfect, pearl-white teeth.

The two men exchanged a surprised look.

"Director Dilby has asked to see the two of you," she said, her customary scowl once again restored.

Archie groaned.

"Don't worry, Dr. Philbin," Patrick said, rubbing his hands together. "This is what makes life interesting. Right, Estelle?"

"I wouldn't know about that, Dr. Denny. But a woman has been calling every extension at the hospital trying to contact you. Something about the paperwork being ready."

Patrick patted his pockets. "It's my realtor. Forgot my phone again."

"Well, you'll have to return her call later. Dr. Dilby is waiting."

Archie groaned again as they followed Estelle into the building.

. . .

Heaving the last of the boxes up to the muscular young man on the back of the pickup truck, Patrick wiped his hands on his jeans and looked back at the house.

"Well, that's everything," Sam informed them as she trotted down the steps. "It's all yours now." She handed Patrick a set of keys and gave him a hug.

The young man jumped from the truck bed and slammed the tailgate shut. "We should get going, Sam. I want to beat commuter traffic."

"Okay, okay." Sam let Patrick go. "But I still need to stop by the church to say goodbye to Father Owen. He hasn't been feeling well." Her forehead creased. "Please don't forget—"

Epilogue

"We will check on him. Don't worry," Patrick promised again. "You sure you want to live with this clucking hen, Stuart?"

Sam's boyfriend feigned a smile and impatiently folded his arms across his chest. "Time's ticking," he urged as he unhappily watched Sam loop her arm around Patrick's waist and turn him toward the house.

"I'm glad I waited for the right buyer to come along. You're going to be happy here," she said, leaning against him.

"I think so," Patrick agreed.

"Maybe you'll even start writing again."

"We'll see. But . . . I'm definitely hosting Christmas, so don't make any plans. It will be a yuletide extravaganza, and I expect both of you to come." He looked over his shoulder at Stuart, who grumbled something and stomped off to the driver's side of the truck, slamming the door behind him.

"Hello, hello," came an excited voice from a second-floor window.

"Did you pick a room yet, Mr. Scarlatti?" Sam called up to him.

Ray Scarlatti's head poked out from Sam's former bedroom window. "I think this one. It's just . . . well . . . do you think it would be okay if I painted it a different color? Though I could live with pink, I mean, I could get used to it—"

"You'll have to ask the new owner," Sam answered, cutting off his excited rambling.

"You can paint it any color you like," Patrick called up.

Mr. Scarlatti smiled and his head disappeared back inside.

"Sam!" Stuart shouted from inside the truck.

"Okay!" She shouted back and sighed. "You guys take good

care of my house." With a quick kiss on his cheek, she turned and climbed into the passenger seat. Stuart started the engine. "Oh!" she called out the window as they pulled away from the curb. "I left you a present on the kitchen table."

He waited until the truck disappeared around a corner, then jogged up the front steps of his new house. "I'll have to get that fixed," he said, nearly tripping on a loose board.

Mr. Scarlatti sat at the kitchen table eating the chocolate bonbons Sam had left for him in the freezer, while Patrick ripped into his present, giddily tearing the shiny gold paper from the box. He slid off the cover and reached inside.

"What is it?"

Patrick sat back and smiled. "It's a diary."

"Whose?" Mr. Scarlatti asked as he licked melted chocolate from his fingers.

"An old friend's."

"Samantha's such a thoughtful girl."

"Yes, she is."

"Dr. Denny?"

"Yes, Ray."

"When do I get to meet our cat?"

...

Clicking on the desk lamp, Patrick laid out a fresh pile of blank paper and repositioned the ink jar. The day outside was waning fast, and he imagined the night descending over the tower and the cemetery. He struck a match and lit Amelia's candle of protection, which he had placed beside Alfred Cummings' diary.

Epilogue

Earthy, wax-scented smoke swirled and rose to the ceiling above him, where shadows began to writhe and dance and conjure fantastic imaginings. He took up his pen, dipped it into the ink, and wrote:

> *Knocking woke him from a most pleasant dream. He stepped over the book that had fallen from his lap and hurried to the door, fearful that the clamor would disturb his young bride, who was enjoying her own sweet dreams up in their bedroom.*
>
> *"Master Cummings," a rustic-looking gentleman addressed him. "Sorry to disturb you at such a late hour, but the trip from Waylingbrooke took longer than anticipated in this almighty awful weather." From his mud-splashed coat, the man withdrew a large brown envelope and presented it with a bow. "Name's O'Brien. I've been sent to secure your services for a small construction project my town is undertaking."*
>
> *Intrigued by the unexpected prospect, Alfred invited the road-weary traveler in and showed him to his homey little parlor. "What is it you that you would like me to build?*

The Author

Tammy Gregg crafts literary Gothic fiction that explores the shifting boundaries between reality and the surreal in small-town New England. Her debut *Why Did God Make the Tree?* is the first of the Patrick Denny novels—interwoven narratives and nested stories within stories that confound imagination, madness, and truth. A lifelong New Englander with degrees in English from Boston University, Gregg draws from the psychological complexity of Nathaniel Hawthorne and Henry James, the uncanny dread of Arthur Machen, and the atmospheric menace of Daphne du Maurier.

www.tammygregg.com

www.ingramcontent.com/pod-product-compliance
Lightning Source LLC
LaVergne TN
LVHW041207250326
834689LV00017BA/163/J